THE WRONG STUFF

ALSO BY SHARON FIFFER

Killer Stuff
Dead Guy's Stuff

SHARON FIFFER

THE WRONG STUFF

STUFF

ST. MARTIN'S MINOTAUR ❦ NEW YORK

www.minotaurbooks.com

Library of Congress Cataloging-in-Publication Data

Fiffer, Sharon Sloan, 1951–
    The wrong stuff / Sharon Fiffer.—1st St. Martin's Minotaur ed.
    p. cm.
    ISBN 0-312-31414-0
    1. Wheel, Jane (Fictitious character)—Fiction. 2. Women private investigators—Illinois—Chicago—Fiction. 3. Antique dealers—Fiction. 4. Chicago (Ill.)—Fiction. 5. Suburban life—Fiction. I. Title.

PS3606.137W76 2003
813'.54—dc21

                                                                2003047025

First Edition: November 2003

10 9 8 7 6 5 4 3 2 1

STILL FOR STEVE
AND FOR AUNT MAXINE,
WHOSE WARMTH AND WISDOM I TREASURE

THE WRONG STUFF

1

Okay, so these are silver plate, and I really don't collect silver plate or silver or anything shiny like that, except maybe hotel silver when I can find it, when it slips through the fingers of the damn Basswood twins who pick for that trendy hotel and restaurant ware shop. What's the name? Oh yeah, "Check Please." Jeez, since that opened up, you can't even find those Buffalo China cups anymore with the brown ring around the top that even Nellie got sick of at the EZ Way Inn. And please, even if I don't collect silver plate, these are candlesticks and you can always find people who want these, especially around the holidays, especially the way Tim will glitz them up, display them surrounded by green boughs and gold ribbons and lit up like Martha Stewart's stock portfolio.

Jane Wheel kept up her frantic inner monologue as she stuffed the last small candelabra into her blue plaid shopping bag. Talking to herself calmed her somehow, made her act rather than react. If she gave herself too much time to think, she'd debate every item, every vintage stapler and Bakelite pencil sharpener that rattled in the bottom of one of her overstuffed bags. This candlestick made six. They were badly tarnished and she didn't have time to check for a mark with Big Elvis breathing down the back of her neck. What was he doing out of the book room, anyway? Had he finally succeeded in steamrollering over every other shopper and taping off the room for himself with a big SOLD sign?

He had about a dozen record albums tucked under his arm and was peering over her shoulder, poised on the balls of his feet, ready to pounce on anything she didn't stuff into her bag. His six-foot-four-inch frame—six-feet-six-and-a-half-inch, if you counted his pompadour—gave him an advantage at these sales. He could see over and reach past almost any shopper who had carved out space closer to the jam-packed tables. Jane smelled him even before he cast his shadow over her. She suspected he didn't brush his teeth or bathe as an offensive weapon in the battle for killer stuff. If he couldn't get there first, he could drive you away faster, overwhelming you with his bulk, his bravado, and his body odor.

What were all these dealers and pickers like Big Elvis doing at St. Perpetua's rummage sale anyway? Jane handicapped garage sales the way a racetrack tout eyeballed the ponies. She studied the classifieds and looked for all the clues that meant a good sale, but not one so good that it promised to be overcrowded—the kind where dealers slept in their cars the night before and collected all the early numbers so a loner like Jane wouldn't even get through the door until the third hour of the sale. Sure, she could doze in her car with the best of them, waiting for the sun to rise and the front door of the sale house to open; but most weekends, Jane preferred finding the sleeper, the underdog, the dark-horse sale, and laying her money down there.

Besides, Jane had a husband and a son who expected her to sleep at home most nights and keep some kind of cereal box in the cupboard and to occasionally check the expiration date on the milk carton. For Charley's and Nick's sakes, she had to maintain the vestiges of normal life, so she picked her sales not only by the most tempting description of items but also by proximity and size. A smaller rummage sale at an out-of-the-way church like St. Perpetua's on Chicago's northwest side might yield more for her than one of the big Northshore estate sales, where dealers had already made deals and pickers like Big Elvis had already homesteaded on the lawn for two days.

So why? she asked herself again, fingering a gaudy pink ashtray from the forties that had SOUVENIR OF CORAL GABLES written across a flamingo's back, slowly turning it in her hand, savoring the fact that another picker was salivating behind her, were Big E and some of the other regulars poking around the tables here? She nestled the ashtray into the bubblewrap she had in one of her bags and backed away.

It was a gorgeous October Friday, all full of sun and crisp air that sliced through your window at 4:00 A.M.— 3:00 A.M. if you had any real driving to do—when a picker's alarm went off. And this was a day when there were at least four conducted estate sales that sounded choice. Two of these were run by professionals who actually seemed to like their work, priced fairly, and didn't stare you down when you were in line to pay, gambling on how much they could demand for the unmarked item you so clearly lusted after. There was even another rummage sale, a much larger one at a church in Glenview, which boasted a furniture tent and a treasure room. It was the kind of Friday morning when Jane should have had St. Perpetua's to herself.

Since Jane had agreed to pick for her friend Tim Lowry

in addition to her mentor, Miriam, whose shop in Ohio she had been supplying with vintage linens, pottery, old tools, school primers, Alice and Jerry readers, Pyrex mixing bowls, bird prints, group photographs, maps, old frames, and anything else that could be spotted, grabbed, stuffed, inventoried, priced, repacked, and shipped, she found herself playing the smart little pig to Big Elvis's big bad wolf more and more. No matter how early the big bad wolf said to meet him at the apple tree, little piggy Jane would get up earlier and beat him there. Or she would try to find a sweeter orchard.

She had been reveling in this sale at St. Perpetua's, spending the time it took to search through books for foxing, the worn brown spots that dramatically downgraded their collectiblity. She had actually taken the time to unfold colorful old tablecloths to look for stains. Her fellow shoppers had been neighborhood people, parishioners, and thrifty mothers looking for bargains on toys and children's clothes. Now she was elbow to elbow with the piranhas of the picking world, whom she had been so smug about avoiding.

The answer to the puzzle hit her as she was in line to pay. As she removed all the objects from her bags for a nun whose speed and accuracy on the calculator only added to her tough-as-nails, all-business demeanor, she glanced at the vintage watch pin Sister Higgins wore right under her name tag. The clock face was upside down to the world, but right side up to the nun, who would have been able to glance down and know in a heartbeat if Little Bobby had actually spent the required five minutes presenting his oral book report. Jane, staring straight ahead at the hawk-eyed nun, after years in the advertising world presiding over meetings she had wanted to be long over, could easily read the time upside down.

Never wanting to look at her own watch, insulting the people to whom she was supposed to be raptly listening, she'd nod seriously, flutter her eyelids, and glance across the conference table at an account executive's Rolex. If the group had been arguing the merits of a tired television campaign for more than sixty minutes, Jane could take action. No one wanted a meeting to last more than an hour, so she could sympathetically look at the speaker, hold up a kindly hand, and ask if anyone had the time since she knew there were other meetings scheduled and her own Timex had once again stopped. Knowing full well the time from the Armani suit's Rolex, she'd listen to someone say it aloud, then stand and shrug, promising to schedule another meeting as soon as possible to clean up the loose ends. How had she lasted sixteen years in that business?

It was 10:45 A.M. according to Sister Higgins's bosom. No wonder Big E and the rest were lurking—they had fished out the other sales and were winding up their morning shopping at St. Perpetua's. Could she really have spent almost four hours at one sale? Even though she was surprised for the moment, Jane knew in the next that she could account for every second. It was, in fact, all the leafing through pages, all the unfolding that she had luxuriated in. The dealers and pickers had ricocheted through the other sales like stray bullets and now had honed in on her territory. It was time for her to go home and unpack the bags. She had promised Charley to meet him there for lunch, and she wasn't sure if there was anything edible in the refrigerator. She'd zip home, unload, wash her hands, and pick up a lunch they couldn't afford at the gourmet shop near their house. Luckily Foodstuffs accepted credit cards. Sister

Higgins and St. Perpetua's had claimed all her cash.

Jane patted her pockets to make sure she had her wallet and cell phone and slid into the car. She flipped down the visor and opened the mirror to check her face for streaks of dirt. When she'd first started making the rounds of the morning sales, she had returned home, looked in the mirror, and seen herself: wild-eyed and glazed with streaks of grime. Pawing through the leavings of others could be a dirty business. These days she stocked the car with a picker's essentials; power bars, water bottles, antibacterial ointment, Band-Aids, and cleaning-up supplies.

She took out a tissue and doused it with some of the liquid "waterless" soap she kept in the glove compartment and wiped her cheek. She saw that she still had the glazed and frantic look she sometimes wore at a sale. Yes, she had gotten calmer and become more professional, but she still could get worked up into a picker's frenzy when she worked a solid little sale like this. And until the last few minutes, she'd felt like she had all of St. Perpetua's rummage to herself—a picker's dream. She closed her brown eyes and took a deep breath before opening them, smiled, and reclaimed her face.

Jane loved her work. Unlike her former days at the agency producing television commercials, when she felt she should be issuing hourly apologies for cluttering people's minds and hearts with meaningless messages, making them want the frivolous, buy the unnecessary, she now did honest work. She recycled, reclaimed, and relocated. She took on the unwanted and the frivolous and gave it meaning. Instead of cluttering people's minds, she now filled them with . . . what? Desire for another kind of clutter? Retro reminders of the good and bad old days? No, absolutely not.

She provided the tokens and talismans that people needed to express their true selves, or at least that's what it felt like on a good day.

On a bad day, the perfect-looking vase in the bottom of the box that might have been a McCoy had a crack and no maker's mark. The ten-pound tin of buttons were all dirty, broken, white shirt buttons and melted sixties plastic—no Bakelite cookie in the bunch. And the sweet little train case with the sticky lock finally popped open at Jane's kitchen table to reveal a dead mouse—or worse. She had found a few other nonvintage, noncollectibles in her travels. There was neighbor Sandy Balance's dead body, and then Oscar Bateman's severed finger. . . . Yes, the picking life had its share of bad days.

Today wouldn't be one of them, Jane was sure. She had a bagful of silver that Tim would love and at least ten great forties' tablecloths, unused, still tagged, that Miriam would pay top dollar for. Jane had also found four wide Bakelite bangles in the bottom of a shoebox full of costume jewelry. She'd paid three dollars for the whole box. It was one of those "Eureka" moments that still had her heart racing. The bracelets weren't carved or fancy in any way, but two were red, one was butterscotch, and one was creamed corn, her favorite colors, and had a lovely thickness and patina. She'd have to test them, of course, but she was sure after she dabbed a bit of Simichrome polish on them, her cotton swab would have the yellowish tint of victory. She felt like singing.

Besides, she reasoned with herself, even the bad days—the body-finding days—had led to the crime-solving days, and she knew that might be leading her in another direction altogether. Det. Bruce Oh had seen the value in her keen eye and sharp sense of objects. He had asked her to consider working with him as a PI. And on a day like today, when she had found all the right stuff and been there first, she thought she just might be able to do it all—be a picker and a PI and live happily ever after.

Jane backed her maroon Altima into the driveway—all the better to unpack the trunk efficiently—but when the garage door opened, she saw that it would be impossible to park her car next to the makeshift shelves where she wrapped and packaged goods to mail to Miriam in Ohio. Charley's old Jeep was already parked inside the two-car space, made barely one car because of the boxes, bags, and stacks of books, records, piles of picture frames, three-legged chairs, and broken dresser drawers that Jane intended to make into shadow-box frames. One corner of the garage was devoted to a pile of more than thirty old wooden shutters that Jane had hauled away from a Dumpster parked at a neighborhood teardown that she thought might make cool CD racks if cleaned and hung properly. She had seen it in a magazine and thought she might turn a few of these into well-crafted, recycled pieces of usable art. When she had some spare time.

Why had she promised Charley a nice lunch on a Friday? More to the point, why had he beaten her home?

Jane, still carrying two plaid overstuffed shopping bags, shouldered her way into the house through the narrow laundry room. The shelves over the washing machine and dryer had been claimed by stacks of vintage cookbooks and boxes of "souvenir kitchenalia" that Jane had to sort before sending out to Ohio. State map tablecloths, dish towels, and aprons; spoon rests in the shape of Florida oranges, California avocados, and Arizona cacti were wedged next to a bottle of laundry detergent and a dusty box of fabric softener sheets that Jane had never opened. She stepped over an overflowing laundry basket and wondered for a moment whether the clothes were clean or dirty.

"Charley?" Jane called. She could hear muffled voices from his study, a euphemism for a closet-sized former sunporch they had converted for him just off the dining room. "Are you on the phone?"

Jane set her bags down on the kitchen table, already covered with the remains of two morning papers, Nick's breakfast, and yesterday's mail. She had also put two old wooden "tills" on the table—thick wooden trays that had carved-out valleys to hold change from what she hoped was an old general store. The one indentation that was so worn that it was mended with a thin piece of board tacked on from the bottom especially charmed her. *It must have held the pennies,* she had thought at the flea market when she first ran her own fingers over the worn wood. Now the spaces held Bakelite buttons sorted by size and color. She was thinking about displaying them somehow, but had not yet determined the means.

Two voices in the study? Maybe Charley had invited a graduate student for lunch. She hoped not. She was still a bit streaky with dirt and still hopped up on rummage sale adrenaline, which was underappreciated by geology graduate students. Now if she had been an antique bottle collector, fresh from some old dump site, they might have gotten excited. Diggers appreciated other diggers. Jane was often confounded by the fact that people's passions for their "stuff" did not always translate into an appreciation for the "stuff" of others. She loved to see Charley all sweaty and excited over a bunch of rocks that he told her were actually the teeth of some extraordinary crustaceous creature. On the other hand, neither he nor his colleagues or graduate assistants seemed to share her excitement over the discovery of a Bakelite needle case with a carved acorn-shaped cap found at the bottom of a moldy sewing box. Go figure.

Besides, she had no lunch to offer. She'd thought she'd have time to wash up and run over to Foodstuffs and buy a few sandwiches and fancy chips, cut up an apple, and pare the mold off the cheddar in the back of the fridge. No, she had already scraped that to pack for Nick in his lunch. When had she last made a trip to the grocery store? It was always tough to keep up with groceries and chores in the fall when every rummage sale, estate sale, and garage sale sounded better than the next. In November, things usually slowed down. They could eat next month. She would make all of Charley and Nick's favorite meals: pot roast and vegetable soup and chicken marsala. Yes, in November she would put on an apron and turn into June Cleaver or Alice from *The Brady Bunch* or whomever they wanted as chief cook and bottle washer. . . .

"Jane? Is that you?" Charley's voice was even, but it had that serious tremor that caught Jane up short. She wiped her hands and walked quickly to the study.

Sitting on the ottoman of Charley's reading chair, red-eyed and tight-lipped, was the last person Jane expected to see there. "What are you doing home, Nick? Are you sick?"

Jane headed for her son, palm outstretched toward his

brow, but he shook his head and turned away from her, swallowing hard.

"Nick tried to call, but you didn't answer," Charley said, "and then he . . ."

As Jane listened to Charley explain, she took her cell phone out of her back pocket and read the THREE CALLS MISSED message scrolled across the tiny screen. In the noise and hustle and bustle of St. Perpetua's, she hadn't heard the ring. She hadn't kept the promise she had made to Nick that she would always answer the phone, no matter what. When she and Charley had separated for some months last year, she had promised her son—it had been their deal—that even if she were about to make the best purchase of her life at the most incredible sale she had ever attended, she would always answer her phone.

Jane was so upset about the fact that she had broken her promise, she realized she wasn't completely listening to Charley's explanation of Nick's presence at home when he should have been at school on a Friday afternoon, especially this Friday afternoon when his favorite teacher was taking his class on a field trip that Nick had been talking about for weeks. Nick wouldn't have missed this Chicago museum visit for anything. In fact, as Jane was trying to listen to Charley, her mind flitted ridiculously to the terrible lunch she had thrown together—those wedges of cheese and the bruised apple—and remembered that the class was stopping for lunch at the Rock 'n' Roll McDonald's. Jane felt foolishly relieved that Nick wouldn't need to open that lunch bag.

"I'm still not understanding. I'm sorry, but . . . ," Jane began, and Nick interrupted.

"They said it was because of insurance. If they didn't have the signed permission slip, they couldn't . . ." Nick stopped and looked away again.

Jane's thoughts cleared immediately. The permission slip. Nick had brought it to her two weeks ago and asked that she sign it immediately so that he could put it right into his backpack. Jane had been filing her sale notes from the last month and couldn't find a working pen. Hundreds of vintage advertising mechanical pencils in a basket on her desk, but not one working Bic. She told Nick to put the slip on the kitchen counter. He reminded her at dinner and she had nodded, seeing the light blue slip under a bag of vintage picture books she had picked up that day at a thrift store. She noticed it again after dinner, but her hands were wet from washing the pans and she asked Nick to move it into the dining room so it wouldn't get anything spilled on it. When she carried in a box of heavy, restaurant-style Buffalo China from the garage to look for a particular size platter that Miriam had called about, she had dropped the heavy carton down on the dining room table and noticed that the slip was now partially covered by the box. She wrote herself a note on a yellow Post-it and stuck it on her purse to remind herself to sign the slip and write a check and give it to Nick. The next day, when Nick saw and asked about the Post-it note, now floating on top of her purse when she dropped him off at school, she promised to go home and get it and bring it back—right after she stopped at the post office and mailed packages to Ohio.

Jane was still standing in the doorway to Charley's study, and she turned and looked at the dining room table. The box of china was still there. She had also put down two more boxes—linens for later sorting. Even with the entire table almost covered, however, she could still see the corner of the blue slip peeking out from under the heavy cardboard carton of dishes.

Jane badly wanted to wake up, to have this whole scene part of an anxious mother's nightmare. She longed to swoon, to pass out and come to and realize it had all been a terrible hallucination. But there is something in the turned head of a child you love so fiercely and whom you have disappointed so thoroughly that doesn't allow you more than a moment of self-saving fantasy.

"I am so sorry, Nick," she managed to say. She was crying, tears were falling, but she managed to keep her voice steady. She knew that it would be unfair to claim any pity, any sorrow. The anger and frustration and disappointment and embarrassment that crowded the airspace in this study belonged to Nick. They were rightfully his, and Jane did not deserve a tearful catharsis right now.

Her own mother, Nellie, a maniacally clean and meticulous little woman who had never found a dirty floor she could not polish, a burned-out pan she could not scour, or a filthy load of laundry she could not whiten, had perpetrated evil in Jane's young life. She had forced Jane to discard her favorite stuffed bear, Mortimer, because it had become torn and dusty. She had failed to attend the second-grade dental hygiene play when Jane played the lead role of the "tooth" and her friend Tim had played "floss." She had told Jane that she looked fat in her prom dress. All horrible maternal crimes, to be sure, but Nellie had never lost one slip of paper, never allowed one homework assignment to remain on the floor, nor had she ever allowed a wedge of cheese under her care to grow mold. Not on Nellie's watch. And now Jane, struggling daily to not be Nellie, to not give Nick any of the hang-ups, fears, phobias, and neuroses that Nellie had so carefully planted and watered in Jane's particular little brain garden, had lost the battle. No, she hadn't become her failed mother, Nellie. So much the worse, she had become Nick's failed mother, Jane.

"Is there anything I can do?" Jane asked. "I could drive you . . ."

Nick shook his head.

Charley, speaking softly, explained to Jane that Nick had also called him at his office, and the department secretary had tracked him down at a meeting. By then it was too late. The buses had to leave and they couldn't make an exception for Nick without the permission slip. The vice principal had been most apologetic.

"I don't know how I'll ever make this up to you, Nick, but I swear I will spend the rest of my . . ."

"It's okay," Nick said, shrugging.

"Of course it's not. I understand," Jane said.

"No, it is okay, it's just . . ." Nick started then stopped. Jane waited.

"There're always kids, you know, who forget or don't remember the money or, you know, don't care anyway, and . . ." Nick hesitated again. "I just don't want to be one of those kids." He looked at his mother dead on for the first time, and she felt her heart crack.

"I know," Jane said. Her mother had cut Jane's long, beautiful hair into a choppy-looking bowl cut when Jane was in the second grade because Nellie didn't have the time to brush it every morning. There were other cropped heads in her class, and Jane recognized them as kindred spirits of a sort. Their mothers worked, too, or had so many other children at home that a braid or ponytail every morning was an impossible task. Yeah, Jane knew they should commiserate in some seven-year-old version of group therapy, like jumping rope to some mother-bashing rhyme, but instead, Jane avoided them. She knew exactly what Nick meant. No, she hadn't wanted to be one of *those kids*. Instead, for her best friend, she sought out Tim, whose mother cut his sandwiches into animal shapes and made homemade treats for the class on his birthday. She became Tim's shadow, and when her hair grew long enough, he taught her how to braid it herself.

"You're not one of those kids, Nick," Jane said. "I'm just one of those moms."

Jane moved all the boxes from the dining room out to the garage only to discover she was out of shelf space. She stacked the cartons into towers, scrawled contents on the sides, and went in to tackle the kitchen, where boxes were both under and on top of the kitchen table.

"I hope you don't take this the wrong way," Charley said, putting down a small and, Jane was sure, neatly and efficiently packed duffel bag, "but I'm not sure just moving the stuff around will do it."

"What?" Jane asked.

"What you want it to do," Charley said.

Jane shook her head. "I'm just cleaning, that's all, just organizing."

Nick came in and sat his equally small and, Jane was

certain, neatly and efficiently packed duffel next to his father's.

"Moving stuff around again, Mom?" Nick asked.

He hadn't meant it as a dig of any kind. He was feeling better—great, in fact—and had become downright philosophical when Charley told him he would wait until after school when the field trip bus returned so Nick could collect his best friend, Parker, and the three of them would head for Rockford, where Charley would give his Saturday symposium and the boys would have a blast at the indoor water park at the resort hotel where Charley had just reserved a small suite.

Nick had even patted Jane awkwardly on the shoulder and told her it was okay, that it was probably for the best. Rockford would be better than the aquarium, and his dad's lecture would be far more interesting than any old volunteer's canned speech to middle schoolers. Charley had promised them a behind-the-scenes tour of the natural history museum and unlimited water slide passes.

Jane was delighted that Nick was happy about the weekend, although she didn't believe for a minute that she was off the hook. She knew that this gaffe wasn't so easily remedied, even though Charley had, for the moment, bailed her out. It was, she knew, one of her major problems—her refusal to be bailed out. She needed to suffer, do some penance, and be absolved in a slower and more torturous fashion. Jane was grateful to Charley, but gratitude did not untie the knots of guilt.

"Try not to put yourself in solitary for too long," said Charley, knowing the only person who could punish Jane to her satisfaction was Jane herself. "Call Tim or something."

"Oh, right. Tim will kill me when he hears this one," Jane said. "He already considers himself a better mother than I am."

When the two had left for Charley's office to pick up his lecture notes, Jane lifted a set of forties' nesting mixing bowls off the top of the small kitchen television she and Charley kept for news watching during dinner preparations. Jane knew she was depressed. Only when she felt hopelessly blue did she allow herself to wallow in daytime television. She stacked the boxes from the kitchen table onto the floor and heard a loud, officious female voice.

"Are you just moving it around? Because that won't solve the problem."

Jane looked behind her. No one. She was alone in the kitchen. The voice she at first thought was either her mother or her conscience came from a tall, thin blonde on television who was sitting next to Oprah, holding a book in her hand.

Belinda St. Germain was the author of *Overstuffed: An Addicts Guide to Decluttering*. She had also written *Breathing Free* and *Stop Kidding Yourself—It Owns You!* Jane spent most of the next hour listening raptly as Oprah's guest described Jane's personality, Jane's house, and Jane's rapidly crumbling self-esteem.

"What's wrong with you," St. Germain barked, "that you need stuff to validate who you are? Get rid of it today before it suffocates you, before it takes over your life."

"Okay," Jane whispered. Feeling slightly hypnotized by her new guru, Jane slipped on her blue jean jacket and decided she should run out and buy St. Germain's books immediately. Of course that would mean bringing in a few more things, additional objects, and the first rule was no more new things; but Jane felt pretty certain that Belinda excepted her own books from the rest of the "rubbish," as she called it.

"What do you really, really, really need?" she asked. "How many pairs of shoes, toothbrushes, tubes of lipstick? How many cans of soup do you need to hoard in your pantries? Do you really shop less when you buy more? No, my friends, you shop more, you buy more, you store more, you are smothered by more, you can no longer breathe in your own space, can you?"

Oprah was nodding, the audience was nodding, and Jane was nodding with them.

When the phone rang, she jumped, and contemplated not answering so she would not miss any more of Belinda's wisdom, but she knew better. Not hearing, not answering the phone, was part of the behavior that had delivered her into Brenda's hands in the first place.

"Mrs. Wheel?"

"Detective Oh?"

"Yes," said Oh.

Jane waited. Oh was always a man of few words and even the few took a while forming themselves.

"Have you considered my offer?"

"Yes, but . . . ," Jane said, "right now, I . . ."

"My wife, Claire, is curious about your decision."

It was unlike Oh to interrupt and also surprising that he brought up his wife. Jane knew that Claire Oh was a highly respected antiques dealer and, according to Oh, quite happy that he had decided to quit the police force, teach courses in criminology and sociology, and open his own consulting business. According to Oh, she was successful enough, her business profitable enough that she would be happy for Oh to teach and not even bother with the *consulting*, which she and everyone else knew was a detective agency and to her was simply police work without the backup.

Since Jane had had a few adventures in her new "picking" career, it seemed that everyone wanted a piece of her. Tim Lowry was ready to make her a partner in T & T Sales, claiming to have trained her eye since they met in first grade. Tim was still Jane's best friend, and she saw him regularly since he still lived in their hometown of Kankakee, Illinois, where Jane went almost weekly to visit her parents, Don and Nellie.

Tim had even introduced her around at his flower shop, another of his many ventures, bragging to his customers that Jane's taste was almost equal to a gay man's, if not quite equal to his. "Because," he said, waggling his finger at Dr. Bernardo's wife, "I'm not just *any* gay man." The woman had left the store giggling, buying twice as much as what she had originally intended. Tim explained to Jane that his success as a florist and antique dealer was largely based on the extraordinary stereotypical act he put on. It was, he often told her, the bane of his existence, to be a well-adjusted and contented gay man in a small town whose residents wanted him to be their town eccentric—"Or village idiot, one of the two," he had added.

Detective Oh's offer was the most intriguing, though, and Jane was still mulling it over. She did love the resolution of solving a crime; the utter satisfaction of it was so intense. As good as finding the Bakelite bracelet in the bottom of the box of junk jewelry? Close, it came close to that. *And besides,* she had been thinking lately, *why do I have to decide? Can't I do both?*

"Your wife?" Jane asked. "I'm not sure why Claire would care about my decision, Detective Oh."

"I am so sorry. I haven't really explained myself. Claire thinks you would be the perfect partner on my new case, so she suggested I call rather than wait for you to call me."

Curiouser and curiouser, Jane thought. Although they knew a lot about each other, Jane and Claire had never met.

"Which is?"

"Pardon?"

"Your new case?" Jane reminded him.

"Yes, of course. My wife, Claire, has been arrested."

"Oh," Jane said.

"Yes?"

"No, I just mean *Oh*," said Jane, "like, *oh my*. For what?" Jane thought she heard a small sigh.

"Oh, yes, of course. What she's been arrested for. Yes," said Oh, and this time the sigh was plainly audible.

"Murder."

2

Clear the mind; clear your desk. Today, right now, throw out three old files, file three documents that you must save, and remove and discard three useless objects from your purse.
—BELINDA ST. GERMAIN, *Overstuffed*

Jane tried her hardest to compartmentalize as she leafed through Belinda St. Germain's *Overstuffed*. A full-size color cutout of St. Germain herself, hair pulled back in a tidy bun, wearing a lint-free Donna Karan suit with sensible but attractive black pumps, stood in the self-help section. Her cold, cardboard eyes stared at Jane. *Any minute,* Jane thought, *she'll start shaking her fiberboard head and picking dog hair off my shirt.* Jane looked around frantically. Where was that "tsk, tsk" sound coming from? Holy Toledo, did she have an "inner Belinda"?

Hold on. First, buy the book and get a grip on the stuff overtaking the house. Second, be a better mother by never losing anything, forgetting anything, missing anything, or being late for anything ever again. Third, become an ace picker without becoming a muttering bag lady. Fourth, become an ace PI by clearing Claire Oh of murder.

"Hold your horses, Jane, just hold your horses," Jane muttered to herself, scanning the rest of the self-help section, causing a clerk to respond with a "Pardon me," and Jane to realize that the muttering bag lady role might already be too ingrained. Jane felt that it was essential she take stock of herself and see if she was up to all this organization and mothering and crime solving. Once again things had turned upside down in her world, a world that should be so much simpler. After all, she was a relatively attractive, healthy, young . . . well, middle-aged . . . well, Nick had recently taken to asking, "How old do you think you're going to live to, Mom, because if you're really *middle*-aged . . . ?"

Okay, she was youngish-middle-aged *looking,* had an attractive professor husband, and a smart (if, on occasion, *smart-ass*) athletic son. She was self-employed, albeit with a made-up career as antiques and collectibles picker, and had a happy, stable home—except for that little misstep when Charley moved out for a while. And the murders. Finding her neighbor's dead body had been a tad disruptive. And then there was the murder in her best friend Tim's flower shop. Uncovering all that stuff about her parents, Don and Nellie and their tavern, the EZ Way Inn, had set her on edge for a while. Yeah, and the severed finger. But truly, until today, until misplacing that permission slip for Nick, she had been pretty well grounded. This, she decided, was her personal tipping point.

Today, for the first time, the suitcases full of other people's photo albums, the stacks of torn quilts and happy, dancing fruit tablecloths, the dust mite–chewed old college yearbooks, and the musty old gas station travel maps seemed overwhelming. Yesterday she could cope with a house filled with what others had left behind. Today she was drowning in debris.

But she could change. Jane could read this book by Belinda St. Germain, digest some decluttering wisdom, and simplify her home, order her life. It could happen. She could do it. Where was her wallet? Jane fished through her bag and pulled out a compact crossword puzzle dictionary, dropped it back in and pulled out an Italian phrasebook. Oh sure, to Belinda St. Germain those objects might seem like handbag detritus—but did she ever have to sit in a car for three hours waiting to get into an estate sale? After she had gotten a number? Well, a picker had to pack like a tourist, anticipating being stranded. Any weekend sale could turn into Gilligan's three-hour tour. Diversions, food, water, clean-up supplies, first aid—all handbag essentials. But right now, standing in line at the bookstore, where was her wallet?

Jane could become a zenlike practitioner of the spare and lean. She could organize her work. She could unpack a box of old photos from a garage sale without sitting down to dust each one and make up a story about the family picnic or the crazy uncle at the reunion. She could resist the old and broken stuff that couldn't be resold, that could only take up space in her basement, her attic, her dining room, her heart.

If Claire Oh could be arrested for murder, anything was possible. Yes, if the world turned upside down and an antique dealer wife of a former police detective could be arrested for murder, Jane Wheel could become a clean and mindful wife and mother, perfectly organized. And she could become a detective and solve the crime.

Aha! Jane found her wallet and fished out a credit card from among the ticket stubs and old receipts. Sure, she could solve Claire's problems. She had, after all, found her wallet.

Jane Wheel, girl hero. Yes, she liked the sound of that.

She hadn't thought of any of the right questions to ask Bruce Oh when he'd told her about Claire's *situation*. His word, "situation." Instead of asking the who, what, and where a good detective might ask, she offered to bring her anything she needed. A toothbrush? Was that what women needed in jail these days?

Oh had assured Jane that their attorney was attending to Claire's release on bond. He told her he would meet her at the coffee shop next to the bookstore to fill her in. In fact, he told her, Claire had insisted that Bruce leave her with the lawyer. She'd asked him to go and persuade Jane Wheel to help her. *Nice to be in demand*, Jane thought. Nick sure wasn't going to be asking for her this weekend. Jane settled into a booth with her bag of books—the collected works of Belinda St. Germain—along with several others on organizing closets and simplifying one's life.

Jane stared into her purse, a large bag made out of an old hand-braided rag rug. Yes, she needed a lot of this stuff, but maybe three items could go. There were stubs of old theater tickets, but those came in handy as bookmarks. After all, she had all these Belinda St. Germain books now—she would need to mark essential passages. An old EZ Way Inn key chain that her parents, Don and Nellie, had given out in the early sixties as customers' Christmas gifts. Six pens. Well, you never knew when one was going to go dry. A wrinkled buckeye that Nick had picked up out of a neighbor's yard as a good luck charm a few years ago, then discarded. Jane had picked it out of his wastebasket, just in case there was some luck left. Surely there must be something in here that could be discarded. . . .

"Mrs. Wheel?"

Bruce Oh, who would forever in Jane's mind be Police Detective Oh, even if he had resigned to teach and consult, even if his identification was now the license of a private investigator rather than a police department shield, sat down opposite her.

He smiled, or at least Jane thought he might be trying to smile. He was not a man of easy expressions.

"Botox would be wasted on you," said Jane.

"Pardon?" Oh signaled to the waitress by pointing to Jane's cup and making a T with his two index fingers.

"You don't frown, you don't furrow, you don't squint, you don't scrunch," said Jane, "and yet . . ."

"Yes?" Oh allowed his lips to turn upward a scant few degrees.

"You are not without expression. How do you do it?" Jane asked.

"Claire says that my eyes tell her everything she needs to know," he said, pouring the hot water in the stainless pot over the tea bag in his cup.

Jane nodded. It was true. At the moment his eyes showed a kind of puzzled pain, as if he was physically hurt but couldn't pinpoint the bruise or break.

"Claire. How does she tell you everything you need to know?" Jane asked.

Jane was looking down at her coffee cup when she asked the question. More precisely, when she heard herself ask the question. How in heaven had she made herself so bold, so prying, so intimate?

Oh seemed more puzzled than put off by the question. "One week ago I'd have told you that Claire spoke directly to me, never holding back."

Oh thanked the waitress who'd brought him more hot water.

"And now?" asked Jane, wondering how Oh was able to silently request tea, receive it in a timely and civil fashion, then be rewarded with a second cup, when she had been trying for fifteen minutes to snag a coffee refill.

"There is nothing direct about Claire right now. She told me to get you on this case. That was the clearest message she sent."

Oh told Jane about the case, which was almost literally a case. The piece of furniture that had started all the trouble was a kind of chest of drawers that Claire had found holding old tools in the basement of a house on Sheridan Road. She'd recognized it as a potentially valuable piece, asked about it, the owners had given it to her . . .

Jane stopped Oh. "Gave it to her? For how much?"

"Nothing."

"How much nothing?" asked Jane.

Oh stared at Jane, one of his I-hear-you-and-I'm-quite-sure-that-you-are-speaking-the-English-language-but-your-inventive-use-of-said-language-is-a-mystery-to-me looks.

"I tell Charley 'nothing' all the time when he asks how much I paid for something. 'How much for that broken lamp with the frayed cord, Jane?' 'Nothing,' I say, when it's just a little. Nothing used to mean under five bucks. Now I've had to keep up with inflation. Anything under ten is nothing now."

"I mean zero dollars, Mrs. Wheel," said Oh. "The person running the sale said she'd check with the owner. It hadn't been priced because they'd thought it was a built-in in the workroom, an old chest holding hammers and nails and brushes. She returned and told Claire that if she hauled it out of the basement after the sale ended that afternoon, she could have it for nothing."

When Jane met Claire Oh later that day, she picked up the story there, at the most amazing part. The "you can have it for nothing" miracle part. After the greeting at the door, Bruce Oh's no-nonsense introduction—Jane Wheel, Claire Oh— and Jane's momentary distraction with Claire's height— six feet, two inches, at least—Claire led Jane into a large room with rich, apricot-colored walls.

Jane saw right away that each piece of furniture—a standing desk under a west-facing window with nothing on its surface except three cut crystal paperweights catching the rays of the setting sun, the down-filled sofa covered in French toile, the two perfectly proportioned wing chairs, the eighteenth-century English landscapes that flanked the fireplace—was perfect and perfectly placed. Everything was elegant, exquisite, and spare. No extras. No cardboard boxes filled with Pyrex mixing bowls, no stacks of *Workbasket* magazines from the fifties. Had Belinda St. Germain already been here? It was only when Claire began to talk, her voice hoarse, her eyes glistening with a picker's frenzy, that Jane recognized a kindred spirit.

"I couldn't believe my luck," said Claire Oh, looking around her living room, drinking it in as if she thought she would never see it again.

"They were *giving* me the chest. And I had already bought the top piece. Somewhere along the line, someone had separated the top shelf from the drawers below. They were using it as a makeshift coffee table and had it priced at ten dollars. I was sure it was the top part of the chest. The carving matched up . . . I . . . I was beside myself. . . ."

Claire leaned forward toward Jane, sitting in the chair opposite her. She held her hands out, palms facing each other, as if she were measuring a drawer. Her hands were square, her nails manicured, but left unpolished. Her face, although pale now—did someone pick up prison pallor after a few hours in a police station—had clearly seen the sun. *Too many years of it,* thought Jane.

Jane realized that she had never thought about Detective Oh's age. He had a face that could belong to someone forty or sixty or anywhere in between. Jane knew the exact year a certain blue dye lot was used on a tablecloth and she could date a McCoy vase within a year, but she always had a hard time with people. Eyes were often so much younger, or older, than the curve of lips. A wisp of bangs often said one year, while the soft, translucent skin around the eyes argued for another. Claire Oh's eyes had youthful zeal when she spoke, but the sag of her jaw, the weathering around her gray-green eyes told a different story.

"A Westman chest and they were *giving* it to me, thanking me for hauling it out of their way," said Claire, her hands still outstretched. For a moment, Jane thought Claire was going to grasp her hands and shake them. Jane understood perfectly the depth of her feeling. Finding something was something. Finding something for nothing was everything.

"I knew it couldn't really be a Westman Sunflower Chest. There are only two of those known to exist. But the wood and the carving, I mean it was under two layers of paint and it was pretty gouged out, the finely delineated feet had water damage from being in the basement, there was hardware missing, but I felt it. I felt the hand of the carver. I ran my hand over the sunflower and I thought, What if there are three? What if Mathew Westman made three?"

"The feel of the wood told you?" Oh asked his wife.

Jane and Claire both looked at Oh, then back at each other.

Jane knew how wood felt, what it held, the story it could tell. Her father, Don, had told her a few months ago that he might replace the oak bar in the EZ Way Inn. Jane had grown up in her parents' tavern, the EZ Way Inn, done her homework by the dim light of the hanging fixture over the pool table. When she was old enough, in the eighth grade, Don had taught her to draw a glass of Schlitz without leaving too large a head of foam, and Nellie, her mother, had taught her the right way to wash a glass. Three times up and down, twisting it slightly over the vertical bristled brushes in the stainless wash tank, dunk twice in the rinse tank, then place upside down on a clean bar towel to protect the rim. The EZ Way Inn was where she had learned everything important. She had learned there what Claire knew, too. That you could *read* old wood, that the feel of it could tell you everything you needed to know.

The bar at the EZ Way Inn was a massive stretch of solid oak with a fat, rolled edge where elbows had softened it, fingers had drummed songs into it, heads had rested on hands, contemplating life's mysteries. As a little girl, waiting for her parents to clean the bar at night or in the morning before opening, Jane had walked the length of the bar, running her hand over that warm, worn wood. Every hill and valley softly carved out of that wood told her a story, sang her a song. There was Henry, who'd liked to sit by the window and always had a Hershey bar for her after school, and Barney who, in his broken Polish accent, had emphasized the importance of music education. That bar was the shadow box, the souvenir album of her family, Don and Nellie and her brother, Michael, and all the other extended family members who stopped by every day when the 3:30 whistle blew at the factory across the street. "Don't replace the bar," Jane had begged her dad.

"Where is it?" Jane asked. She vaguely remembered that she should be asking questions about the murder, the *who*, *what*, and *when* of why she was in the Ohs' perfectly appointed living room in the first place, but all she could think about was touching one of the carved wooden sunflowers on the Westman chest.

The room off the Ohs' kitchen, in the hands of parents and children and cats and dogs, would have been named and used as the family room. A television and squishy couch, upholstered in a color that wouldn't show spilled cocoa, would have taken up most of the sunny space.

Bruce and Claire Oh, however, had kept this room spare. The mullioned windows were bare of curtains; however, the carefully placed trees and trailing vines on the outside of the glass offered natural privacy. The walls were painted a deep tan; the trim was a rich cream. A thick carpet, patterned with florals and vines, the colors all softened by at least a century, anchored the room. Two buttery leather chairs sat on either end of a mission library table. A reading room? A meditation space? *Belinda St. Germain would give her eyeteeth for this room*, thought Jane. *There's not one wasted object, not one piece of filler.* Even the large chest of drawers sitting in the middle of the rug seemed as if it might belong there, as the object of display in a small, elegant museum gallery.

Jane approached the chest and stroked one of the

large, carved sunflowers on the drawer. She knelt to feel the carving of vines trailing down the chest's heavy legs and feet. Instead of a griffon's claw or a hairy paw for the chest's feet, Westman, if it was indeed Westman who was the maker of this magnificent piece, had continued his garden design and carved ivy leaves encircling the legs and clinging sensuously to the ball feet. Jane stood up and ran her hand along the top of the shelf, which was now reattached to the three-drawer body.

"Someone had pried off the shelf and used it as a narrow table. Probably in a child's room for a while," Claire said. "There was paint and waxy stuff all over the surface, maybe crayons. I saw it and spotted the sunflower carvings at the top of legs, and I knew a master hand had touched it."

The way she said it, "a master hand," made Jane stand up a little straighter. Yes, that was what one, sometimes, some lucky times, saw across a room—the work of a master hand.

"What I didn't see right away was that the table was actually the top shelf of a chest. The top surface was narrow, but that could mean it was handmade and offsize, that's all. It was only when I saw the chest that I put it together," said Claire. "I guess I mean that literally as well as figuratively." She smiled, almost apologetically, at Bruce Oh, who had barely spoken since Jane had entered the house.

"It's beautiful," said Jane, knowing that any word was inadequate when used to describe treasure. She felt the pull of the chest and continued to stroke one of the larger carvings on the drawer.

Jane knew that wood could talk, tell stories. She believed that the carved chest had whispered just loud enough for the right person to hear, "Take me home, Claire. I'm something."

"Yes," said Claire, walking around to the back of the chest, turning and looking back at Jane and her husband. She was taller than the chest, tall enough to look across the top of it. Claire leaned her chin on the shelf, half closed her eyes, and sighed. "It's a fake," she said.

3

How many pairs of shoes do you own? Don't check yet. Got the number? Now go to your closet and count. Twice as many? Three times as many? Why do you own what you can't even remember you have?

—BELINDA ST. GERMAIN, *Overstuffed*

"A beautiful fake," said Claire, "but a fake nonetheless."

Jane looked back and forth from Claire's eyes to the drawer pulls and the sunflower carvings and shook her head.

"I'd bet my . . . ," Jane began to say.

Claire stopped her. "Don't. You'd lose it." She came back around the front of the chest and pulled out the drawer. "You can see where they aged the wood, but it's a little too even, too neat. Dovetails are all large and too perfect. Look how it fits."

Claire slid the drawer back in place.

"Perfect, isn't it?" asked Jane.

"Yes," Claire said. "It shouldn't be though. A drawer from an authentic piece wouldn't go all the way in, wouldn't be such a perfect fit. There would be more ventilation space left at the back. There are other clues, too. . . ."

Bruce Oh, who had quietly brought in a tray with coffee, set it down and motioned for Jane to come over and sit.

"Claire rarely makes mistakes," he said.

"But when I do . . . ," Claire said, letting the thought trail.

"If Mrs. Wheel is going to help . . . ," said Oh.

Lost in the land of ellipses, thought Jane. *Somebody better finish a sentence around here.*

"What is it you think I can . . . ?" Jane began to ask.

Claire cleared her throat and straightened herself to her full six plus feet. Jane had always mistrusted people that tall. The truth was, and she knew it, she was jealous. Jane worried that the tall were able to see everything she, as the smaller than average, missed: dust on top of the refrigerator, cobwebs on the ceiling, the frailties of the human heart. Right now, even though Claire Oh was clearly in distress, Jane was certain she would never lose her keys, mismatch her socks, or mislay a permission slip.

"I called my helper, Stanley, to bring the truck over, and we loaded up the chest together. I kept it here, at home, in the garage. Horace came to see it. He agreed with me that it was a Westman—or the closest thing we were ever going to find. Wrote me a check for a deposit, and I told him I'd drive it up to Campbell and LaSalle myself for the cleaning and restoration."

Claire looked Jane over from top to bottom. "Do you know about Campbell and LaSalle?" she asked.

Jane was surprised at how thoroughly she resented Claire Oh's question. Yes, she was a picker not a dealer, and yes, she liked the old and worn more than the old and precious, and yes, she was wearing a boxy, vintage wool jacket over a pair of skinny jeans instead of the slim, gray Armani skirt and silk blouse that Claire was wearing. Yes, even after some jail time, Claire Oh had the dealer look, the I-know-the-value-of-everything-you've-ever-touched look, and yes, she had on Manolo Blahnik heels, too, but did that give her the right to assume Jane would not know that Campbell and LaSalle were the premiere restorers/refinishers/rebuilders in the country? Just because the jewelry Jane was sporting was a Bakelite pin with dangling butterscotch cherries instead of the forties Cartier diamond watch that Claire wore on her left wrist? Jane reminded herself that she really liked Bruce Oh, and he had asked her to come and talk to Claire.

"Who is Horace?" Jane asked.

"Horace Cutler's a dealer in fine European antiques. This wasn't his cup of tea, but he had a buyer. Everyone was going to make something on this," Claire said, patting the surface of the chest.

Everyone but the owner, Jane thought, but didn't say anything out loud. After all, would she refuse if someone running an estate sale gave her something? Just asked her to haul it away? No. But what if she thought the something was *something?* Would she tell?

"I checked it in with one of the carpenters at Campbell and LaSalle and told him I wanted the minimum amount of work done. Clean it up, put it back together, save the age, you know, the patina," Claire said.

Jane nodded. She and her pal, Tim, when out of earshot and sight of Charley and Nick, played a pretend game. Tim would link his arm though Jane's at a flea market, and they would discuss their imaginary daughter, little Patina. "Would Patina like a little dressing table for her room?" "Is Patina still collecting poodles?"

Tim always said that as soon as he met the right man,

they'd get themselves a poodle and name it Patina just to satisfy all of his Kankakee flower shop customers who weren't happy having a gay florist unless he made them laugh and sang them show tunes. Tim often used Jane, not as his beard to pretend he was straight, but rather as his foil for outragious behavior. Jane was stuck playing Cher to his Elton.

"They want me drooling over Liza and nibbling quiche," Tim had said the last time Jane was in the store. "If they saw me with you, eating a pizza, drinking a beer, and not ratcheting my voice up to an octave above Q for queen, they'd go back to buying their flowers at the Jewel."

"I drove up to Michigan and picked up the chest myself," Claire said. "I just glanced at it, and it looked gorgeous. I delivered it to Horace's gallery. His assistant signed for it. I came home and changed for the Hospital Auxiliary antique show at the Community House and when I got there, Horace was already waiting for me at my designated space, screaming at my assistant that the chest delivered to him was a fake and he wanted his deposit back immediately. He said he had already sent it back to the house." Claire continued rubbing the wood as she talked. "He went even crazier when he saw me. Called me lots of names. Screamed at everyone passing by that I was a liar and a cheat."

Bruce Oh, silent for so long, went over to his wife and patted her hand, which, Jane realized, was moving a bit obsessively over the carving. He led her over to the couch, and when she had sat, Oh took up the story.

"Mrs. Wheel, you've been at shows like that. The first night is a benefit. Well-dressed people, drinking champagne, an elegant evening. Mr. Cutler's screaming cut through the crowd like a knife."

"What happened?" asked Jane.

"Security came and escorted him out," said Claire. "Here was this elegant little man, dressed in an impeccable suit, yelling like a crazy person. Said his credibility with his customer was ruined. Shouted that he'd get even. He actually said he'd"—Claire stopped for just a second, swallowed, and continued—"he said he'd kill me for this."

"My god, what did you say?"

"Not if I kill you first." Claire shook her head. "I was being flippant, of course. I'm regretting the bravado now.

"I returned a few cases to my booth at the antique mall that night like I always do so they could be locked in the safe I keep there, just jewelry and a few smalls. The back door was locked. I let myself in and there was a light on near my booth. Horace was there. Dead on the Kilim rug, right in front of the Pembroke table.

"How did you know he was dead?"

"The lack of breathing, the pool of blood, the seven-inch blade with the carved bone handle sticking out of his chest," Claire said, shrugging. "The dagger was a tip-off of sorts."

Oh again laid his hand on his wife's.

"I'm sorry," she said. "I've had a very bad day."

"It's okay," said Jane, thinking she had been right about tall people. They were supercilious and got away with it because they could see farther than the average joe—or jane.

"But what about the timing of all this? How long had he been dead? Did you call the police right away?"

"The police walked in right after me. The alarm had been tripped. I turned it off before I came in, but it had rung at the police station because of a front window being tampered with," Claire said. "It was a scene from a television program. I was kneeling over the body of a man that at least thirty well-dressed, reliable witnesses had heard me say I'd kill."

"Network," Jane said, looking past Claire, locking eyes with Bruce Oh.

Oh looked at her blankly.

"Last scene before the first commercial break," Jane said. "Network television program." She shook her head. "Not even HBO."

Jane placed four large boxes on the dining room floor. Belinda St. Germain had told her at the end of chapter one that sorting was a top priority. The categories that St. Germain had defined—trash, charity, deep storage, and finally, the well-placed essentials—had to be slightly amended for Jane's work and home space. "Trash," after all, was such a relative word. Everyone knew the hackneyed mantra of the garage sale crowd—one person's trash is another person's treasure—but it got more complicated for a picker. Jane labeled her boxes with the following—"Might be for Miriam,""Maybe I should ask Tim first,""Not Yet," and "Almost Trash."

Sorting out what was going through her mind also benefited from a kind of labeling. Actually, Jane realized, her thoughts were working more in her old ad exec mode of pro and con listing before going forward with a pitch.

Reasons to take the case:
+ Makes me a real detective.
+ I like Bruce Oh.

+ I'll learn more about antique furniture, which will help me be a better picker just in case this whole detective gig doesn't work out, which it probably won't.
+ My role as a mother is up for grabs.

Reasons not to take the case:
+ My role as a mother is up for grabs.

The pro list clearly outweighed the con list, however that one con was a lulu. If she ran off to play detective, wasn't she in even more danger of losing permission slips and packing defective lunches? Perhaps Belinda St. Germain had a point when she stated that sorting through one's stuff—learning the difference between the right stuff and the wrong stuff—was a lot easier than figuring out the rest of one's life.

Maybe Jane needed to start with the stuff. She stood knee-deep in a pile of used wool sweaters that she thought someone might want for felting, shoeboxes full of old snapshots of someone's California vacations, and two laundry bags full of silk flowers that she thought Tim might be able to use for decorative somethings. Since she had moved these piles in from the garage in order to sort them into the boxes that she had also dragged in and marked, the dining room was already more impassable than it had been that morning when Charley and Nick had pointed out the errant permission slip on the table.

When her cell phone began playing "Jingle Bells"—Nick must have been at the tone menu again—she forgot how much she hated the device and lunged for it gratefully.

Anything to focus on other than these piles of . . . these piles.

"Yes?"

"Whoa, girlfriend, you actually sound like someone who answers a cell phone, instead of searching for it in your purse until it stops ringing."

"Timmy, do you ever use fake flowers?"

"I hot glued them to a foam-core sandwich board once for a Halloween costume," said Tim.

"So I should put them in the 'Almost Trash' pile, maybe?" Jane asked, more to herself than Tim.

"I was going as a garden plot," said Tim. "It was pretty cool."

"So you do want them?"

"Want what?"

"Never mind," Jane said. She looked at the mounds of stuff in front of her and made her decision. "I thought we might go on a road trip bright and early tomorrow."

"The Waukesha auction?" Tim asked.

"Nope, Michigan. Campbell and LaSalle."

Tim laughed. "You're kidding, right? You don't have any furniture good enough for Campbell and LaSalle."

Was she wearing a "kick me" sign?

"Tim Lowry, you know I don't have the money or the truck to get big pieces of good furniture, but that doesn't mean I don't know what they are or that I don't recognize quality. It doesn't mean I'm small time or . . ." Jane stopped. Of course she wanted to accept Claire Oh's case. She needed to take control of her life again. She took a deep breath, mustering her dignity and calling on the ghost of her former professional self for help.

"Tim, Detective Oh asked for help on a case, and I said yes. I mean I've decided to say yes. And since I also said yes to being your partner, you can be my partner this weekend. You can set us up at Campbell and LaSalle, can't you?"

"Of course I can. I've been going there for years," said Tim. "I didn't mean to imply anything about . . . it's just like you said, that you don't have the big cash flow or the truck for a Campbell and LaSalle job. No need for the thin skin."

This was great. Jane had been a detective on her first real case for only a few minutes, and she already had smart-ass Tim apologizing. She made a mental note to get business cards printed as soon as possible.

Jane filled Tim in on her conversation with Claire Oh. She had barely begun her description of the Westman chest or the alleged Westman chest, when Tim stopped her.

"Horace Cutler, yeah, I heard all about that. So that's who killed him? Wow!"

"Tim, don't be ridiculous. Claire Oh did not murder Horace Cutler," said Jane.

"Okay, you're right. Forgot for a minute that you're Jane Wheel, girl detective. But let me ask you this. If you read what happened in the paper, big-deal antique furniture forgery catfight and one cat ends up dead with the other one kneeling over him, you'd pretty much take it as fact, yes?"

"Well . . ."

"But because this is Bruce Oh's wife, you have some weird karmic debt that you're paying off to him?"

"Bruce Oh is a quiet, intelligent man, who is wise and thoughtful and clever without having to show off about it by spouting song lyrics and puns, like some people I know," Jane said, "and his wife wouldn't . . ."

"Hey, your husband Charley—remember him—is a wise and thoughtful man, and you do all sorts of irrational things. You buy truckloads of vintage junk that might make you some cash if you turned it around, but you adopt it and give it its own room."

Jane took a deep breath and looked around the room. She was drowning in stuff; her family was drowning in stuff; she was pulling them under. Yes, she was an irrational woman married to an intelligent, logical man. But she wouldn't kill anyone. Claire was not what Jane had expected, not who she wanted her to be, but Jane didn't think Claire would kill anyone either. But. But what? There was something.

"Claire didn't kill Horace Cutler, Tim. She's . . . she's not . . ."

"Ye-e-e-s?" said Tim, drawing the word out like a cartoon shrink.

How could Jane explain this? Before she had met Claire Oh, she had had such a clear picture of her—and for the silliest of reasons. Detective Oh's neckties. He wore these funny, gorgeous vintage ties that he always seemed vaguely embarrassed about. He'd wave away Jane's compliments, explaining that his wife bought them and insisted he wear them. Jane had pictured her, had actually tried to pick her out at estate sales, and had thought of her as this plump, homey, funny collector, a bit more advanced than Jane, but lovely and warm. Claire Oh was supposed to be the counterpoint to Bruce Oh's careful reserve. She was supposed to be the yin to his yang, the jazz to his classical, the Mrs. Columbo to his Peter Falk. No, that wasn't quite it . . . but Tim was waiting.

"Claire Oh did not murder Horace Cutler," said Jane, "but I will admit this. I didn't exactly warm up to her. There's something about Claire that just rubbed me the wrong way, something . . . I don't know, like she was a snotty cheerleader or something and I was the editor of the yearbook or . . ."

"You *were* the editor of the yearbook," Tim reminded her.

"Yeah, but I *chose* that. I could have been a . . ." Jane stopped herself, remembering that she was a mature adult, a career woman, a wife and mother, and soon to be an organized, uncluttered detective and picker. Besides, Tim was the one person in her life who would know for sure that she couldn't do the splits at age fifteen—or at any other age for that matter. She wasn't going to convince Tim that she *chose* not to be a cheerleader.

"That's all beside the point," Jane said. "Maybe if it weren't for Detective Oh, I wouldn't want to do this, but . . ."

"Let's face it, honey, if it weren't for Detective Oh, you would have drowned in Bakelite buttons by now. The fact that he sees your talent for finding things, your instincts for what's valuable, as important job skills is what's given you the confidence to move from junk collector to . . ." Tim stopped.

"Yes?" Jane asked, waiting to hear Tim use her new professional title of detective.

"A junk collector who's about to visit Campbell and LaSalle."

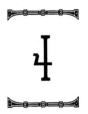

4

When someone asks you for a pen, do you rummage through your purse and come up empty-handed? Do you empty your bag later and find three pens and two pencils, ink dry, leads broken? Wouldn't one working, well-placed writing instrument be enough?

—BELINDA ST. GERMAIN, *Overstuffed*

"It's in here someplace," Jane said. She was searching for a small notebook that she always kept for jotting down items she was currently looking for at sales. She decided to take notes as Tim told her about Glen LaSalle and his partner, Blake Campbell. "Jingle Bells" sounded from somewhere in the bottom of her large, leather bag.

"Isn't it a little early to switch your ring to Christmas carols?" Tim asked.

"Oh, Nick does that. He switches the sound so I never know it's my phone. I'll be grocery shopping and the phone will ring and everybody in the produce section is slapping their pockets and digging through their briefcases, and I'll be thinking, Can't be me, my phone doesn't play "Take Me Out to the Ballgame," and sure enough, when I'm hunting for my checkbook, I'll find that I've missed a message."

Jane abandoned the search for her notebook and

looked at her phone. It was vibrating as well as playing music. "Nick must have set all systems go," she said.

"Hello?"

"Yeah, hold on."

Jane sighed. Only one person she knew called her on the phone, then sounded so busy and irritated when Jane answered that she was often confused about who called whom.

"Hello, Mom," Jane said, even though she could hear her mother talking to someone else.

Jane's mother, Nellie, came back on the line. Jane couldn't prove it, but she thought just maybe the phone vibrated not because of a preference setting but because it was reacting to the dialing style of Jane's mother.

"You're coming home Thanksgiving, right?" Nellie asked.

"Mom, don't we have a month or so? Yes, we'll be there," Jane said.

"Yeah, she could bring it then," Nellie said, but clearly to someone other than Jane.

"I could bring what?" Jane asked, trying to cradle the phone and talk while removing all the pens and pencils from the bottom of her bag.

"She sure as hell isn't going to ask you for food. Remember when you made that pumpkin pie?" Tim asked, laughing.

"Hey," Jane said, punching him in the arm, "I used a real pumpkin, not canned. It was special."

"Rind and all. God it was vile."

"Charley said it wasn't too bad. He liked that it didn't come from a can. Besides, the instructions were so frigging unclear," Jane said, remembering the masses of pumpkin entrails covering her kitchen floor.

"What the hell are you talking about? Who's there with you?" Nellie asked.

"Pumpkin pie and Tim. We're driving to Michigan," Jane said.

"Stop talking while you're driving. Jesus, Don? Don? She's on the phone driving her car again."

Jane could hear her father's voice in the background.

"Your dad says to pull over."

"Mom, listen to me. I'm not driving. Tim is. We're on our way to a furniture place in Michigan. What is it you want?"

"Furniture place? What the hell do you need any more furniture for? Where's Charley? Where's Nick?" Nellie asked Jane, then called to the others in the room, "She's in a car with that Tim going to Michigan."

Nellie had met Tim when Jane brought him home from first grade. It was one of those rare days when Nellie, because of a doctor's appointment or some other outside force, had left work at the EZ Way Inn before six o'clock at night and ended up at home by four, so when Jane fished her key out of her plaid book bag, Nellie was already opening the door. It was a special day when Nellie was home, and Jane could still conjure up the joy she'd felt at having a mom there, in the house, just like on television.

"Who's that?" Nellie had asked, jerking her head at Tim, and Jane had told her that Tim was her best friend. Jane remembered that Nellie had been most suspicious. "A boy is your best friend?" Tim had shaken hands, hung up his coat on the peg by the door, and removed his shoes. Nellie, who might write "Catholic" on a form that asked for religious faith actually worshipped only two things—cleanliness and hard, backbreaking work. She watched Tim carefully and nodded.

Tim walked right over to the cupboard where Jane kept all of her paper dolls, neatly stored by Nellie in the folders they came in. He removed the June Allyson folder and asked, "Should we finish cutting out the hats and other accessories?" Nellie had nodded again, and taken Jane's coat from her. "We won't be worrying about that one," she had said and had fixed them a plate of cookies.

"Just like on a television show," Jane said, remembering out loud how much that afternoon resonated.

"What the hell are you doing with Tim? Where's your husband and son?"

"Rockford. Charley's giving a lecture at the museum there, and Nick went with him. What is it you want, Mom?"

"Hello, honey," said her dad, Don, who had picked up another phone. "What's Charley talking about?"

"You watch out for that Tim," Nellie said, ignoring her husband on the extension.

Jane laughed.

"I mean it," Nellie said. "Maybe he's just been biding his time, waiting for the right moment."

"Whoa, Mom, I'm pretty sure about Tim," Jane said, still laughing.

"You take canned pumpkin out of the can so it would make sense that you take the real pumpkin out of the shell, right?" Tim said, still reliving the great pie disaster of 1999.

"My mom thinks you've been playing possum all these years, might really be after me," Jane said, tears starting to roll down her cheeks.

"Listen to me, Jane, you think you know everything,

but men are only after one thing," Nellie said, "and maybe you don't know that Tim as well as you think."

"And what might that one thing be, Nellie?" asked Don. "Because if that's the case, I'd like to tell you if I got it or not."

"Stop right there, you guys," said Jane. "Way too much information. Just tell me what you want, Mom. Why did you call?"

"Bring home Grandma's sewing chest."

"What?"

"That table that folds out. Aunt Veronica wants to see it," said Nellie.

Jane was relieved. It didn't actually sound like she had to lose one of her favorite pieces of furniture; she just had to take it home for a visit.

"Veronica remembers a secret drawer and I told her she's senile, but she won't take no for an answer."

"Especially when it's so beautifully phrased," murmured Jane.

"What?" Nellie asked.

"I'll bring it," said Jane.

"Yeah, and watch out for Tim," said her mother.

"Have a nice weekend, honey," said her dad.

Jane ate the last bite of her hamburger and drained her beer. She and Tim had stopped at a roadside restaurant, the first nonchain place they had seen since getting off the highway.

"Almost as good as the EZ Way Inn," she said.

"What was Nellie saying about me anyway?" Tim asked.

"She thinks you might have had a lifetime plan of pretending to be gay just to somehow trick me into bed," said Jane.

"How the hell did she figure it out?" Tim asked.

"Do not ever underestimate the paranoia and conspiracy theory that we like to call Nellie," said Jane.

"For forty years I've pretended to like other men, for god's sake. I've even had long-term relationships. I mean, I am nothing if not thorough. I even became a florist," Tim said, eating french fries off of Jane's plate.

"You've learned the words to show tunes; you've dressed meticulously and expensively; you've rehabbed architectural landmarks."

"I pretend to like to take long walks by the river, read poetry, and refinish chairs. I don't watch football on television. I polish my silver," said Tim. "I can make drinks in a blender."

"Let's face it," said Jane. "We're describing the perfect man here. If Nellie were right, I'd leave Charley for you in a minute."

"No you wouldn't," said Tim, his voice soft, taking her hand.

"No, no I wouldn't," said Jane, looking into Tim's eyes. "But I want to grow old with you, too. Is that crazy?"

"Not entirely," said Tim. "I know the feeling. Tell you what. When we get to Campbell and LaSalle, you can check out the new-age yuppie communal way of life and decide if you dig it. If yes, maybe the Wheel family of three and the Lowry party of one and a few other well-chosen people we can stand to be around for more than ten minutes ought to buy some land together and work out our own little sunshine acres for our soon-to-be senior years."

Tim handed Jane a booklet. It was made of high-quality paper, a marbled tan, with deep brown lettering. In elegant block printing across the top, it said CAMPBELL AND LASALLE.

"Read it," said Tim, when Jane looked at him. "I'm going to go out to the car and call the shop."

Glen LaSalle and Blake Campbell have spent twenty-five years crafting furniture and building a community of artists. On thirty acres of woodlands, they have created an idyllic setting for the woodworkers, blacksmiths, carvers, painters, historians, and artists who have come to work and found a place to live, breathe, and thrive in a world devoted to the fine creation and restoration of beautiful artifacts.

"In a world of fast fixes and hasty repairs we at Campbell and LaSalle take a different path. We believe in the value of time and perfection. We will fully research your piece of furniture, your silver, your jewelry, your painting, and decide, with you, the extent of restoration, reclamation, and rebuilding you, and we, feel is necessary to maintain the dignity of the piece."

Campbell and LaSalle invite you to call for a consultation. A list of accommodations in the area follows.

Jane studied the map of the Campbell and LaSalle community. Tim had told her there were several rustic but beautifully appointed cabins on the property that those in the know used when they brought in big pieces for consultations. Writers and painters whom Glen LaSalle and Blake Campbell deemed worthy were also welcomed to use the place as a kind of artists' colony. Many contemporary novelists gave effusive thanks to Campbell and LaSalle for "allowing them the opportunity to work in beauty and silence" or for "giving them the space for their work to grow."

"Here's the thing," said Tim, when they were back on the road, "there isn't even an application process to live at Campbell and LaSalle. Can you imagine? You're a struggling writer, maybe one novel well-received critically but dying on the vine as far as bookstores and stuff, and you get a call from Blake Campbell inviting you to come and live up there for a month, rent-free, board-free? You get a cabin and peace and quiet and meals . . . they have an incredible chef. You just have to fit in with the 'spirit.' "

"What does that mean?" Jane asked.

"Hard to say. Kind of a hippie, yuppie, snobby, work ethic? You know . . . casual dress, work clothes, as long as you look like you picked them out from Ralph Lauren's country collection. You know, you're there for the art and you're not attached to material objects, but at dinner there's a lot of one-upping on the wine and the sauce for the duck and all that bullshit."

Jane sat farther back in her seat. She should still be sorting through her purse. She hadn't even discarded one item let alone three. She hadn't finished sorting through the boxes at home either. If Charley and Nick came home right now instead of Monday as planned, they would find the house even more chaotic than when they'd left.

Belinda St. Germain was reassuring in her book. "It sometimes gets worse in order to get better," she counseled, along with other darkest-before-the-dawn clichés, but Jane forgave her the bad writing. Belinda, after all, had something to teach Jane, and Jane would, by golly, learn it.

Sorting and discarding. She could do it. Right now, she

would practice by sorting out her feelings about Claire Oh. One-upping? Is that what Tim had said about the Campbell and LaSalle dinner table? Was that what was bothering her about Claire? Before Jane had met her, she had been certain she would like her, that she would be a kindred spirit. After all, Claire dressed Bruce, and Jane knew how she felt about Bruce Oh—respectful, fond, curious. Right now, she was extremely curious about how he had hooked up with Claire. He was so fair and unpretentious and straightforward. Claire seemed judgmental, like someone who just might send the wine back at Campbell and LaSalle.

When Jane had asked Claire if Horace might have switched the chest himself, had a duplicate made, Claire had laughed.

"Why would he go to all that trouble? If he claimed publicly that it was a fake, he wasn't going to be able to sell it."

"Or quickly produce an authentic one for sale," added Oh.

"Would he have wanted the real chest for himself?" Jane had asked.

"Not his style. Didn't collect American," Claire had said.

Jane wasn't convinced. She had heard so many people profess to collect only one kind of object, one artist, one author, but when you saw them at a sale, their eyes were everywhere. Appreciating the value of one piece led to the appreciation of another—and another.

Belinda St. Germain might be hammering away at "the glory of absence" and "the space of spaciousness," whatever the hell that was, but Jane knew the beauty of bounty. Jane, like every other picker she'd watched work a sale, had the indiscriminate lust for all of it.

"If I'm not near the Roseville I love, I love the McCoy I'm near" was one of the songs that played in her rummaging brain at a sale.

If Horace Cutler had seen the beauty and workmanship in the Westman chest and wanted it for himself, why not pass off a copy to someone else? He'd have the chest and make the money from the sale of the fake. Oh and Claire were right—why would he create a public performance at the antiques show?

Jane sighed and went back to sorting through her purse. Trying to do a Belinda St. Germain purge before they arrived at Campbell and LaSalle might give her more closure than trying to figure out who had killed Horace Cutler and why Bruce Oh had married Claire. Holy Toledo, is that what people said about Charley? Why in the world did he marry that Jane?

"Look at this beautiful handkerchief," Jane said.

Tim looked over quickly. "GET WELL?" he read aloud.

"Yes, it looks like a child embroidered it, doesn't it?"

"I guess that won't make it into the trash pile," said Tim.

"No, of course not. Can you imagine how much work that was? Maybe for her mom who had the flu? That isn't the kind of thing that's trash, Tim," Jane said. She shook an old Sucrets tin.

"Jeez, they haven't put Sucrets in tins in years, have they? Do they still make Sucrets? That can go, right?"

Jane opened and closed the tin. She held it out open to Tim, on its side. "I thought it would make a sweet little picture frame, sort of a craft project for . . ." Jane stopped.

Tim laughed. "When is the last time you did a craft project with Nick?"

"I might want . . ."

"Jane, he is more interested in sports at school, science with Charley, and building a bicycle out of old parts with me than making a picture frame out of a cough drop tin," Tim said, then added more gently. "He's growing up, dear."

Tim was right. Jane knew it. But still, that tin might come in handy for something. She dropped it back in her bag along with the lucky buckeye and Belinda St. Germain's book, which made it even heavier than usual. Tim had slowed the car down and turned onto an almost hidden road. They approached a tall, intricately worked iron gate. An iron stand, hidden by clematis vines and climbing roses, still lush with fall blooms, housed the state-of-the-art intercom system. Tim gave their names, and the gate swung open.

"Welcome to Campbell and LaSalle, honey," said Tim.

"Remember the commune down at school? When you came to see me at college and we visited my friends who were living in the Bucky Fuller dome they had all built together?" Jane asked, hanging out her window, looking at the lush woods, trying to spy some of the hidden cabins Tim had described.

"Yeah, your friends' kids wandered around looking like feral cats. Frightening place."

"Didn't little Moonbeam or his sister . . . ?" Jane asked, starting to laugh.

"Yes, the little animal child peed on my shoe. The mother said it was because he liked me and wanted to mark me as his own."

"I still get a Christmas card from his mother. Moonbeam goes by Bob now. He's in mergers and acquisitions."

"Still peeing on people."

"Oh my," Jane said. Her mouth remained open as she stared at the main building of the Campbell and LaSalle complex.

The first impression given by the lodge, as it was called in the brochure, was somewhere between the most inflated, nostalgic, selective memory of the perfect summer camp and a presidential retreat. Set among majestic pines, the low, rambling log building was both impressive and inviting. Was it a Northwoods Camp David or 4-H Camp Shaw-wa-na-see? The twig furniture on the long front porch gave it the perfect look, but the piles of cushions and padded footstools emphasized that it wasn't only for a photo shoot. People could actually wrap themselves up in one of the Pendleton blankets stored in an open chest under the eaves and watch the sun rise over the tree line. Or set? Jane looked up and noted that the sun was still high overhead, not giving her much of a clue as to which direction the lodge faced. She always liked to know her directions and usually considered long, twisting driveways her personal enemy; but here, she realized, she felt less lost than enchanted.

As soon as Tim stopped in the large circular drive, she opened the door and listened. At first, nothing. Then a distant sound of water. A rushing creek? A waterfall? Was it just the trees breathing in the wind? Jane got out, closing the car door as softly as she could manage, not wanting to disturb this scene.

There was a corkboard, tastefully framed in hand-carved twigs hanging on the massive front door. A note was pinned there with what Jane would swear was a pine needle. The paper was most certainly handmade, delicately imprinted with ferns and wildflowers.

To our arriving guests—
Please make yourself at home on the grounds. Wander, breathe, enjoy. We at Campbell and LaSalle maintain a creative midafternoon silence between the hours of one and four. If you encounter an open studio, an individual artist might be happy to share his/her current work with you. If a door is closed, please respect the privacy of the resident. At four, return here and we will be happy to serve your needs.

"Do you mean, if customers show up, they have to wait until four P.M. to pick up a piece of furniture? Or to have an appraisal done?" Jane asked. "They can run a business like that?"

"This is not just any business," said Tim. "It is, my cretin junker friend, Campbell and LaSalle, as every brochure and hand-lettered note is going to remind you. The 'we at Cambell and LaSalle' is going to wear pretty thin by tomorrow afternoon, I guarantee you. But they do cast a spell, yes?" Tim asked. "Note that we're whispering," he added.

He was right. Jane couldn't make herself disturb the silence. Yes, it seemed a bit pretentious, but then again, Campbell and LaSalle seemed to have earned the right to set this stage. The property was magnificent. Jane gestured to a path and Tim nodded. They knew each other well enough to know that both would want to explore. Both would hope for the open door.

No luck at the first cabin. WRENS' NEST had blue shutters

with cutouts of birds in flight and an inviting windowbox filled to overflowing with blooming fall pansies. A copper kettle filled with what appeared to be kindling sat next to the front door. Unfortunately, it was a *closed* front door.

Jane and Tim saw similar still lifes on the front porches of BLUEBERRY HILL, LADYSLIPPER, TWO WINDOWS, and FRIENDS' RETREAT. All had closed doors.

At the end of the path was a large barn. A small sign at the entrance read THE WOODSHOP. The huge, garage-sized doors at one end were closed, but another smaller set of Dutch doors stood open.

Jane headed for the open door and Tim followed.

"It's more than a woodshop," said Tim, "it's practically Blake Campbell's laboratory and emergency room. He sees each piece of furniture that comes in here like a patient. He does triage, research, and treatment here."

Jane saw immediately what Tim meant. One-half of the barn was a workshop: row upon row of woodworking tools all hanging or standing in place, including two large workbenches and power tools. A large, tented area looked like the private operating room of a mad scientist. Another wall of shelves held solvents and finishes and brushes. The upper gallery of the barn housed a library as large as that of a small liberal arts college.

No one seemed to be around, but the door had been open. Jane walked up the open stairs to the gallery of books and noted that, for as many research volumes and histories, there were an equal number of art books and hundred-year-old magazines encased in protective plastic. The research library was not limited to academic art history but encompassed all the popular looks of the day, the year in question.

On top of an oak library file was a framed card that said, "We at Campbell and LaSalle research the history of each precious object with our minds, our eyes, our touch, and our hearts." Jane felt Tim behind her, breathing over her shoulder as he read the card.

" 'We at Campbell and LaSalle' have a giant hand-carved hickory stick up our ass," Tim whispered.

" 'We at Campbell and LaSalle' could use a Grey Goose vodka on the rocks," Jane whispered back.

Jane noticed that one of the larger furniture volumes was open on top of a large partner's desk. There was a small business card stuck in the page, and she could see pictures of chests with arrows and annotations. Maybe someone had been looking up Claire Oh's Westman chest? As she moved around to the other side of the desk to get a better look, Tim called to her to come down with him.

"I hear someone in the back office," he said. "Let's go introduce you to Blake."

Jane decided she could revisit the gallery later. It seemed much more interesting to meet half of the "we at" boys.

When they entered the office, beautifully appointed as Jane knew it would be, they found it empty. What Tim had heard was music from the CD player. Mozart, of course. Jane felt certain that the *Best of Motown* or *Willie Nelson's Greatest Hits* were rarely played at Campbell and LaSalle.

A smaller door at the back of the office was open to the outside, and Jane walked out following a trail that led to a sparkling creek. Jane could see it shining like a ribbon at the end of the walk. The sun, the trees, the beauty of this place began to overwhelm her. Jane thought about the most recent nugget of Belinda St. Germain's treatise that she had read.

> Does a tree need one more leaf to make it more perfect, more complete? Look to nature to find what you need as opposed to what you might want. A brook is a small treasure when it has the right amount of water, a danger when it overflows its banks. We think of a flood as an aberration, a crisis. What about the flood of useless items overflowing your kitchen cupboards and closet shelves?

Belinda had a point. The trees were perfect, the brook babbled, even the stones in the path seemed the perfect mix of pattern and randomness. The sun, sinking lower in the sky, sent the light slicing through this clean and crisp air, providing picture-perfect illumination.

Yes, Belinda. Jane thought, *I don't need anything in this moment except what nature has given me: trees, water, stones, light.* Even the red wool plaid shirt by the water's edge seemed a welcome splash of contrasting color on the landscape. *Oh, Belinda, if only you were here to see this man drinking in the clear water, in this perfect setting,* thought Jane, noting that the only sounds were the whispering leaves and the few faint notes of Mozart that filtered down from the barn.

Jane watched the man at the water's edge. The realization that he wasn't drinking, wasn't moving, wasn't breathing, washed over her slowly at first, then flooded her system. She ran to his side and pushed him over, getting his face out of the water. She listened for breath, then started hitting his chest, breathing into his mouth, hoping she remembered her CPR class instructions. She heard footsteps behind her, turned, and saw Tim punching numbers on his cell phone. Someone new came up behind her, moved her aside, and took over the CPR, pleading with the plaid-shirted man between breaths, "Come on, Rick, damn it, come on."

Jane turned to Tim, who had just finished giving directions over the phone and whispered, " 'We at Campbell and LaSalle' seem to have a dead man on our hands."

5

I once visited a client who described herself as completely happy while shopping. The happiness turned to depression as soon as she returned home and found that she had no proper place for her new "find." How many objects can you see, just by looking around in your own space, that have no "proper place?" Does it make you feel disturbed, claustrophobic, out of control?

—BELINDA ST. GERMAIN, *Overstuffed*

Blake Campbell stood in front of the large, stone mantel in the great room of the main lodge and faced those assembled. Although he claimed to have been sleeping when he was summoned from "quiet time," he now looked alert, competent, with a sad-but-of-course-I'll-cope-someone-has-to-lead-the-troops tightness around his perfect mouth. Jane had never seen anyone in person who looked and sounded more like a model, and she had been in advertising for over fifteen years. Still, she shook her head and whispered to Tim that she had never even seen a head shot as perfect looking as Blake Campbell in the flesh.

"He's always reminded me of a sketch—no flesh and blood. Like those Hamilton cartoons in the *New Yorker*. The rich, naïve narcissists," said Tim, adding, "he's a nice guy, though. I've always liked Blake. His looks have worked against him actually. And his name. And his money. No one takes him seriously."

"My favorite was when the man and woman are in this barn looking at a hen and the guy is holding an egg up and saying, 'Nature never ceases to blow my mind,'" said Jane.

Tim looked at her.

"My favorite Hamilton cartoon," Jane said. "Who's the reality check?"

Jane gestured toward another man who walked in and stood next to Blake Campbell. For every impeccable cashmere strand woven into Blake Campbell's Missoni sweater, this man had an answering unraveled acrylic thread dangling from his generic V-neck. The unshaven scruff that added just the right touch of Hollywood-style ruggedness to Blake Campbell's face, made this man look unclean, unkempt, and vaguely unhealthy—more like someone who had been in bed with the flu for a few days. He had an I-must-cope look in his eyes as well, but it was more of an I've-always-had-to-clean-up-the-messes-haven't-I stare.

A third man entered and Jane recognized him as Glen LaSalle. She had heard him give booth lectures at several antique shows. He'd appeared on several of the shelter and appraisal programs that had sprung up on television, following in the well-made footprints of the *Antiques Roadshow*. Average height, thinning hair, and serious glasses, he had the professorial look of the expert. Most recently Jane had encountered him when he'd pushed her aside and took over the CPR for the plaid-shirted man down by the stream.

"Funny how Glen LaSalle is the spokesman of Campbell

and LaSalle. You'd think Blake would be the figurehead," said Jane.

"Too pretty. I told you, no one takes him seriously, even though he's just as much the brains. He's certainly the chemist in the operation," said Tim.

Although Blake and the scruffy man were in front of the crowd of anxious residents, artists, and clients who had assembled when the "gathering bell" had rung, it was Glen LaSalle who began addressing the group from his position by the side door.

"Sorry to disturb quiet time, but we have some terrible news," Glen began. Two uniformed policeman came into the room through the side door opposite LaSalle. Jane, as she watched the faces of the listeners, saw worry turn to fear in an instant.

"One of our guests has had an accident," Glen said, then stopped. He looked like he wasn't sure what or how much to say now that he had started this whole thing and looked first at Blake, who gave the slightest shrug, then at the man next to Blake.

"I'm Sergeant Murkel and I apologize for my appearance. I was off duty when I responded to this call. I'm afraid that one of the resident artists here, Mr. Rick Moore, was found dead at approximately three-ten P.M." Murkel went on to explain that although it was much too early to say anything definitively, Mr. Moore appeared to have drowned.

Jane watched the jaws drop, the fidgeting hands still, the eyes blink, the breathing quiet as the eleven people in the room took in the news. One woman, age thirty-something to fifty-something with straight hair hanging to her waist, took the hands of the woman and man on either side of her on the leather couch and bowed her head, as if leading them in prayer.

"Drowned?" Tim whispered to Jane. "The creek is only ten inches deep."

"He was lying facedown in it. I didn't really get a good look, but he didn't look banged up and the bushes and plants weren't trampled like there had been a fight or anything. No blood. His clothes weren't torn. The only thing at all . . ."

"Jeez, what are you like when you *do* get a good look?" Tim asked. "You scoped out that scene like it was the flea market table at the St. Stan's rummage sale."

". . . strange," Jane continued, paying no attention to Tim's interruption, "was that he didn't have shoes on, just big, thick walking socks, the kind padded on the bottom and the instep, but no shoes. In fact, one of the socks had snagged and was practically off. His left foot was bare."

Sergeant Murkel had said that he and the other officers would like to speak with everyone. They were going to set up an office of sorts in Blake Campbell's studio, which was located between the barn woodshop and the gallery, which was directly behind the lodge. Jane took out the Campbell and LaSalle booklet Tim had given her earlier and studied the map on the back. Although it wasn't to scale—every building and landmark was more spread out than this cozy little drawing implied—all the visitors' cabins, artists' residences, and work spaces were drawn in. The lodge faced east, and the gallery was just west of it. Jane tried to memorize it like a watch face. If the lodge and gallery were at twelve o'clock, then the barn was at ten. That would put Blake's studio at eleven, just behind the trees from where Jane had found Rick Moore.

Jane saw Blake wave and nod to someone in the doorway to his right. Jane supposed it led to the kitchen since the young woman standing there wore a white canvas apron over her tight blue jeans. Blake then signaled to Glen, pointing toward the kitchen and nodding.

"Cheryl and the staff have tea prepared, but instead of setting up in here as usual, we're going to ask that you please serve yourselves from the kitchen and be as comfortable as you can here in the great room while the police finish up their business," said Glen, and after one beat, "Rick loved tea time. Especially the way we at Campbell and LaSalle celebrated it every day. I think we should all go on and enjoy it now."

" 'We at Campbell and LaSalle' love our tea?" Jane asked. "He's an animated brochure."

"I'm going to cut him some slack here," Tim said. "I think maybe there's just some comfort in retreating into a script."

At least the script had merit. Jane realized that she had never seen a tea table laid out quite like the spread at Campbell and LaSalle.

There were the sandwiches: smoked salmon and heavenly date bread and butter; cucumber, cress, thinly sliced radishes, again with that real, pale butter that made you forget your name when it melted on your tongue; and, as a matter of fact, tongue; and pastrami, shaved so thinly and placed so delicately on rye rounds, painted so beautifully with a brown mustard, that each little morsel was a work of art; and the chicken salad and curried egg salad on dense white bread cut into shapes of hens and eggs.

The sweet trays were laden with slices of cake and scones; tiny muffins that looked carved out of some rich marble; butter cookies and fruit tarts; and whole multi-tiered trays reserved for chocolate: dark chocolate mint cakes, éclairs, slices of seven-layer cocoa bliss. Bowls of whipped cream and fresh fruit were interspersed with the trays.

"The berries alone are exotic. Where in Michigan in late fall do you get strawberries that look like that?" Jane asked, overwhelmed with the bounty laid out before her.

"Glen and Blake are both loaded: family money, earned money, inherited money. They're green magnets. This property belonged to Blake's grandfather. It was the family compound, hunting lodge, and summer camp. He and Glen decided to run this place from here and make it a mecca for artists and people who appreciated fine things," said Tim, heaping his plate with sandwiches.

"Are they a couple?"

"Not everyone who dresses well and has taste and good manners is gay, my dear," Tim said, adding, "more's the pity. Glen was widowed years ago. His wife was a painter who died in a car accident. Blake's never married, but as you can imagine, there are several willing consorts-in-waiting."

Jane looked over at Blake, who was drinking tea and talking to the long-haired woman speaking directly into his ear. He was bending close to her, listening intently, and nodding. The police were circulating, asking guests one by one to step out into Blake's studio for interviews.

A blond young man, wearing jeans so covered in paint splatters that it looked more like a purposeful fashion statement than the garb of the workingman, came over to Tim and began talking as if they had been studio mates for years.

"I warned him about that tent, but no, he was such a know-it-all, really more like a got-to-know-it-all, I guess. He kept saying he had to learn the process. That was his thing, the process," he said, shoving a curried egg salad sandwich into his mouth.

"I'm Jane and this is Tim," said Jane. "What are you talking about?"

Tim turned to her, his back to the blond, and mouthed more than whispered, close to her face, "Very subtle PI technique," and turned back to the man now working on the smoked salmon.

"We just arrived. We were walking around, and Jane found Rick down at the creek."

"I'm Mickey. Painter," he said. "Sorry I just launched in on you, but Rick, man, if anybody was going to fuck up around here . . . oh, sorry," Mickey said, bowing his head to Jane.

She was touched. When did any man, especially such a young man, show respect by censoring language anymore? Her own son, singing along with rap on the radio, half the time sounded like he was raised in a sewer. Jane never knew whether it was better to inform Nick that he was saying/singing things in front of her that he shouldn't or better to ignore it so he would never know what most of it meant. Wishful, dreamy parental fog was the place where she most frequently found herself. But here was Mickey, in his little Eminem blond crew cut, apologizing for dropping the F-bomb. Nice to know that people still believed in civil discourse.

"It's okay, nothing I haven't heard before," Jane said, smiling.

"Cool," Mickey said, looking down at her feet. "They just looked kind of new, and sometimes chicks get freaked out when accidents happen, you know?"

Jane looked down and saw the salmon and crème fraîche on the toe of her left boot and wondered how long she would have to wait before frantically cleaning it so the potent combo of oil and butterfat would not leave a permanent stain.

"So as I was saying, if anybody was going to fuck up around here, it would be me is what all these uptight fuckers think, not Rick. He was always careful. You know, read the labels and directions and all that bullshit."

Tim nodded. "So you think it was related to the chemical . . . ?"

"Yeah, sure. Rick was spending so much time in Dr. Campbellstein's laboratory, we were calling him Igor," Mickey said, snorting and dropping chicken salad on Jane's other foot. This time he just smiled, looking like he might high-five her.

"Mickey?" The woman with the long, straight hair called and gestured to Mickey to join her and Blake at the sweets table.

"Good thing," said Jane. "He looked like he might want to turn me into a canvas for a food-fight series. What chemicals are you talking about?"

"I heard a few others talking about Rick Moore. He did a lot of work aging and coloring wood for restorations. He was experimenting with some of Blake's recipes. They figure he was overcome and disoriented and headed outside."

"And ended up facedown in the creek?"

"If your eyes were burning from ammonia or if you couldn't breathe or were gagging, it might seem like the thing to do . . . get up close and personal with a cool drink of water."

"Pardon me? Tim? We've met here before. Roxanne Pell."

Jane hadn't noticed Roxanne before. She must have been standing in back when Murkel spoke to them. Jane would have remembered her. A striking redhead, tall, slender, with a quality that Jane would have to call poise. Comfortable in their own skin was how Charley characterized people like Roxanne. Their acceptance of self gave them their beauty. Jane, for just a moment, wondered if it was too late in life for her to get some of this kind of confidence for herself.

". . . and this is Jane Wheel. She's joining my business, and I wanted her to see for herself where very lucky pieces of furniture and art get their new leases on life."

"I am so sorry about your unfortunate introduction to Campbell and LaSalle," said Roxanne, shaking Jane's hand. "Nothing like this has ever happened before. Even with all the woodworking we do, we haven't had so much as a cut that needed stitching. This is painful for all of us."

"Was Mr. Moore here with a family or friend?" Jane asked.

Roxanne shook her head. "He came for a month or so every year. More if we had a special project for him. One of Blake's people, although he participated in every aspect of craft. He could build, and he did exquisite carving. He painted, too. Called himself an amateur, but some of his landscapes were quite fine. Glen wanted some of his pieces for the gallery, but Rick was shy about it, just liked the process. He wanted to learn about finishes this time, so Blake was working with him."

"I'm not sure I understand. Is this a school, too?" asked Jane.

"This is, let's see, an art gallery, a summer camp, a retreat, a shrine, a commune." Roxanne paused and looked at Tim. "What else, Tim?"

"A congregation, a country club, a finishing school, a vocational high school, a gourmet paradise," said Tim, gesturing toward the rapidly emptying chocolate tower and excusing himself to partake.

"Campbell and LaSalle is many things to many people," Roxanne said, "it's so hard to characterize."

"What about you? What's your field?" asked Jane, not sure if that was the kind of thing one was supposed to ask at Campbell and LaSalle.

"I'm a secretary," Roxanne said with a smile.

Jane tried not to look surprised or skeptical.

"Really, I am. I also paint a little, and I'm trying to write short stories. My degree is in art history. But I keep the books, do the mail, assign the cabins, hand out the keys, answer correspondence. That sort of thing. Actually, I guess I'm more like a cross between a concierge and a head counselor.

"And every couple of years, I get engaged to Blake," Roxanne said, smiling, "whether I need to or not."

"Are you now?" asked Jane, trying to imitate Roxanne's teasing tone.

"I don't think so," said Roxanne. She looked down at her left hand. There was a pale circle around the left finger of her otherwise tanned hand. "I think I took the ring off a few weeks ago. I can't remember if it was because of a project

I was doing or if it was because Blake disappeared into himself." She shook her head. "When he becomes immersed, he doesn't even remember his own name, let alone mine. Makes me feel foolish to be wearing an engagement ring."

"Sounds like a difficult relationship for you," said Jane.

"Sometimes, but as long as there is Campbell and LaSalle, the entity, to attend to, I keep busy. As long as I can immerse myself, I can spare the genius every now and then," said Roxanne. She smiled and patted Tim's arm, who was back with his treats. "Anyway, I'm glad you're here, just sorry about the business with Rick."

Roxanne helped herself to a truffle and quickly named the people in the room for Jane. She had just finished when a commanding, husky voice boomed out.

"We'll gather at eight then?"

Jane turned to see the long-haired woman, whom Roxanne had referred to as Martine when she'd given Jane the rundown, addressing the group at large. Martine turned and walked out, her hair hanging down like a cape across her shoulders.

"Martine's a poet. She's also studying to be . . ." Roxanne broke off and looked over toward Blake and Glen, who were deep in discussion. "I'm sorry. I should find out about calls I'll have to make. I'm not sure I ever heard Rick talk about any family, but there must be someone I'll have to talk to." Roxanne squared her shoulders. "Martine is going to lead a life celebration for Rick at eight here in the great room. Dinner will be at nine-thirty. Hope it's not too late. We always keep a more European clock," Roxanne said, smiled, and glided over to Blake and Glen, pulling a small tablet and pen from her pocket.

Jane thought she looked like one of the elegant house servants on *Masterpiece Theater. She should be wearing a big ring with keys and tools for keeping the castle running,* Jane thought, *like a head housekeeper or headmistress or . . .*

"Your lips were moving," Tim said. "Put this in your mouth so you don't give yourself away."

"As what?" Jane asked, taking the éclair and doing what she was told.

"Junk picker in hog heaven. When your lips move, you want something. It's your tell. I've told you a million times you give yourself away."

"What do I want here?" Jane asked. *Besides Roxanne's hair,* she thought, but didn't say. She looked around. The furniture was vintage Arts and Crafts, the paintings, the candlesticks, the pottery, everything everywhere you looked was stunning. But it was also perfectly placed. Nothing could leave. It was impossible to want to take anything away from this setting.

"Nothing," she answered herself. "Reading Belinda is working."

"Liar, liar," said Tim. "You want plenty. You want the biggest thing of all."

"Yeah?" said Jane, wiping her mouth with one of Campbell and LaSalle's fine monogrammed napkins. "And what might that one thing be, smarty pants?"

"Answers."

Yes, Jane supposed she did want answers. Was the chest Claire Oh had shown her the same one she had brought to Campbell and LaSalle? Was it, or one of them—if there were two—or some part of it, authentic Westman? And how many questions was that anyway?

But something else nagged at her. As a picker, as a detective, as a wife, as a mother, as a friend, as a woman, she had to face a fairly huge question. Had she become cold-blooded, coldhearted? What was it about Campbell and LaSalle that had allowed her, encouraged her, to consume and enjoy an elegant high tea one hour after finding the body of a dead man?

6

How would you feel if every window, every door was blocked? You cannot see outside; you cannot walk outside. There is no light, no escape. Your unnecessary possessions and disorganized clutter block the way. When you strip away the debris, you let in the sunshine. You are free.

—BELINDA ST. GERMAIN, *Overstuffed*

No, Jane wasn't sure she wanted answers. Well, yes, eventually she did. But as she had told Tim, the most important thing was to figure out the right questions.

"Trying to sound like Guru Belinda or Yoda?" Tim had asked.

Now, settling into her simple, yet elegant quarters in one of the small visitor's cabins, she tried to sort out her current calendar of events. Claire Oh had been so certain of the chest's authenticity when she'd first found it, when she'd brought it to Campbell and LaSalle. Why, then, was she so quick to believe it was a fake when she saw it again? Despite the drawers and dowels and patination and all the false things she had pointed out about it, she still stared at it, stroked its carvings . . . she still believed in it somehow. That's what was so puzzling. And if all those signs of forgery were so obvious . . . ?

Of course, it was so obvious. Jane jumped up out of the mission rocker provided as her casual chair and dug through her bag to find her cell phone. The first time she dialed Oh's number, the phone went into "roaming" and clicked off. She walked to another corner of the room, turned her head, spun around, and dialed again. This time it went through. She smiled to herself. Tim made fun of her movements with her phone, called it "the cellular ballet," but it worked, her voodoo with electronics. It was her only weapon against the avalanche of new products and wireless wonders that flooded the market monthly. She might not understand them, but she could woo them.

"Oh," Oh answered.

How could Jane break him of that disconcerting habit?

"It's Jane Wheel, Detective Oh. Is Claire around? I have a question," Jane said.

"Resting, but I'll . . ."

"No," said Jane. She paused. If she was going to be any kind of detective, she would have to get over this self-effacing, shy, don't-want-to-bother-anybody attitude.

"Actually, it is important and I'm not sure I'll be able to get through later. There's a memorial service and a late dinner and I . . ." Jane stopped when she thought she heard a click on the phone. "Hello?"

"Who died?" asked Claire.

"I thought you were sleeping, Claire," said Oh.

"I heard the phone. Who died?"

"Rick Moore, a woodworker, painter, everything guy who was here as a guest artist, and I found him . . ."

"Mrs. Wheel, you didn't find another body?" asked Oh. Jane thought she heard a small sigh.

"Rick?" said Claire.

"You knew him?" Jane asked.

"He was a regular up there. I knew them all," Claire said.

There was a click, and Jane wasn't sure who had hung up.

"Hello?"

"I'm here," said Oh. "Claire hung up."

"Here's what I want to know. Claire showed me all the evidence that the chest was phony: those drawers fitting too well, the machine cuts. They were so obvious, why didn't Claire notice them right away? Before delivering the chest to Horace Cutler's gallery?"

"Good question," said Oh.

"I'll give you one answer I came up with: because she didn't want to see them. When you spot something that you think might be the real thing, the genuine article, sometimes you stop yourself from seeing everything . . ."

"Yeah," said Tim, who had walked through the screen door from his adjoining cabin, "historical blindness."

"Yes," said Jane.

"What?" asked Oh.

"Sorry, Tim just walked in. It is a kind of blindness. You want so much to be the one who found the Revere candlestick or the Meissen teapot or the Faberge egg . . ."

"Or Tiffany lamp or authentic Galle," added Tim.

"Right," Jane said.

"What?" asked Oh.

"Stop talking, Tim, it's confusing," Jane said. "Detective Oh, if Claire fell deeply enough in love with the chest, believed it to be a Westman chest, it's possible she could have missed something; but now that I'm at Campbell and LaSalle . . ."

"Right," said Tim. "You're absolutely right."

"Yes," said Jane, beaming.

"I'm sorry, Mrs. Wheel, but I'm missing something," said Oh.

"Campbell and LaSalle would not have missed anything on this chest. They would have authenticated it or exposed it or whatever it is they do when they consult or evaluate. No one here would have missed the kind of things Claire pointed out to me," said Jane. "Someone would have told Claire that it was a nice, old, well-carved piece, with some new parts added or whatever, and they would have asked her how much she wanted done on it, as a piece of furniture. They wouldn't have authenticated it as a Westman chest unless they believed it was one."

"Did they?" asked Tim.

Jane looked at him blankly.

"Was it delivered to Horace Cutler?" asked Tim.

"No, Claire said she drove up here and picked the chest up herself and brought it to Cutler. His assistant signed for it, and she didn't see him again until that night at the charity show."

"When Claire picked it up, they must have gone over the work with her, showed her what they did. No one here would have missed anything like the joins in the drawers," said Tim.

"She was in a hurry to get back for the show that night. She had been on the road since before dawn. Maybe, in her hurry, she just had them load it . . ."

"Janie, would you not want to see it? Your baby? All put together, all dressed up?" asked Tim.

"Mrs. Wheel," said Oh. It was the loudest Jane had ever heard him speak.

"I'm so sorry," Jane said into the phone, "I got lost talking to Tim."

"I am still missing something," said Oh.

Of course he's missing something—everything. His wife either really missed the boat, or she deliberately tried to pass off a fake to Horace Cutler. Jane was trying to figure out how to present this to Oh as a kind of nonjudgmental, hypothetical question or comment.

"We need to look at the papers, the research, or recap of the work done at Campbell and LaSalle," said Jane.

"Damn. Keys," Oh said, not exactly directly into the phone.

"What?" Jane asked, thinking that it was the first time she had ever heard him use a four-letter word. Damn counted as a four-letter word, didn't it?

". . . what I'm missing," said Oh.

"I'm sorry, I'll fill you in on what Tim and I were talking about," said Jane.

"Not now, Mrs. Wheel. What I'm missing at the moment is my wife," said Oh, "and quite possibly, yes, damn it."

"Detective Oh?"

"My wife and her car are gone, Mrs. Wheel," said Oh. Then, remembering his impeccable manners, "May I call you back later, please?"

"I didn't even get to the other possibility," said Jane, holding the now silent cell phone. Claire might have been blinded to the problems of the piece, but what if she wasn't. What if she had just decided to fake it?

"Tim, maybe Claire knew the chest was good and old and almost good enough and got somebody to patch it up . . ."

" 'We at Campbell and LaSalle' do not patch . . ."

"Wasn't Rick a carver? Didn't Roxanne or Mickey say he was a carver? Maybe he was in on some . . ."

"Didn't you hear Oh? Case closed," said Tim.

Jane looked around the small cabin. Gorgeous wood floors with a small, hand-hooked rug on the side of the iron bed. There was a featherbed and a down comforter and several plump pillows. The bathroom was small but perfectly equipped. A row of pegs on the wall held large white towels, and a hunk of handmade soap was threaded through a piece of braided twine. There was even a petite fireplace, kindling and wood in a brass bucket on the terra-cotta apron; and in case more mood lighting was required, there was a row of fat beeswax candles along the oak mantel.

"It's like a honeymoon spot," Jane said, shaking her head.

"The proximity to the neighbors might cramp some people's style," said Tim.

Jane looked out the wooden screen door. A small porch held three rockers and a wooden lounge chair. Directly across the porch was an identical screen door leading to a twin of Jane's cabin. Tim assured her that his was equally charming.

"The details are their trademark," said Tim. "I'll bet that soap-on-a-rope thing was some craft project at their school, and they even grew the frigging hemp."

"When did you start saying 'frigging'?" asked Jane.

"About the time you did, when you pointed out the lyrics to some of the rap Nick was singing along to. Is that it? Singing along with rap? Or do you rap along with rap?" Tim asked.

"What did you say?" Jane asked.

"My name is Timmy L., and I'm here to say," Tim began in his best gangster voice.

"Before. Why did you say the case was closed?" Jane asked.

"We got the ex-cop's wife / going on the run / she knew the chest was fake / and she got herself a gun." Tim seemed to be trying to dance, but he looked more like he had been bitten by a poisonous insect.

"Shut up, Tim," said Jane. "It's not that simple."

"Let's hear it," said Tim. "Let's hear you complicate it, babe."

"We're talking about Claire Oh, who herself is a respected dealer. If she knew she had a fake, even a good fake, why would she try to pass it off on Horace Cutler? That's the hitch there. If she was going to be crooked, why not go to a customer who trusted her and would pay her the money and never question the authenticity? And more important, why go to all the trouble and expense of bringing it through the university of fine wood here at Campbell and LaSalle just to substitute another chest? Why not just have some guy in Chicago do it, who would just fix it up and follow her orders?

"And the time frame is another thing," Jane said, sitting down on the bed. She had packed only six items in her suitcase, having accepted the "essential packing challenge" in chapter 3 of Belinda's book, so was already settled in her little cabin.

"Claire picked up the chest here and dropped it at Horace's place, then went home, showered, changed, and made it to the antiques show on time. There was no time to stop anywhere else, to make a switch, to stash a big piece of furniture. And that's another thing," Jane said, bouncing on the bed. "She drove up alone. She couldn't have done anything with that piece alone. It's way too heavy for one person to move."

"How much was the appraisal? How much did she sell it to Horace for? What was he charging?" Tim asked.

Jane shook her head.

"It's not an exact science or anything, especially since there hasn't been one on the market. There are only two and one is in a museum, so"—Tim said, looking as if he were running a calculator behind his eyes—"I'm guessing a big American piece like that could go as high as two hundred thousand dollars if there was enough buzz generated in advance."

"You know what's bothering me more than anything?" asked Jane.

"That you didn't bring pajamas?" Tim asked.

"Couldn't work them into my six. I really wanted to bring this sweater. I've got a silk undershirt on I can sleep in. In fact, I layered a lot since she didn't say . . ."

"Spare me those details and tell me what's bothering you more than anything."

"Right. It's the ties," said Jane.

"How will I know when you get Alzheimer's? Will you tell me how I'm supposed to know when you actually stop connecting the dots?" Tim asked, throwing up his hands.

"Even though I had never met Claire Oh before, I liked her because of those ties she buys for Detective Oh. You know the ones, the bowling pins, the Dr Pepper bottles, those great old novelty ties she finds at sales."

Tim nodded.

"That said something to me about who she was, what kind of person she was. I mean, she found great ties and she got him to wear them," Jane said.

"I expected to really like her, maybe be a little jealous because she obviously is so much higher on the picker food chain than I am; but still, I expected her to have a sense of humor, a sense of, I don't know . . . whimsy or something."

"And she was flat," said Tim.

"As a pancake," said Jane. "She was as snobby and ordinary as any dealer, as . . ."

"As Horace Cutler, probably," said Tim. "He was a piece of work. All fake-almost-Oxford sounding, even though he came from Iowa or someplace.

"I don't think I've met the real Claire yet. Something's going on with her that's got Oh puzzled, too. I would bet . . . ," said Jane, stopping when she heard a gentle knock on the cabin door.

The rumpled policeman who had introduced himself at the "gathering" before teatime poked his head in. "Hey, you're both here; that's great," said Sergeant Murkel. "Sorry it's taken me so long to get over to talk to you."

"I did give a statement to someone before tea," said Jane.

"Yes, yes, I saw that, but I just had a few more questions, a few loose ends to tie up," said Murkel.

Jane nodded. She didn't know everything about police investigations, but she certainly knew about loose ends. They were practically her specialty.

"Mrs. Wheel, why did you say you were up here at Campbell and LaSalle?"

"I didn't," said Jane. "I wasn't asked. But I'm happy to tell you. Tim has several pieces up here, and he's training me in the antique-dealing business, so he thought it was time I saw where good furniture goes to be reborn."

"Unfortunate you had to be the one to find Mr. Moore."

Jane looked at Tim. She knew it was only a matter of time. She was about to be punished for relishing that tea. She was going to have to admit that she had a knack for finding dead bodies: Bakelite, McCoy, bodies—practically her specialty, too.

"Yes," said Jane, "I wanted to ask you about that. Do you know exactly how he drowned?"

"Drowned? Who said that?"

"You did. At the lodge. And he was facedown in the water when I found him," Jane said.

"Hmm," Murkel said. "Yes. Does the fireplace work?"

"I think so," Jane said, wondering if he really wanted information or just wanted to see what the guest cabins looked like.

"It appears that Mr. Moore drowned, yes," said Murkel, his eyes still roaming around the cabin.

"Was he working with chemicals or something that caused him to . . . ?" Jane stopped.

"If I need to talk to you again, will I find you here? You're staying for the weekend?" asked Murkel.

"Blake said there'd be no problem if we didn't have a problem," said Tim.

"And you don't have a problem," Murkel asked, looking at Jane, "with finding a dead man and all?"

"What was that about?" Tim asked after they heard Murkel step off the porch and into the dark. "Does he think *you* drowned the guy?"

Jane had to admit it was odd, creepy. He seemed to be looking for something in the cabin. He didn't give anything away, but he certainly seemed curious. And if Murkel was suspicious, shouldn't Jane be suspicious? Claire Oh had found Horace Cutler dead. Jane had found Rick Moore dead. Claire knew Rick Moore, therefore . . . there wasn't any transitive or intransitive property to connect this up. But Jane could feel some kind of web spinning over her head, something that included all of them.

As usual Tim did not approve of what Jane planned to wear to the evening service for Rick Moore, or life celebration, or whatever it was Martine had planned for the evening. There wasn't any choice, though. Jeans and a black sweater would have to do. Between Jane's plain taste for functional and easy clothes and Belinda's packing instructions, Jane didn't have a lot of options.

"What would anyone expect? Who knew there would be a memorial service?" Jane asked.

"I don't know, but everybody around here seems to be taking it in stride. That Martine had it pretty well planned by the time I had gotten to the sweets table at tea," Tim said.

"Yes, everyone did seem fairly calm, except maybe Mickey. He was a little wired. What about Claire's reaction? asked Jane.

"What?"

"She said she knew Rick Moore. What would you say if I told you somebody you knew had died?"

"How terrible, what happened? How did he die?"

"Yeah, unless . . . ," Jane said.

"Damn it. There's a spot on this shirt. I'm going to run next door and change. I'll be ready in a sec," said Tim.

Jane nodded. She didn't want to finish her thought out loud anyway. But to herself, she continued, *Yeah, unless you already knew.*

7

After craning my neck to see around a centerpiece at a dinner party, I finally asked permission to move it. I not only couldn't see the other guests, I couldn't even hear them. The cacophony of "things" present on the table, in the room, drowned out any meaningful conversation. Ah, for the simple table. . . .

—BELINDA ST. GERMAIN, *Overstuffed*

Jane was glad she hadn't removed her flashlight from her bag. It was one of the objects that she had, at first, considered an "expendable" in the Belinda St. Germain vernacular. She hadn't actually removed any items from her bag yet. She had, however, added the following: a Campbell and LaSalle brochure and map, several large paper napkins from the roadside grill she and Tim had stopped at on their way to the compound, Belinda St. Germain's miniworkbook to keep track of things she thought of that could be "subtracted from the multiple lives" she led, according to St. Belinda, as Jane was now beginning to think of her, and this flashlight that she had brought in from the car. Yes, it made her bag even heavier than before, but Jane was just enough of a camper to think a good flashlight is worth the trouble of carrying.

Tim had laughed when she shined the light on the path in front of them.

"Why, Nancy Drew, you think of everything!"

"Look, Bess, I know we look like the cover illustration from *The Hidden Staircase*, but I don't want to break my neck here. These little prairie lights or whatever they call them are sweet, but they don't really illuminate the path enough for me," said Jane.

The paths were dimly lit with small lights that blended into the landscape. The idea, Tim had told her, was to use as little light as possible, so the starscape would be visible for all. The sky was magnificent, clear and without that hazy Chicago skyline glow. Jane could see the constellations more clearly than she ever had. Unfortunately she didn't know her Orion from her Cassiopeia, and she made a mental note to see if the old star finder she had bought for Nick at a sale was still in the zipper pocket of her leather travel bag. She had put it there for one of their family trips to Kankakee to visit Don and Nellie but had been so distracted by Nellieness when there that she never took a moment to look up into the night sky. When visiting her mother, Jane was more likely to be looking into Conrad's *Heart of Darkness* (ah, the horror, the horror) than the *Good Guide to Starry Nights*. Or, as Nellie always told her, "Don't look up, look down. You're much less likely to step in shit." *No wonder I am able to be such a swell mother to Nick, I am awash in maternal wisdom*, she thought.

Unlike Kankakee, however, Campbell and LaSalle *was* the kind of place that promised you great rewards if you took the time to look up. Uh-oh. She was beginning to sound like the brochure. Ah well, if she could find the star map, she'd stick it in her pocket and tomorrow night dazzle Tim with her we-at-Campbell-and-LaSalle-know-our-stars stuff.

"Do you know who lives in that cabin?" asked Jane.

Tim shook his head. "I haven't quite got the lay of the land yet. I think I know who's here; I'm just not sure where.

"I'll take who for starters," said Jane.

"Why?"

"Why what?" asked Jane.

"Why who?" asked Tim, clearly enjoying playing Abbot to Jane's Costello.

"Well, I've been thinking about the Westman chest—or whatever it is. Let's just say it was the real deal when Claire Oh brought it here, and, at a glance, it seemed to be the real deal when she picked it up. She delivered it to Horace without really examining it because she was in a rush to get to the show. Someone here might have made the switch, I mean if it's really worth so much money. There are trucks loaded with furniture coming in and out all day. There are plenty of opportunities to get a piece in and out of here. During that afternoon quiet time, it's a graveyard," said Jane.

"Literally," said Tim.

"So if someone wanted to make a switch, give Claire Oh the fake chest, there would be plenty of opportunity," said Jane.

"Opportunity, maybe," agreed Tim, "but what's the motive? Antique forgers are people who want to make money, and how is someone from Campbell and LaSalle going to sell a Westman chest without any publicity? An auction would be the way to go for the big bucks, and that would take a buzz. If Claire and Horace were to come forward and made a scene, that would be the ball game."

They were almost at the entrance to the lodge. Jane

wasn't so sure that what Tim had just said was right. It wouldn't be the ball game at all if someone just wanted the Westman chest for a personal collection. Jane knew there were people out there who didn't mind keeping something in a vault, as long as they were the ones with the combination. After all, weren't there stolen works of art that people bought and kept to stare at in private? They couldn't display them because everyone in the art world knew they were stolen, but weren't some paintings worth having to some people, even if they were for their eyes only. Perhaps especially if they were for their eyes only?

So there was the possibility of a Campbell and LaSalle switch. But why would that have led to the murder of Horace Cutler? He had already made a scene about the chest being a forgery, so it wasn't to shut him up. Someone at Campbell and LaSalle might have wanted their switcheroo kept quiet for a while, but Horace hadn't publicly accused them; he had publicly accused Claire Oh of cheating him. It would be up to Claire Oh to prove that the chest she had brought to Campbell and LaSalle was a different one than the one she had picked up. She would have been the one to point the finger and cause a scandal. Jane had to call the Oh house again and see if Claire was back. She wanted to ask her if anyone knew about the chest going to Campbell and LaSalle. For that matter, did anyone else know about the chest itself besides Horace Cutler? And did Claire know who had worked on it here at Campbell and LaSalle?

The great room was already full when Jane and Tim entered. Martine was standing in front of the stone fireplace. With a dozen lit candles behind her and that great mane of hair caught up in a high, braided tail, she looked like some kind of priestess about to announce tonight's sacrifice. Mickey, seemingly unaffected by the goddesslike performance about to begin, was helping himself to a scotch from the enormous walnut sideboard. As soon as he saw Blake though, Jane watched him leave his drink and cross the room to him. Blake looked in his direction as Mickey talked, waving a card that looked like it had paint chips on it, but Blake didn't seem to look *at* him as much as *through* him. Mickey looked ready to start dancing or waving his arms in front of Blake's face to get his full attention.

Tim took Jane's elbow and escorted her over to the group of Campbell and LaSalle guests and staff whom she hadn't yet met. At its center was Glen LaSalle.

"I'm so sorry that your first visit to Campbell and LaSalle is marked by Rick's tragic accident," said Glen.

Jane nodded, agreed, everything in keeping with the finder-of-the-body etiquette that she was beginning to know quite well. Perhaps she, like Brenda St. Germain, could find her writing niche with books like *How to Break the News That the Man Isn't Breathing*. Why was she feeling so flippant about this? Could it have anything to do with her antipathetic reaction to Martine, who was dramatically serious enough for the whole bunch of them? No one here seemed to be mourning Rick Moore. They just seemed somewhat troubled that it had happened here—and during quiet time. Didn't the man have any real friends or family?

"Glen," asked Jane, as he started to move away, "who were Rick's pals here?"

"Pals?" asked Glen. He shook his head. "We," he hesitated and Jane was positive he was about to say the obligatory "at Campbell and LaSalle," until he caught himself, "are all artists here, and we respect privacy. Rick was devoted to his work, our work, and to bettering his craft. He spent so much time in the archives in Blake's woodshop that you'd think he was studying for his Ph.D. We were a family . . . ," Glen said, then shrugged and gave Jane a small smile. "Did we all really know each other? As with most families, I would have to say no."

Jane turned to Tim when Glen had moved away. "So who were Rick's pals? I didn't catch the answer."

" 'We at Campbell and LaSalle' don't have pals," said Tim. "Get with the program. We do, however, have bedfellows. Strange ones, at that. Martine, for example, has been the consort of both Glen and Blake. Roxanne, as she told you, has been engaged to Blake about a dozen times. Mickey, I believe, sees Annie, the textile artist over there, but only when she's not with Martine. Keeping it straight so far?" Tim asked. "Although no one around here does, if you get my drift.

"Geoff and Jake have been here forever. They started out as master carpenters, building most of the cabins on the property—the ones that weren't here from the old family compound days. Under the influence they've become master restorers and rebuilders. They also work together making custom furniture for a rarified list of clients. They keep to themselves, worker bees more than *les artistes*."

"How about that incredible man over there?" Jane asked. A tall man in a flowing, embroidered caftan stood by the sideboard talking to Mickey. "Not many guys could pull that look off, but he's an exception."

"Silver. One name. Like Madonna or Cher or . . ."

"Or Charo?" Jane offered.

"You will never be able to lie about your age if your popular cultural references date you, dear. But yes, like Charo. Silver founded the literary magazine *YES* about ten years ago, and his loyal readership has kept him in caftans ever since."

"Really?" said Jane. "How can anyone support himself running a literary magazine?"

"Only one caftan. No expenses. He mostly lives here and in other writers' colonies. Gets a grant here and there. Operates as a poet in the schools; gets gigs at small liberal arts colleges. He told me his whole routine one night over some of Campbell and LaSalle's expensive brandy. He's a master guest, you know. Adds class to parties and fund-raisers, won a state arts council award for his poetry a few times during the last decade, just enough name recognition to keep him in the literary loop and just enough obscurity to keep him pure."

"Has he ever hooked up with anyone here?"

"He and Martine look like they borrow each other's clothes occasionally, but I think he's a true loner. Likes his persona to stay mysterious and his overhead to stay minimal."

"Would you like a drink or anything? Martine looks like she's winding up for a long one," said a deep voice behind Jane's right elbow. She turned to see a very pleasant-looking man with brown curly hair and a lazy smile. His brown eyes looked right into Jane's as he introduced himself.

"I'm Scott Tailor," he said. "Spelled like the seamstress."

Jane shook his hand.

"I didn't see you here before, Scott," said Tim. He seemed genuinely delighted to see him now.

"I was out brush hunting the past couple of days. I got

back for dinner and heard about Rick," he said. He shook his head and Jane felt obliged to mutter something soothing, so her "So sad" collided with his "So stupid."

"What?" Jane asked.

"First thing we tell everyone is to keep windows open. All the time. No matter what. Stupid shmuck has been working with finishes long enough to know that breathing that stuff can kill you, especially if you're working in the ammonia tent."

Jane shook her head.

"It's a method for treating wood. Arts and Crafts period. Set up an ammonia tent and let the furniture 'cure' in it to get the right color. We don't even use it that much."

"I've been telling Jane about the Campbell and LaSalle family, and here you come along acting like the disgruntled brother-in-law. No sympathy for the guy?"

"Oh sure, sorry. But come on. He's been coming here on and off for years, following Blake around like a puppy. Shit, if Blake ever stopped fast, you wouldn't be able to find Rick, he'd be shoved right up his . . ."

"So he should have known better?" Jane asked.

"He did know better," said Scott. "And to go and drown when Martine is in residence. She drools for an opportunity like this. You know, she's in training to become a life coach or some bullshit thing like that, and this is right up her alley. Last year she was studying addiction counseling; but she said it was too constraining, and she had so much more to give." Scott drained his glass and poured another. "I'm not kidding. You'd better get a drink. She's an all-purpose triple threat. She will drive you to be addicted to something to escape her; then she'll track you down and counsel you out of it; then she'll make your life a living hell by coaching you through it."

"If she's so awful, why does she have such a position of honor here?" asked Jane.

"Honey, this might be the twenty-first century, but this is still a bunch of old hippies living on a commune," said Scott. "She's phenomenal in the sack."

Scott winked and moved to an overstuffed chair with an ottoman and made himself comfortable. He burrowed into the cushions, put a tolerant smile on his face, and gave his full attention to the front of the room where Martine had raised her arms and begun intoning a welcome.

Tim motioned for Jane to take a seat in the back near the sideboard while he quickly poured two tumblers of Grey Goose over ice. He threw in olives and a little olive juice and handed Jane her dirty martini. Scott watched out of the corner of his eye and nodded his approval, slightly raising his own glass in their direction.

"Do you know him well?" Jane asked Tim.

"Yeah, great guy. Plays the melancholy clown around here. I think he's in love with Roxanne, but it's hard to tell without a scorecard. And she's only got eyes for Blake and this place. He's a terrific painter."

"Oh, my friends, my fellow travelers in this human realm of joy and pain, let's bow our heads together, let us create a silence in which our hopes and wishes can float up, out, around, into the realm above our lowly path, into the realm where our friend Rick is now watching us." Martine spoke these words in a kind of deep, full-throated chant, not unlike some of the poets Jane and Charley heard when they attended university functions for visiting literary artists. Jane always returned from them muttering how much Charley owed her for that one night of pretentious drivel that she would not be able to reclaim. Charley was usually able to call upon one of the nights he had spent at a wrap party for the commercials she had produced in her past life as an advertising executive as a fair exchange in the wasted-minutes-of-our-lives category. Her firm had made it a habit to use any excuse—a finished commercial, a client-pleasing campaign launch, a Clio nomination—to book a table at some trendy downtown restaurant and proceed to drink the night away. She had left that quasicorporate/quasicreative life with a taste for designer vodka and no regrets. As a matter of fact, as she sipped her drink, she realized she might have enjoyed those writers' nights with Charley a lot more if they had had a drink or two to get them through the poetry slams.

"We all knew and loved Rick, a quiet man, a fine craftsman, a determined scholar, and we invite his spirit to stay here, with us, at Campbell and LaSalle, to inspire us and guide us . . ." Martine looked up, her eyes closed, her arms outstretched.

"Eeny-meeny-jelly-beany, the spirits are about to speak," whispered Tim in his best Bullwinkle J. Moose voice.

Jane laughed, sloshing the ice cubes in her glass.

Martine looked straight at her, suddenly all business. "That is a wonderful idea," she said, still looking at Jane. Jane did a *Who me?* kind of take, looking behind her to see if anyone was signaling something to Martine. But, alas, no. Martine, it appeared, had honed in on Jane.

"We must all speak tonight. We will share our stories and our memories of Rick, and in that way keep him with us. Our newest guest, Jane, was the last to arrive here and sadly was the last to experience the earthly manifestation of Rick and perhaps the first to experience his new being as a spirit among us. Please share," Martine said, again holding her arms out, this time in supplication to Jane.

Jane felt the flush moving up from her toes. Who was this woman but the recreation of her seventh-grade teacher, who had constantly called her out and embarrassed her for talking when she was merely laughing at one of smart-aleck Tim's remarks. Jane tried to shake her head in a serious and spiritual manner, one that conveyed the message that she was too overcome to speak, but Martine's eagle eyes bored into her. Jane knew that she would not let go until her talons wrapped around Jane's neck and lifted her high in the air—Jane, the little rabbit in the nature documentary that was such easy prey, and so easy to drop from the mountaintop.

Jane cleared her throat and raised her own hands to gesture, then realized she was spilling expensive vodka on her jeans and, oh for the love of mike, was that an olive rolling down her ankle? Martine was standing about four feet away from her and without looking down, she grasped the hands of the two people who sat on either side of the aisle that they had made for her when she began walking to the back of the room. Annie and Mickey, willingly or not, now had their hands raised to Jane.

Jane glanced at Tim, who gave her an innocent and hopeful smile.

"Well, I didn't know; I mean he was already . . . ," Jane said, then felt a curious vibration before she heard anything. *Thank god*, she thought, *it's an earthquake*. But the floor did not seem to be moving, the glassware on the sideboard was still, and she realized the vibration was coming from her own pocket and she briefly thought that a heart attack was just as good as an earthquake. Maybe better. It was then she heard what everyone else in the room seemed to be listening to so intently.

"Jingle bells, jingle bells, jingle all the way."

Jane had not turned off her cell phone.

Jane looked around the room. Tim and Scott were both laughing, their shoulders heaving silently. Roxanne had the courtesy to turn away. The rest just looked at her with a mixture of curiosity and horror.

"I'm going to have to take this," Jane said. "I promised my son I would always pick up, see, and . . ."

Jane got up and backed out of the room, holding the cell phone in front of her like a weapon. *Stay back everybody,* she was thinking in her best Edward G. Robinson silent-to-self voice, *the first one of you who makes a move gets a speed dial right in the kisser.*

As soon as she was out of the main room and into the large, tiled foyer, she looked at her phone. Not Nick. Nellie.

"Mom, I can't talk; I'll call you back," she whispered.

"What?" Nellie shouted. "Are you still driving?"

"I'll call you back," Jane said.

"You don't have to come back; it's not even broken, the doctor says," said Nellie, "although he's an old quack."

"What?" Jane shouted, forgetting that she was supposed to be talking in a church whisper.

"I'll call you back. Your dad's trying to watch his program."

Jane stood with her mouth open, thinking that her

mother might be straying off the earthly human path herself and into some kind of voodoo realm and perhaps Martine might like to conjure her spirit; and just when she thought she couldn't feel any more confused or discombobulated, she looked out the window into the dark Michigan night.

She was still holding on to her glass of Grey Goose in her left hand, so she took a long swallow. It had no effect. What she saw out the window stayed perfectly still and perfectly visible. Peering in, with her eyebrows raised and a perfectly manicured finger held to her lips, was Claire Oh.

8

In my past life as a collector, an acquirer, and a rabid consumer, I often felt like a lost and lonely pioneer, hacking my way through a forest, no clear path ahead, no horizon line to guide me.

—BELINDA ST. GERMAIN, *Overstuffed*

Bruce Oh had definitely noticed changes in his wife's behavior during the past few months. First, she had been leaving her cell phone turned on at all times, running to answer it no matter what the call might be interrupting. Second, she had been using her alumni status at Northwestern University to check out library books, big, heavy books that she took up to her study and read for hours each night. Third, and most telling he now thought, she had stopped buying him vintage ties.

That might be explained away by a dearth of vintage ties on the market, an explainable absence of clothing of any kind at the estate sales she had been attending. But not only had she not presented him with any new old patterns or colors to set his teeth on edge, she hadn't noticed the plain conventional ties he had taken to wearing each day. She hadn't commented or insisted that he should stop being so predictable. In fact, his wife had stopped looking at him altogether.

Claire had not been herself and he knew it, but Bruce Oh had felt that it would be unfair and judgmental to pry into his wife's individual life. Their marriage was founded on a kind of mutual respect for privacy. Bruce Oh went off to work every day and became Detective Oh, and Claire went off to work each day and became Claire Nelson, dealer in fine antiques. They came together each evening and shared a peaceful dinner, perhaps with a few amusing stories or remarks about their respective days, but mostly they talked about world events, philosophy, their garden, their extensive summer trips. Bruce meditated in the morning and the evening; Claire practiced yoga. To outsiders, they might seem too quiet, too uninvolved in each others' lives, but Bruce Oh had never felt that way. Their communication was crystal clear. Respect without demands. Admiration without question. Interest without judgment.

Yes, Claire did have the tie fixation. That was a bit of whimsy that amused them both. Until it disappeared, Bruce Oh had thought of it as a minor part of their relationship. He now realized that it was crucial to their intimacy. When Claire had stopped looking at his reflection in the mirror, standing over his shoulder and shaking her head about how he would never take the world by surprise if he insisted on wearing navy-blue-and-maroon stripes instead of purple squares inside of lime green circles, he had felt a loss as great as if his wife had confessed to an affair. Yes, he should have been more alert when his wife stopped caring about his neckwear.

An even more interesting puzzle, he realized, was why he was now lamenting Claire's loss of attention to his sartorial habits when he should be paying more attention to the cloud of suspicion surrounding his wife. Hadn't she just been questioned about the murder of Horace Cutler? Hadn't she now disappeared from the house without saying a word to him? Shouldn't he be in furious motion trying to find her since she had been released into his custody?

No, Bruce Oh could honestly say he was never in furious motion. That was not his style. He sometimes sat at the table in his study, staring out at the willow tree, waiting for the answers to come. If he told others at the police department that he practiced clearing his mind to allow answers to come to him, the more polite officers would have waited until he was out of sight before laughing and making mock bowing gestures to each other. Most of his coworkers, though, would not have hidden their skepticism. It wasn't that Oh did not use conventional police methods—he most certainly did— he just opened himself to other channels of thought.

For example, now as he sat ruminating on the tie-selection business with Claire, he realized that he could pinpoint exactly the day Claire had stopped supervising his daily choice of clothing. It was almost two months ago, two days after she had walked away from the Lake Forest estate sale where she had stumbled upon the Westman chest. This piece of furniture, this "find of a lifetime" as Claire had characterized it, had taken over his wife's life. She had become consumed in researching the chest and its probable/possible maker, Mathew Westman. She had spent her days talking to museum directors, dealers in antiques, historians, appraisers. She had spent her nights studying pictures of hardware, dowels, pegs, nails, and the tongue and groove joinings of Early American drawers in the big books she had hauled home from the university library.

From her office doorway, he had watched her tap her foot nervously while waiting for a fax to come through, a page explaining and illustrating patterns of oxidation on wood. She would pull the sheet out of the machine, raise herself up to her full height, tap a finely sharpened pencil against her teeth, and finally say, "aha," or some other likely exclamation, favoring him with a vacant smile as she walked past him in the hall.

How could she have noticed the tie he was wearing? She hadn't even known her husband's name for the past two months. If asked for the name of the man she had been living with, she would have to answer, Mathew Westman. He was the man who now commanded her full attention.

Bruce Oh had not remained sitting still, staring out the window at his willow tree, while trying to put puzzle pieces in place. Uncharacteristically, he had been roaming through the house. He now stood in front of his rival's masterwork.

Earlier, he had watched Jane Wheel watch Claire stroke the carved sunflowers on the drawers. He had read the desire in Mrs. Wheel's eyes—she, too, wanted to touch those carvings, feel the work of a master carver. What was it that these two women saw or sensed from this piece of wooden furniture?

His wife, who had studied art history in college, was a savvy businesswoman, and he knew she viewed the chest as the find of a lifetime, a career maker. Mrs. Wheel, well, she would probably tell him all about the warmth and feel of the wood, the passion that had gone into the making of the piece, the people's lives that this chest of drawers had witnessed. That was the kind of thinking Mrs. Wheel followed. That was a difference between the two women.

Claire tried to find the right object to place in people's lives while poor Mrs. Wheel got stuck creating a life for the inanimate object.

He would do it. He would touch those flowers and try to feel what they had. He placed his right hand on the sunflower on the top right-hand drawer and followed the raised wooden stems and leaves down the side of the chest. Perhaps he was getting it because he began to feel strange. A wave washed over him, something he had never felt before. What was this strange sensation? Ah yes, he felt ridiculous.

The carving was intricate, and he could feel each petal sharply delineated. He put a hand on each side of the top drawer and felt the wooden edges. Something struck him again, this time a more curious feeling. Something Mrs. Wheel had told him about the feel of old wood and something he felt here did not match up. And something about that disjointed feeling startled him back into the present moment.

He walked back into the kitchen and looked at the notepad next to the telephone. "Gone for milk" was written on the lower half of the top sheet of paper. Claire had printed it in block letters, using a great deal of pressure. There was something odd about the note. First of all, they rarely left each other notes. It was too late for the small neighborhood grocery to be open. And, even stranger, they didn't drink milk. If Claire were truly herself, she would have come up with a much better lie than that. Something more, though . . .

It struck him. Claire always doodled while on the phone. She was listening on this extension when Mrs. Wheel phoned and told them about the death of Rick Moore at Campbell and LaSalle. Where was the page with her drawings, her little cats and dogs, her trees and houses? When she didn't draw pictures, she printed words over and over, using different lettering styles. Where were her doodles?

Oh walked over to the trash can, thoughtfully concealed in a pull-out bin in the food preparation island. On top of the yogurt carton, orange peels, and coffee grounds were two pieces of crumpled notepaper. Oh smoothed them out and read the name, RICK MOORE, printed in large capitals. Surrounding the name, Claire Oh had doodled what appeared to be tiny spears or featherless arrows. Bruce Oh tried not to lose himself in what the drawings actually represented. What seemed most important was that fifteen small sharpened points were all aimed at RICK MOORE.

9

"As Granny St. Germain used to say, "too many cooks spoil
the broth." Well, I'm here to tell you that too many spoons,
ladles and bowls in your cupboard do exactly the same thing."

—BELINDA ST. GERMAIN, *Overstuffed*

"If I meet one more person here who is described to
me as a 'master' something or other, I'm going to scream,"
Jane whispered to Tim.

Roxanne had moved away with Geoff and Jake, who
seemed shaken but not stirred. They had both commented
on how painful and disruptive Rick's accident was and
would be to their own work, but neither seemed to be particularly sad. Rick Moore's death was a troubling event, but
Rick Moore's life didn't seem to be anything people much
cared about. Neither the "tragic accident," which now
seemed to be the official title, nor the memorial service had
diminished anyone's appetite. Apparently, right after Jane
made her exit, Martine wound up her performance and a
late cocktail hour began. As soon as Jane had clicked off the
phone and moved over to the window, she heard people
remarking on the beautiful trays of appetizers being wheeled
in from the kitchen.

Jane did not tell Tim that she thought she'd seen Claire

Oh's face peeking in at her. She excused herself and went outside, claiming she needed to return the phone call that had come in and needed to search for better reception. She circled the entire lodge, checked the benches in the garden, and walked over to the guest parking area to see if she recognized a new vehicle. She didn't notice any changes. Maybe Claire's face was just a smudge on the window, a passing shadow, "a bit of undigested beef?" Claire Oh starring as the Ghost of Christmas Past?

Jane decided to make a few calls. No answer at the Oh house. No answer on Charley's cell phone, so she left a good-night-and-have-fun message for him and Nick. Too late, after she had hung up, she realized she should have asked about Charley's speech at the museum. Ah well, as soon as she was organized, uncluttered, and the perfect mother, she would work on being a more solicitous wife. How many roles is one woman expected to perfect at a time?

Jane hit number seven on her speed dial and waited for Nellie's familiar snarl.

"Yeah?" asked Nellie, already in the middle of a conversation with Don about whether something should be soaked.

"Mom, what happened?"

"I dropped a bag of onions on my toe is all," said Nellie, "and your father is acting like I got gangrene or something."

"Let me talk to Dad."

"I'm on the other line, honey," said Don. "Your mother is exaggerating. I just think she should maybe soak it or something."

"Can't hurt to do that, Mom, why don't . . . ," said Jane, cut off by Nellie's insistent, "There's not a thing wrong. I've done this before. It turns all black, then the toenail . . . ," who was in turn cut off by Don's, "Oh, for god's sake, Nellie, spare us the details. I just want it to feel better."

A moment of silence while everyone decided whom to interrupt next.

"Daddy, has she seen a doctor?" asked Jane.

"I talked to him on the phone and he said if I could move it, it wasn't broken," said Nellie.

"But you can't move it," said Don.

Jane wondered if her parents ever talked to each other when she wasn't on the phone and they were on separate extensions. It seemed to her that real communication only took place while she played switchboard operator.

"Now," said Nellie. "I can't move it now, but I could then. There's the water boiling. I'll be back."

Jane heard the extension fall to the floor. Was her mother the only person left who didn't walk from room to room with a cordless?

"Jane," said Don, "are you there?"

"Yes, how bad really?"

"Black and blue, maybe broken. I'll take her in tomorrow. She wanted to slice up the onions for vegetable soup, and I told her to wait until I got the dolly to carry in the bag from the back porch, but you know her, impatient."

Jane stopped looking behind the bushes and into cabin windows as she was walking, hoping for another glimpse of Claire Oh while her parents used her to witness one of their nightly wrangles.

"A dolly? How big of a bag are we talking about?"

"Fifty pounds," said Don.

Jane hesitated. She knew her parents were too old to

run the EZ Way Inn, to work both days and nights, to cook lunches for the factory workers and run bowling leagues in the winter and golfing leagues in the summer. Her dad, Don, shouldn't be tapping beer kegs and lifting cases of bottles, and her mother, Nellie—well, there were many things Nellie shouldn't be doing, but trying to move a fifty-pound bag of onions was high on the list. As a dutiful daughter, shouldn't she be forbidding them to do such hard work, such heavy lifting? On the other hand, in their few free hours, they fought like cats and dogs. At the EZ Way Inn, they worked like a well-oiled, if often grouchy and cantankerous, machine.

"Where the hell are you anyway?" Nellie asked, back from stirring her cauldron on the stove.

"Mom, don't lift those heavy bags anymore. Get Duane or Carl to carry stuff in the night before."

"Are you still off in the woods with Tim?" asked Nellie, ignoring Jane's suggestion to use their occasional nighttime bartenders for anything more than verbal abuse.

"Yeah, I'm on a case," Jane whispered.

There. She had said it. Didn't that make her a real detective?

"Well, stop it. You can't put a round peg in a square hole, you know. Get back to your family. Where's Nick?" asked Nellie, while Don shushed her, telling Jane to be careful.

"He's with the good parent," Jane said, promising her father to call the next day, not saying anything directly to her mother.

What did Belinda St. Germain have to say about emotional clutter? Jane hadn't read that far, but she wondered if there was a chapter on how to be wife, mother, daughter, picker, and detective all at the same time. It seemed to Jane that if you have to carry around that kind of personal baggage, you ought to at least be able to pack it up in a collection of vintage leather train cases with lovely red or butterscotch Bakelite handles.

Jane was starved, and she knew they must be serving something wonderful over in the lodge. She decided to dash into her cabin, run a brush through her hair, and put on a bit of lipstick. She hadn't brought enough clothes to be able to actually change for dinner, but she thought the celebration of Rick Moore's life might have taken a small but cosmetically repairable toll. When Martine had called on her to speak, she had felt her hair stand on end. Maybe she could calm it down.

The hand-crafted lamp on the dresser was turned on. Its leaded-glass shade cast a soft glow over the cherry surface of the dresser. There was a wooden hand mirror face down next to her makeup bag. She picked it up to check the damage, feeling like she might be grateful that the light was low. She wasn't, though. The dim light might lessen the laughter creases around her mouth and the newest crinkles around her eyes, but it also made it more difficult to read the words printed on the mirror. As neatly and carefully as one can manage using a worn-down tube of Clinique–Angel Red, someone had printed:

R.M. MURDERED

Jane continued to look into the mirror. Peeking around the lipstick letters were her brown eyes; and since they were hers, had been hers forever, why did they now look so foreign to her? Who was this middle-aged, middle-class woman, middle-of-the-road person who found herself at the center of murders? Okay, *maybe* murders, *possible* murders. Oh, what the hell, couldn't they all forget that alleged-possible-maybe crap? This was a murder. Period.

Jane had known it when she'd seen Rick Moore lying facedown in that stream. He was in his stocking feet, or one stocking foot, at least, and that was enough for her. She had heard Murkel or one of the other police officers say that Rick's lack of shoes showed how desperate he was to get out of the barn and how disoriented, but that isn't what Jane saw. If Rick had been working around all those toxic chemicals and varnishes and finishes that everyone talked about, he would be wearing shoes. Any master carpenter—and god knows, they were all masters around here—knew that you didn't set foot in a workshop without shoes and socks on. Shoes and socks? At least. Steel-toed work boots more likely.

Besides, the mirror said so. Mirrors don't lie. They are the unforgiving reflection of your age, your joys and your sorrows, and they even have been known to mouth off about who is the fairest in the land. Even if it wasn't written here in exactly black and white, it was printed in a decisive silver and red—murder! Claire Oh was somewhere on these grounds trying to clear herself of Horace Cutler's murder because it must be linked to Rick Moore's death, and she was asking for Jane's help. Jane wished that Claire had used her own lipstick, since Belinda St. Germain's packing tips didn't allow for a spare tube and Jane's Angel Red was now a stump of its former self, but she was delighted to get the message. She felt she had known all along.

The real reason that Jane agreed with the sentiments in the mirror were simple. She and Tim had come to Campbell and LaSalle to solve the murder of Horace Cutler. Nobody had thought his death was an accident. No one had suspected that he had broken into the antique mall and fallen against the silver dagger, which had jumped out of the display case. And Horace's murder likely had something to do with the Westman chest, and the Westman chest had a lot to do with Campbell and LaSalle. So if she and Tim were there to investigate a murder and someone else was found dead . . . ?

Didn't anyone watch television? Didn't anyone read mysteries?

Rick Moore was a master carpenter, a sycophantic student of Blake Campbell. Surely he would have known about or even worked on the Westman chest. Jane had to get into the barn workshop and do a little research herself. It would be easier if she could find Claire Oh and talk to her. She had a feeling that now that the stakes were raised, now that Rick had ended up facedown in the stream, that some of Claire's cool, calm superiority might disappear. Murder, suspicion of murder, and fear of murder all had the effect of making someone not quite so tall.

Dinner was in full swing at the lodge. Conversation had passed from "So sad about Rick" to "Are you consulting on the Bleakman vanity?" as smoothly as the soup course had flowed into the salad course. Jane slid into the seat next to

Tim, realizing that it wouldn't be so easy to bring up Rick or ask about what he had been working on.

"What?" Jane asked, as Tim looked her over and shook his head.

"You were gone long enough, so I naturally assumed . . .," Tim said and ended with a shrug.

"What?"

"Honey, a simple comb through and a little lipstick wouldn't have been the end of the world," said Tim. "That's all I'm saying."

"Damn right, that's all," said Jane.

"Is Nancy on the trail of someone?" he asked, raising an eyebrow.

Jane smiled and reached for the bread basket. "You have salad dressing under your eye," she whispered.

Blake Campbell was sitting alone in an armchair with a pleasant if vacant look at the group assembled in the great hall of the lodge. The dinner table was still filled with people, but a few were standing, stretching, and beginning the after-dinner mingle.

Jane sat down next to him, trying to keep her wits about her. She was never her best around extraordinarily handsome men. She didn't feel particularly attracted to them, but she did feel something. So many actors and models had come her way when she was producing television commercials that she had begun to see a common need, a similar longing in the beauties, both male and female. Like the very rich who never knew if people wanted them for themselves or their money, she supposed they never knew if someone wanted them for themselves or their incredible looks. And here was Blake, so full of the right stuff—the looks, the money, and by all accounts, the talent and intelligence. He had it all, including that needy, lonely look she'd seen in so many pairs of eyes all wanting her to hire them.

Jane offered her hand and reminded Blake that they had been briefly introduced during the frantic events of the afternoon.

"It's not the way I'd like to see anyone introduced to Campbell and LaSalle," Blake said with a sigh, "but you seem to have weathered the shock." He hesitated, then turned up his smile a notch brighter and two degrees warmer. "Quite beautifully," he added.

Another problem with the chronically handsome— they were so good at acting charming that it was hard to tell when they were simply *being* charming. Jane decided that she should not be a detective at this moment, analyzing every smile and sigh. She would find out more playing the picker-in-training-to-be-a-dealer role.

"I'm wondering if I'll still be able to begin my assignment tomorrow?" Jane asked.

"Assignment?"

"Tim is training me to leave behind my junker ways and become a dealer. He not only wanted to show me around here and introduce me to the best restorers and furniture experts, he gave me a little homework. He wanted me to research a piece of furniture," said Jane.

"Final exam?" Blake asked, clearly intrigued.

He likes tests, Jane thought. *He's bored out of his skull.*

"Sort of," said Jane. "I have a small drawer from what might be a traveling desk or maybe even from some type of game table, and I'm supposed to find out everything I can about it. Tim said that between the library you keep and the experts I would find here, I should be able to give him a detailed description of the piece, age, maker, a few of its adventures, even the specifications to have it rebuilt if I wanted."

"Lowry thinks very highly of us here at . . ." Blake let himself trail off.

"He said if he was a sick boy he'd go to the Mayo Clinic, but if he were a sick highboy, he'd ask to come to Campbell and LaSalle," said Jane.

Blake grimaced and groaned, but he was clearly flattered. "As far as I know, Rick's accident doesn't affect access to any part of the facility. I don't want anybody experimenting with the ammonia tent without my supervision, of course. You can use the library in the barn and talk to anyone who has the time and inclination, except during quiet time, of course."

"Getting to know my prize pupil?" Tim asked, handing Jane a glassful of what she assumed was vodka. The olives were a tip-off. She hadn't noticed his approach, but it seemed that he had been keeping an eye on her. Maybe he was afraid she would fall under the Blake Campbell spell.

"An excellent student, I think," said Blake, standing. "I'll be at your disposal all day tomorrow."

"Except during quiet time," Jane said.

Jane and Tim watched Blake walk to the back of the room, touch Roxanne briefly on the shoulder, nod, then leave by the huge double doors.

"You get along with him, don't you, Tim?" Jane asked. When he nodded, she added, "because he sure left fast enough when you came up."

"He's not running from me," Tim said. "I was talking to Scott, who said that Mickey's been chasing him all over the place trying to get put on all the projects that Rick left. You know, now he wants to be the apple of Daddy's eye."

"It's funny. Everybody talks about how close Rick was to Blake, how he followed him around and all, but Blake doesn't seem particularly broken up," Jane said. "No one seems very sad."

"Is that what you were doing with Blake? Gauging the mourning level? Looked more to me like you were establishing the old teacher-student-flirtation strategy," said Tim, taking a large swallow of his drink. "Very clever."

Jane nodded and took a large drink herself, nearly choking.

"Water? With olives in it? What the . . . ?"

"I thought of it myself. Make you look like you're drinking and relaxed and all, but really you're as sharp as a tack and gathering clues," said Tim.

"As far as sidekicks go, my friend," said Jane, wiping her mouth with a C & L hand-embroidered cocktail napkin, "you are on thin ice."

Tim hung his long arm around Jane's shoulder and gave her a brotherly hug. "You can't fire someone you never hired, babe. Besides, you'll see that I'm right. This is a hard-drinking, high-living crowd. You watch old Silver and Martine knock 'em back. If you look like Miss Priss, they won't trust you."

"Now smile and eat your olives like you mean it," Tim added.

Jane laughed and fished out her cocktail pick, which had three bleu cheese olives speared on it. She ate them all—better them than drinking the olive-flavored water—and sashayed out with Tim. She had to get back to her cabin and get prepared for her long day of study at Campbell and LaSalle. At the door, Scott stood sentinel.

"Calling it a night so soon?" he asked.

"I have a full day planned tomorrow," said Jane. "What time does everybody get up around here?"

"We at Campbell and LaSalle," said Scott, in a deep announcer's voice, "work as hard as we play. The workshops and studios start opening up around seven. There's a breakfast buffet laid out from five-thirty to eight. Busy little bees here at blah, blah, blah."

"See you in the morning then," said Jane.

When she reached the porch steps, she turned back to wave good-bye to Tim, who had decided to have yet another nightcap with Scott. The two of them had already disappeared inside.

Martine now stood there, watching Jane leave. She flashed her a smile that Jane decided could be interpreted as either playful or wicked. Then Martine reached over her left shoulder and picked up her fat, long braid with her right hand and waved it at Jane.

Wicked.

10

If you save it because you think, someday, you'll wear it, use it, donate it, repair it, mend it, mount and frame it, paint it, reshape it, or make it into a lamp, stop lying to yourself. Toss it.

—BELINDA ST. GERMAIN, *Overstuffed*

Back in her cabin, Jane tried to wait up for Claire. She reorganized her makeup case, not that there was all that much in it. She emptied out her purse and searched for items she could discard, but found herself actually looking desperately around the cabin for things to add. There was a lovely notebook, an old-fashioned light blue parchment cover, college-ruled, in the nightstand drawer, and she slipped it into the outside pocket of her bag. She would need it for note taking tomorrow. Besides, you can't have too many notepads, no matter what Belinda St. Germain says. She also took a pen and highlighter she found in the bottom drawer of the chest.

She washed her face and, studying herself in the bathroom mirror, wondered if after thirty-odd years of avoiding the issue, it might be time to do something about her eyebrows. She flossed. Twice. She found a package of emery boards in the bathroom cupboard and filed her already short, rounded nails.

She paced. Finally, she closed her eyes, just for a minute, to rest.

When she opened her eyes again, something almost like light was peeking in through the shuttered front window of her cabin. It was very early morning light, but it irrevocably signaled the break of day, and she knew she had missed her chance to meet with Claire Oh.

Claire would not come out of hiding during the day, would not risk being seen at Campbell and LaSalle. For all their talk about isolation and creative space and private workspaces, Jane had seen copies of the major newspapers in the library in the lodge. She had overheard Annie ask at the dinner table if anyone else had heard more about Horace Cutler, the dealer who had been murdered in Chicago. And, she had added, hadn't he had work done at Campbell and LaSalle?

If anyone had read the papers, they had to have seen Claire's name mentioned. Jane was pretty certain that she wasn't supposed to be leaving town, let alone crossing state lines to sneak around and use up lipsticks to write secret messages. Jane hadn't been a detective long, but she was quite certain that Claire's behavior, if made public, would be frowned upon by law-enforcement officers.

It was only 5:30 A.M., but she would be able to get a bite to eat and check out the library in the barn. She pulled on the same dark jeans she had worn the day before, knowing Tim would mention it, but she was at the mercy of her six-item packing challenge. She was beginning to have some doubts about some of Belinda's manifestos, but she owed it to Nick to try and discipline herself into a decluttered world. She also owed Nick and Charley a phone call, but it was too early. She'd try to get them before Charley's speech or panel or symposium or whatever he was at the museum for—she really should know this stuff. And, she promised herself, after she finished her business here, she would.

Too early to call Bruce Oh, too, since it was an hour earlier in Illinois. She would phone him right after breakfast, though. Perhaps Claire had driven the two and a half hours to Michigan last night to leave Jane the message, then returned home. Actually, with no traffic and what would most likely be Claire's disdain for speed limits—after all, a moving violation paled with being a suspect in a murder case—she could have made it to Campbell and LaSalle and back in less than four hours. She also could have told Jane over the phone in less than four minutes that she believed Rick Moore had been murdered. What was Claire's reason for contacting Jane via lipstick and mirror? Because she didn't want to alarm her husband? She was already a suspect in another murder, plus he was the least alarmable person Jane knew. More likely she didn't want to *inform* her husband.

Of course, Jane thought as she investigated the breakfast buffet, delighted to see that she had the huge great room all to herself, she was assuming that it was Claire who had sent her the message. Her lipstick had been functional when she'd left the cabin, and when she and Tim had arrived in the great hall, they were the last residents of Campbell and LaSalle to show up. The first thing Jane had done when they entered was take roll. Now, after helping herself to slabs of multigrain toast that she smeared with freshly ground nut butter and homemade strawberry jam, she walked over to the table and re-created last night's gathering.

Glen LaSalle and Blake Campbell had been up front talking to Martine before the service began. Roxanne was part of that group, too. She and Tim met Scott near the door. Mickey was fixing a drink and had gone to sit by Annie after talking to Blake. Geoff and Jake were already seated by the time Tim and Jane had sat down in the last row. Everyone had been in front of them except Scott, who was off to the side. No one had left before Jane went out to make her phone call and wander the grounds.

Jane was sitting in a high-backed chair with her back to the buffet table and the kitchen door. She heard someone come out and add a platter to the table, but did not turn. Kitchen staff? She would have to find out how many people worked in service here. She had seen Cheryl, the head chef, and she thought she had heard two other names mentioned as kitchen apprentices. The appetizers and dinner had followed so quickly after the memorial, though, it would be hard to believe that anyone cooking or serving could have taken a break from the kitchen during the Martine extravaganza.

Jane brought her plate back to the dish cart and placed it on the lower shelf as a small, hand-printed card instructed. She helped herself to coffee and took her seat, settling in just as she heard two people enter through the side door that led to Roxanne's office.

"Ask anyone anything, Sergeant. Don't be surprised if no one saw Rick during those afternoon hours, though. Most people are in their cabins or studios during the afternoon. And no one's cabin looks out at the parking lot. In fact . . ." Roxanne broke off her sentence, and although Jane couldn't see Murkel, she assumed he nodded at her to continue, because she cleared her throat and went on.

"Rick Moore had a pickup truck that he parked on an old access road in the woods about a quarter mile from his cabin. He didn't even use the parking area or the main driveway in and out of here. Not only would no one have seen him leave, no one would have even heard him if he'd left for Chicago during quiet hours."

Jane wasn't sure how long it would be before they realized she was sitting there, and when they did, she didn't want to appear like she was eavesdropping. Out of habit she had picked up a newspaper by the front door and carried it with her to the table. Neither she nor Charley liked to speak before several cups of coffee, and neither found it rude to read at the breakfast table. Jane lowered her head and lost herself in the classifieds of the *South Haven Daily*. Not a great ruse, but the best she could do. She quickly circled a few of the garage sale ads so it would look like she had been studying the paper for some time.

"So Moore could have left between three and four, made it to Chicago, and returned sometime that night? No one missed him at dinner?"

"Rick wasn't very sociable. He often ate in his cabin or worked through dinner."

"We have a positive ID on him and his truck, and we'll get the rest of the crime-scene test results later this afternoon. Puts a different light on what happened here yesterday, that's for sure," said Murkel.

"I don't really see that," said Roxanne. "And I'm sorry, but you'll need a warrant to go through his things. We're a retreat, of sorts, and . . ." Jane couldn't hear the end of Roxanne's sentence.

Murkel said something as he walked toward the front

door, but Jane couldn't hear him either. Geoff and Jake must have walked in as he walked out. Jane heard Roxanne greet them and say she'd be back in a minute. That gave Jane the break she needed to stand and refill her coffee. She nodded to the two men filling their plates with fritattas and slices of bacon, not knowing from the night before who was who. They had been introduced as Geoff and Jake, and both had nodded at exactly the same time. Jane hadn't had time to ask the sorting-out questions before Martine had begun chanting.

Roxanne reentered the room through her office, and Scott came in through the front door. Jane was certain during all the good mornings that Roxanne had no idea that Jane had overheard the earlier conversation with Murkel. Scott sat next to Jane and suggested she try one of the muffins with her coffee, something about Michigan blue-berries. Roxanne asked them to excuse a moment of morning noise while she hammered a small nail into the wall by the kitchen.

Scott smiled, watching her rehang the twig-framed bulletin board that displayed the day's menu. "Better not let Blake catch you," he said.

"That's why I'm doing it this early. He'll never know."

"Roxanne's the only one who gets away with using regular nails around here," Scott said, by way of explanation. Geoff and Jake were oblivious to both the hammering and the conversation. They only had eyes for their fritattas and a drawing of a vanity they had placed between them and seemed to be studying and making occasional marks on between bites.

"Blake doesn't want anyone tempted by contemporary

tools," she said, sitting on the other side of the table with her cup of coffee.

"Or with modern glues, brushes, anything," added Scott. "Amazing we're allowed to eat with forks."

Roxanne smiled. "When he's not around, I replace some of those square hand-cut nails with big round-headed modern ones so the hanging wire on the boards won't slide off. I feel sneaky doing it, but those twig frames are fragile. A mirror broke in one of the cabins last week, too, slid right off the *authentic* nail."

"Was it Rick's?" Jane asked.

Roxanne looked startled. "Yes, how did you know that?"

"I was just thinking about seven years' bad luck," said Jane.

"A bit of an understatement, isn't it? Death being the ultimate bad luck and all," said Scott.

"I suppose a picture hanger would be out of the question," said Jane.

"Bite your tongue," said Scott. "Roxanne's the real fixer around here; she just doesn't get any of the credit."

Roxanne covered her eyes and bent her head. "We at Campbell and LaSalle do not *do* picture hangers, dear," she whispered, sounding exactly like Glen LaSalle.

As if the imitation invoked the man, Glen walked in with Martine and Blake. Roxanne picked up the nails she had taken out of her pocket to illustrate her small chore and stood to greet them and, Jane was sure, inform them that Murkel had found out something about Rick Moore that might make for some C & L unpleasantness. Jane noticed that Roxanne had missed two nails, one new and the old square one she had removed, and Jane quickly picked them up and put them into her bag. It was the least she could do for her since Roxanne had showed enough trust to confide her handyman/woman secret to Jane.

She could return them later to Roxanne and find a way to learn we-at-Campbell-and-LaSalle information that might be more pertinent to Jane's investigation. Roxanne had told Jane that she kept the books and ran the business, so she must know about pieces checked in and have access to all the billing records. With Roxanne's help, Jane could find out exactly what happened to the Westman chest when it was in residence at Campbell and LaSalle.

Jane put on her best lost-in-artistic-thought face and nodded to Blake, Glen, and Martine, who were serving themselves at the buffet.

"Good luck on your mission," said Blake.

Jane was startled for just a moment. She then remembered her story about Tim's research assignment and nodded. He flashed her one of his dazzling smiles, and Jane was grateful for her experience with good-looking people. A less prepared woman, she knew, could be totally corrupted by those perfect teeth and warm brown eyes and that tumble of gray-flecked brown hair. Even with her experience and the steel armor woven while sitting through hundreds of commercial casting sessions, Jane felt a bit woozy.

When she reached the barn, she decided to look around the work areas before climbing up to the library. Like a three-ring circus, it seemed that there were three distinct staging areas. Each area had a full array of tools and brushes hanging from a rack above a workbench. Looking up, Jane saw a curtain–rodlike device, similar to the track that runs around patient areas in hospital emergency rooms to afford patients a modicum of privacy. Apparently, furniture projects were afforded privacy here at Campbell and LaSalle. More than once Tim had referred to it as a kind of clinic for valuable antiques. This workspace expanded the thought.

Jane smiled, picturing Blake in a white medical coat, soft paintbrush hung around his neck like a stethoscope, questioning a chest of drawers. "And how about your middle drawer, dear? Has it been sticking? A little painful opening the top one?" Picturing Blake at all made her feel slightly guilty, and she decided it was time to call Charley. She dialed her husband's cell phone as she climbed the open stairs to the gallery library that ran around three sides of the barn. At the north end the gallery expanded into a wider loft area with plenty of room for three leather club chairs and a few worktables with green-shaded library lamps. Jane listened to the ringing phone as she took out volumes on Westman and Early American restoration. She wasn't even sure she knew what to look for.

"Hi, Charley," she said at the beep. "I'm in the most stunning little library here at Campbell and LaSalle. You'd love this place. I hope you and Nick are having fun. I haven't gotten a chance to reorganize the house yet, but my purse is . . . ," Jane began, then remembered that she hadn't decluttered her purse either. "Charley, I forgot to ask what your speech was about, so call me when you get a chance, I want to hear all about it. I . . ." She stopped when she heard the time's-up click.

This time she had asked about Charley's speech but hadn't left enough time to say I love you. What was it with her and phone messages? She admired those who could concisely get their message across and end the communication gracefully. She always said something like well ... um ... okay then. At any moment she sounded like she was going to break into la-di-da, la-di-da, like Diane Keaton playing *Annie Hall*. Or worse yet, she said thank you at the end of the message even if someone had asked her for a favor that she was agreeing to do. Okay then ... well ... thank you. Why oh why did she feel in control and intelligent when she had a notebook and pen in her hand and become a blithering idiot when faced with a cell phone or a Palm Pilot? Maybe St. Belinda had some insight into that in the chapter titled "Ending the Paper Trail." Jane would skip ahead and read that one next, if she could remember where she had put the book.

Mathew Westman, according to the book titled, *The People's Craftsman,* was not only famous for his solid, well-made chests and cupboards but also for making decorative items like frames for mirrors and document boxes. He liked to try his hand at inlay as well as carving and was considered a dilettante by other furniture makers of his day. It seemed to Jane that he was a bit too curious and facile with his carving tools to be taken seriously. *Even back then, people seemed to insist on specialization,* Jane thought. It didn't seem fair to her. She still recalled the joy and stimulation that working on two vastly different accounts had brought her when she was at the ad agency.

The large beer company for whom she had produced two highly successful campaigns had insisted that she work for them exclusively and drop a smaller mom-and-pop account she had nursed along for years. When she had tried to explain to both the client and her boss that it kept her fresh to go back and forth, to take two paths, to reach into two different parts of her brain, they had laughed and told her she was being sentimental. The smaller account went to a creative director and account executive with much less experience. When her firm lost the account, no one seemed to miss The Carpet Pros. Jane took it as a personal blow. She could work *big* better when she worked *small* at the same time. And she had learned how to do what she did by working on The Carpet Pros's account. They had watched her grow from the new kid into a professional, and they had each respected their history together.

Of course Mathew Westman loved to carve frames and smaller objects. It allowed him to continue to learn. It honed his skills, kept him fresh, and allowed him to experiment. The book didn't exactly say that, but Jane figured it out.

The book did state that Westman's masterpiece, a set of heavily carved drawers with a kind of shelved cupboard on top, now known as the Westman Sunflower Chest, had been made for a wealthy family in Massachusetts and had been handed down through that family until it was donated to a museum in 1987. One other chest had been authenticated as a Westman and was believed to be an earlier version and was privately owned. There was wide speculation that a few other Westman chests survived; however, none had surfaced. The rumors seemed to be based on the belief that a prolific carver such as Mathew Westman would not content himself with only a few models. His early mirrors and other decorative pieces, including a group of ornate shadow boxes, followed in an extensive series, which showed a playful experimentation with design and balance.

The frustrating piece of information about Westman was that he'd kept no catalogue of his work—at least, none had been found. Only a few flyers with sketches from his workshop remained, so there was no way to actually pinpoint numbers of pieces and styles. The author did say that Westman was often quoted about building "good pieces for the people, not just the wealthy," hence, the smaller items, the mirrors and whatnot shelves that were affordable to many. *Interesting distinction,* Jane thought, *that even then the wealthy couldn't possibly be "the people," too.*

Westman's son, James, showed promise as a carver and builder and was part of Mathew Westman's shop for at least six years. He grew ill and died while still a young man; and, according to this biographer, Westman, the father, never got over the loss of his son. Some of the pieces he built after that were apparently rejected because his carvings, which had always been incredibly realistic, became more strangely personal.

One family for whom he had carved a bed refused to keep it because of the faces carved into the bedposts. They described it as a scary sight, the eyes that peered at them in the night, and insisted that it be taken back. The rumor was that Westman had gone to their home and chopped the bed frame into pieces right in front of the whole family, hauled out the wood, and burned it all behind his own house.

The madness that seemed to overtake him in his grief might not have been good for business in his own day, but currently, any mirror or piece of furniture that had the feverish face of Mathew Westman's son carved on it was quite desirable. It would not fetch as high a price as a Westman Sunflower Chest, but any picker would be wise to study the carvings of son James's face and learn to recognize the Westman hand.

Jane, curled up in one of the leather chairs, felt the warmth of the sun from one of the high windows that surrounded the gallery loft but still shuddered. She had always believed, insisted to others, that every object told a story. Every crocheted pot holder, every tattered first edition, every Bakelite dress clip held a secret. Somehow, actually knowing the secrets of the Westman carvings did not satisfy her the way her own made-up stories did. There was a safety and an anonymous thrill in speculating on the life of an artist, a maker, a former owner of a now collectible piece. There was nothing safe about knowing the truth.

A piece of paper fluttered out of the pages of the book and sailed first up, then down and under Jane's chair. She closed the book and set it on the library table and got down on her knees to pick up the paper. Reaching under the chair, she felt the paper on top of something else parked there. Resting her head all the way down on the floor, she peered underneath the chair.

"Ear to the ground, nose to the grindstone, that's what I like about you, Nancy Drew," said Tim, setting a mug of coffee down on the library table after locating a vintage-looking tile that was clearly marked REPRO/SAMPLE to use as a coaster. He had come in quietly, not to surprise Jane, but because the sound of his own footsteps might aggravate the pounding in his head.

"What size feet do you have, Tim?"

"Honey, I'm mighty hung over, so if you're playing some kind of mind game, I don't . . ."

"What size?"

"Eleven and a half," Tim said, and flopped into the chair opposite Jane's.

She stood, pulling out a pair of well-worn Birkenstock sandals.

"It was a quick look and all, but I'd say Rick Moore was about your size. I looked at his feet because he had no shoes on and because, when everyone gathered around, it was all I could see." Jane held up a sandal, then put it next to Tim's foot. "Pretty close," she said.

Tim massaged his temples. "Common shoe size, and who cares anyway? What's it prove?"

"They're Rick's, all right. These are the Arizona sandals. I have them and so does Charley. The tan lines I saw on Rick's bare foot match up with the straps on these," said Jane.

"Impressive, but I repeat, what's it prove?"

"That Rick Moore wasn't experimenting with solvents or standing too long in the ammonia tent. All those little hand-lettered signs around here? There are at least five downstairs that list the rules, which include number one, leave the windows open at all times and number two, heavy work shoes and socks must be worn in the work areas.

"Rick Moore was wearing Birkenstock sandals because he wasn't in the workshop; he was up here reading in the library," said Jane. "And he got comfy in this chair by taking off his sandals and scooting them underneath."

Tim sighed the sigh of a man too long at the Grey Goose and too soon out of bed. "I suppose you know what book he was reading, too," he said, stretching.

"As a matter of fact, he was reading this biography of Mathew Westman," Jane said, handing Tim the paper that had fallen out of the book.

Dear Rick, Dear Rick, Dear Rick, Dear Rick, Dear Rick, Dear Rick
Take care of it, take care of it, take care of it
Blake, Blake, Blake, Blake. Blake, Blake, Blake, Blake, Blake, Blake

If it was a real note, it was long on salutation and close and extremely short on content. It seemed like more of a doodle, a handwriting practice sheet.

It had been crumpled, then smoothed out. The note, or whatever it was, was unsigned.

11

Hanging on to that history textbook from junior year at college? The one that you thought you'd use as a reference, delve into as part of your commitment to lifelong learning? You will never, I repeat, never, read that book again. Toss it.

—BELINDA ST. GERMAIN, *Overstuffed*

Jane's everyday bag was an oversized leather tote that could hold a normal-sized purse plus a change of clothes—and maybe a lunch. On more than one occasion, it had also held Nick's soccer cleats and a warm-up jacket and a water bottle. Jane had no trouble slipping the book on Mathew Westman and what she believed were Rick Moore's Birkenstock sandals, Arizona model, deep into her bag. And in the small, zippered pocket, she placed the note she had found.

"Take care of it"? What was *it*? The fake Westman chest swapped with the real Westman? Was *it* the worry about Horace Cutler screaming his head off at the antiques show? Was Horace Cutler going to be taken care of? Permanently?

Jane looked at Tim shielding his eyes from the morning light streaming in through the high row of windows that surrounded the gallery loft. She would give him two minutes to recover, then she would need his help. Jane dialed Bruce Oh's number. No answer. She left a quick please-call-me-immediately message, feeling a little smug that she had actually said what she had meant to say and gotten it in before the beep. Only a beat later she realized she hadn't left her name, but she was pretty sure Oh would recognize her voice or be able to check caller ID or some new people-finding phone feature that she hadn't yet heard of. For god's sake, there was no anonymity left in the world at all; surely Oh could figure out who had called him and from where. Unless Oh didn't check messages at all because he was out looking for his wife, who might not have returned home last night.

"She's here," said Jane. "I have got to talk to her."

Tim groaned. Hangover or no hangover, she needed him to search Campbell and LaSalle. Dragging her heavy bag and Tim by the hand, she hurried him over to the lodge. No one was at the breakfast table, so she parked Tim in an armchair and rushed into the kitchen.

Cheryl looked up from a notebook where she was listing ingredients from a large cookbook propped up on the cooking island.

"Sorry to bother you, but my friend, Tim, needs a remedy quickly. Could I mix something in the blender?"

Cheryl shrugged and nodded, eyes back on her book. Jane helped herself to tomato juice, Tabasco, and an egg. Nellie's secret hangover ingredient—for Don and others since she never indulged—was usually unavailable, but this was a gourmet kitchen, stocked and loaded, so Jane took a shot.

"Any anchovies?" she asked.

Cheryl was now interested. She opened the cupboard

and handed Jane a tin, which Jane quickly opened. She threw one of the salty strips into the blender with the rest of the ingredients and pulsed. She tossed in a few ice cubes and pulsed again. Sniffing the drink, she added a few more shakes of hot sauce, then poured it into a glass.

"Thanks so much," Jane said, running water into the blender and replacing the pitcher of tomato juice in the refrigerator.

"What is that a remedy for?" Cheryl asked.

"Vodka," said Jane. "My mom's recipe. She hates drinkers, but she owns a bar and plays nurse to a lot of customers the morning after. Says it'll kill or cure. I've never tried it myself."

Jane smiled, thinking that the kill or cure part was probably what Nellie prized in this recipe. Knowing her mother, she was sure that Nellie would be just as happy to see it kill . . . well, just happy to see it kill.

Tim was desperate enough to drink it down with two aspirin and a B-complex vitamin that Jane fished out of her bag.

"What's in it?" Tim asked, wiping his mouth.

"Last night I saw Claire Oh's face in the window right out there," Jane said, ignoring his question and pointing to the small windows flanking the front door of the lodge. "I think she's still here on the grounds somewhere. You have to find her."

"What . . . ?" Tim began again.

"I have to get into Rick Moore's cabin now. Murkel was talking to Roxanne, and something's simmering about him. Before it gets closed off to me, I have to get in there and see if I can find out what he was working on."

Tim was still trying to figure out what Jane had made him drink, but somehow he felt a little better and decided maybe it was better not to know. In fact, she had told him it was Nellie's recipe and perhaps that was all anyone was supposed to know. He saluted her and headed out to cover the grounds.

Jane went directly to Rick's cabin.

Jane prided herself on being able to figure people out by their possessions. She wandered into estate sales, fingered the old clothes in the backs of closets, counted up sets of towels and sheets, peered into the back reaches of kitchen cupboards to find the mismatched glasses, the hidden talismans of everyday lives. Jane Wheel, completely at sixes and sevens in the housewares section of a department store, unable to make a single decision about a new purchase, could look around someone else's kitchen and tell you every item that was either well-used, well-loved, or merely kept out of duty and obligation. She often felt, standing in the middle of someone else's house, that she could step into their lives, inhabit their world, and pass for that person by simply slipping in among the objects. So why, in her own house, in her own life, did she so often feel like a stranger, an imposter?

When Nick was an infant and she took him shopping or for a walk in the park, she would often look over her shoulder, thinking someone would surely spot her and report her as someone posing as an adult, as a mother. She and Charley joked about it. They'd named it—this nagging fear and self-doubt—the baby inspector. "Watch out," they would say, when one of them had forgotten to bring Nick's hat and a breeze blew up, "the baby inspector will see."

She had outgrown this lack of confidence though; she was sure of it. Except for this recent little glitch of losing the field trip permission slip, she had done nothing in the past few years to warrant a visit from the baby inspector.

So why did she feel the hair on the back of her neck stand up when she slipped into Rick Moore's cabin? She was comfortable among the possessions of others, yes? She could assess his personality, his strengths and weaknesses, by what he'd kept, what he'd saved. And it was important to find out who he had been and what he had known. It might explain why he was dead.

There was a small worktable opposite the bed. Jane went over and sat in the chair that was pulled up to it. A leather portfolio, scuffed and worn, lay on the table. Slowly and carefully, Jane opened it. She actually laughed softly when she saw the first page. A list of paint colors, drawings of finishing brushes. What had she expected? Bats to fly out and announce who'd murdered Horace Cutler.

There was a small appointment calendar, a giveaway from a hardware store. Jane looked through it quickly. Dates of antique shows and flea markets were noted. The Chicago show where Horace had made a scene at Claire's booth was noted with the others. There was also a phone list in the back. At least forty dealers in the Chicago area alone—Horace and Claire among them—but nothing starred or underlined. What was Jane hoping for? A yellow highlighter marking victims? Victims of whom? What? Jane saw Tim Lowry's name listed and smiled. He'd be pleased that even though his business was officially in Kankakee, he had made it into the ranks of the Chicago dealers.

Jane noted that Rick's wardrobe was a definite Belinda

St. Germain "Do" rather than "Don't." In his closet he had two pairs of identical blue jeans, three plaid work shirts, a navy hooded sweatshirt, and on the floor, heavy work boots and a pair of beat-up, cheap running shoes—efficient and economical.

Something was missing here though. Jane had to sit again in his chair and try to feel what had made this man tick. No reading material on his bedside table; no photographs or knickknacks, even though he had occupied this cabin for a month or two at a time. He had lived on the very surface of this place, had barely made a ripple in the air in this cabin.

What had everyone said about him? A consumate craftsman and student of Blake's. He loved Campbell and LaSalle and yet, it appeared to Jane, he had hardly put any roots down in this spot. When Jane had walked into her guest cabin, she had felt it as so homey, so welcoming. One had to make an effort to make one of these guest rooms feel cold and sterile. Rick Moore had succeeded. This cabin had no personality. Where was he? Jane couldn't accept the fact that, even though he was dead, he didn't exist. She had known far too many people who went on long after they were gone, making themselves known by the pot holders they had crocheted or the photo albums they had tended.

Jane looked out the back window of the cabin. Unlike hers, this one had a back door. She stepped out and was struck by the fairy tale view. This was the Woods with a capital W. Hansel and Gretel could surely get lost there and emerge, tired and hungry, at Rick Moore's doorstep. *They wouldn't find much to nibble on here,* Jane thought, then somehow nibbling reminded her of breakfast and breakfast took her to Murkel's talk with Roxanne, and Roxanne's words sent her out the door and down the path that must lead to the access road.

There it was: Rick Moore's *real* home, a blue pickup truck with a camper top over the rear bed. Jane knew right away that this was where Rick lived. She opened the driver's side and felt the warmth of habitation. Piles of papers, books, a stack of restorers' catalogues, one devoted solely to hinges. On the passenger seat, a handmade, well-worn wooden box. Rick Moore's tools. Jane opened it as carefully as she would a jewelry box containing precious gems. At least a dozen brushes, some with only two or three hairs in them, it seemed. Carving blades, antique nails, crude, wooden-handled objects that Jane thought beautiful but utterly confounding. These must be the allowed tools, the ones that Blake and the others permitted their craftsmen to use when doing restoration work. A piece of paper was folded up in the bottom of the box, and Jane smoothed it out, half expecting to see old spidery penmanship and have the paper crumble into dust, but it was a contemporary page ripped out of a college-ruled notebook. On it was a hurried sketch of a young man's face—scary, creepy, a sad and haunted face. When Jane looked closer, she realized it looked frightening because it wasn't the sketch of a real person but a sketch of a carved face. Someone had drawn a detailed picture of a Mathew Westman carving, a carving of his dead son. The sketch was annotated with numbers and blade descriptions. It reminded Jane of a paint-by-numbers drawing. Someone had written meticulous instructions on how to carve a disturbed Mathew Westman face. Were they Rick's own notes on the carving? Or were they Rick's instructions from someone else?

Jane shoved the paper into her pocket. She would sort out who had instructed whom to do what later. She crawled into the back of the truck and flashed her narrow beam of light into the corners. She opened a small metal box and found some hinges, a few brass drawer pulls, and a few pieces of carved wood. Jane held them up close and smiled in spite of what they told her. It felt so good to see them again, to run her fingers over the wood, these beautifully carved petals . . . flowers identical to the ones that bloomed on Claire Oh's Westman Sunflower Chest.

Jane saw a large manila envelope marked IMPORTANT and grabbed it, crawling backward out of the truck. Flashing her light around one last time, she saw some clothes rolled up into a ball in the corner. They looked filthy, covered with paint or stain, and she noticed a drop cloth and rags on the same side of the truck. She didn't need to go through Rick's laundry just yet. It would be just as interesting and much less messy to read the contents of the envelope that he had marked important.

Jane brushed herself off and pulled out a sheaf of papers printed out from a Web site. The first page had a picture of a chair and a bold headline, but Jane didn't have time to read it. She heard voices and footsteps that were far too heavy to belong to Hansel and Gretel. Stepping in among the trees, she hoped she was as invisible as she felt.

Glen LaSalle and Scott Tailor stood in front of the truck, peering into the windows. Although they talked quietly, Jane could make out most of what they said.

"I don't like robbing the dead," Scott said, "but Rick wouldn't want his tools out here, rusting or getting ripped off by teenagers coming out here to get high."

"If that makes you feel better about what we're doing, by all means cling to it," said Glen, sounding amused, "but no teenagers come out to Campbell and LaSalle to drink six-packs. It's two miles to the blacktop from here and only a few people even recognize this as a limited access road."

Jane couldn't see their faces, but she tried to imagine Scott's expression. She didn't think he looked pleased. "Rick didn't have anything in his life but his work and those tools. They belong in the barn, not in some police evidence room or wherever those idiots would toss them."

"Yes," Glen said, "you're right about that."

Jane heard them open and close the truck door, then heard their footsteps fade away in the direction they had come.

Two miles to the blacktop was too far for Jane to walk now. It would take too long and put her out on the highway too far from Campbell and LaSalle's main entrance. She would just have to wait a few minutes and take a chance walking back the way she had come. She needed to get back to see if Tim had found any trace of Claire. Perhaps she had lipsticked another note for them to find. Jane wanted more than a scrawled word or two now. If Rick Moore had been murdered, she needed to find out why—or how. She would settle for how since any of the big questions often led to the biggest answer of all—who.

Oh. The cell phone began its "Jingle Bells," and Jane realized how lucky she was that it hadn't rung while Scott and Glen were standing five feet away from her at the truck. Nick would have to show her how to set the phone to vibrate and not ring. She thought she had done that, but now it vibrated *and* rang. She was afraid that if she tried to do anything else to it, it would light up and whine like a siren. She answered, sure that Bruce Oh had gotten her message and would be able to help her answer some pressing Claire questions.

Instead of Oh's polite but clipped voice, Nellie was yelling at Don to turn down the television. Only when Jane yelled into the phone three times did Nellie turn her attention back to the phone call. "What are you yelling about? Where are you?"

"Mom, I'm still in Michigan, and you yelled first," said Jane.

"Yeah, well, I broke my toe. At least that's what that quack Bernard says, and your dad wants you to come and work with us for a few days," Nellie said.

Jane could hear her father in the background shouting that he did not want Jane to come to Kankakee; they could manage fine. Then she heard her mother tell him that Jane liked to come and work at the tavern, and her father answered that Jane had better things to do with her time. She was a professional. "A professional what?" Nellie asked Don. "Junk picker? Private eye? Washing some dishes; making some soup. That is real work, and it wouldn't hurt her to pitch in." Jane's dad answered back that Jane pitched in all the time, but it wasn't necessary now since he could handle the next few days and he had help lined up for the following week.

Jane knew that this argument about her, around her, over her, could go on for days, and she would not be required to say one word. She clicked the "end" button. An hour or so from now, when Nellie noticed that her daughter was no longer on the line, she would call back. Nellie, unfortunately, in many more ways than one, had Jane's number.

Back at Rick's cabin, Jane picked up her bag that she had left by the door, stuck in the envelope from the truck, and went in search of the hungover Tim. If he had found Claire, she could cut to the chase fairly quickly. Had Claire been in cahoots with Rick Moore to fabricate a fake Westman chest? Jane had pocketed one of the carved sunflowers from Rick's truck, and she pictured herself holding it out to Claire, asking if this were the work of a master's hand. Who else knew about the Westman forgery? Was that the person who'd murdered Horace Cutler? Had Rick Moore really been murdered? What was behind all the we-at-Campbell-and-LaSalle hocus-pocus? How deeply was Claire involved in all of this?

And why was Jane—a modern woman, a youngish-middle-aged, attractive, intelligent picker PI, whose own son told her she was stylin' when she wore her new boot-cut jeans—using a word like "cahoots"?

12

If there were a fire in your home, heaven forbid, what would you save? If you said anything, and I mean anything, other than your spouse, your children, your pets, and yourself, you still have much work to do.

—BELINDA ST. GERMAIN, *Overstuffed*

Tim stumbled over a tree root in front of Annie's cabin and fell headfirst into a terra-cotta pot filled with violet pansies, tiny bronze mums, and purple-and-chartreuse sweet potato vines. The inner hangover sufferer in him swore and cursed aloud, but his inner florist was quite impressed with the fall arrangement. The timing was right for the flowers, but it seemed late in the season for these vines to be so strong and healthy. Since his nose was practically in the pot, he sniffed to see what these plants were being fed.

"How do I crack wise about this? Let me count the ways . . . ," said Scott, who had walked up behind him on the path. "Do I start with a pun about nosing around or getting back to the land or ask about you falling for someone or . . ."

"You speak softly," said Tim. "Better yet, you do not speak at all."

Back on his feet, Tim looked Scott over. He thought

they had gone at the vodka bottle drink for drink, but Scott seemed clear-eyed and chipper. His downright morning perkiness only added to Tim's distress, although he had to admit that whatever poisonous cocktail Jane had served him had helped him approach normal. He wasn't feeling quite right, but he could see it from here.

"We at Campbell and LaSalle can hold our liquor, my friend. You've been too long at the shopkeeper's life and forgotten how to party like it's 1999."

"Eighteen ninety-nine is more appropriate for this crowd," said Tim, regaining his balance and gesturing at the antique brushes Scott was holding in his left hand.

"You like?" Scott asked, beaming. He held them up as if they were a bouquet of roses. "Hog bristle for varnishing; sable for detail work. This one is camel, but not from a camel . . . it's made from Russian squirrel. Blake thinks good old American squirrel hair is too coarse, but I aim to prove him wrong on that. I like this one for oil and glazings . . . pure badger. And for lettering, ah, my sweet little ox. See, the hair here is taken from behind the ears."

"And you thought it was funny to see me sniffing flowers," said Tim.

"Hey, man, a craftsman is only as good as his tools," said Scott, slipping the brushes into the pocket of a short canvas apron. "What do you want with Annie?"

Tim hoped he didn't look as blank as he felt. He had managed to search the grounds of all the cabins looking for signs of Claire Oh without running into anyone at home or on the paths. He didn't really have a story prepared for why he was making the rounds. He had been a fairly facile liar all his life, but now that Jane was drawing him into her midlife-crisis career of intrigue, he felt more pressure. He seemed to remember that a good rule of thumb when telling a convincing lie was to stick as close as possible to the truth.

"Aspirin. Jane didn't have any, so I thought I'd see if Annie had a well-stocked medicine chest before bothering Roxanne up at the lodge."

"Sorry, pal. Annie won't have any corporate OTC meds around. She's strictly homeopathic, aruyvedic, organic, vegan, aromatherapeutic."

Tim shrugged it off. The fall had actually helped clear his head, and he could feel the fog lifting. "How about you? Coming to pay a call on Miss Annie?"

"I'm doing a little color consulting. She's doing some textile design that is supposed to complement a line of furniture that Geoff and Jake have been cooking up," said Scott.

"Lots of entrepreneurial work going on here lately," said Tim. "Used to be perfection and restoration, one piece at a time."

Scott nodded. Over drinks the previous night, Scott had talked gossip about collectors they both knew, craftsmen they had encountered at Campbell and LaSalle, but he hadn't really touched on any of the work being done here.

"Used to be that everyone was happy to sit at the feet of Glen and Blake, but we aging hippies need to have some security. It's not as if our independent contractor status around here pays for dental insurance."

"I'm not sure I follow," said Tim, both of them heading up the path to Annie's door.

"A lot of us started coming here in our twenties, right after college. It was like that big commune in Tennessee somewhere, except here you got great gourmet meals instead of beans and brown rice, no one made you till the soil, and there was no leader who had to approve marriages or asserted his right to sleep with your girlfriend. Hell, I helped build a lot of these cabins in those days. Blake and Glen both had family money to burn, and we just sat around talking about making the world a more beautiful place and refining our spiritual selves by creating beautiful objects," said Scott.

"Blake and Glen weren't gurus?" asked Tim.

"Yeah, maybe, I guess. But they were more like designer gurus than spiritual leaders . . ."

"Ralph Lauren instead of Ram Dass?"

"Exactly," said Scott, laughing. "And they always paid well for the work, and nobody needed much to live on anyway—enough for a pair of tickets to see a Dylan concert or maybe a down payment on a VW bus."

"I get it. Enough to keep you in designer tie dye, but no one saved for a rainy day," said Tim.

"Rainy day? It's one thing to have no health insurance when you're twenty-five and going to live forever, but now . . . Have you ever had to pay for a root canal? Holy shit, man."

Tim looked at Scott's expensive boots and the cashmere v-neck he so casually wore under the apron as work clothes. He thought, but didn't say aloud, that Glen and Blake had cultivated a talented bunch of artists and had instilled within them exquisite taste.

"And I laughed at my dad when he suggested dental school," said Scott.

After Tim had said hello to Annie and tidied himself up from his brush with the planter, he left Scott with her for their color consultation. "Color consultation"? Tim wondered if that might be a C & L euphemism for a different kind of consultation altogether. Annie was a beautiful girl, all dark hair and pale skin, violet eyes, Elizabeth Taylor in *National Velvet*. Her gorgeous eyes though, when she answered the door, were red-rimmed. Was there someone at last shedding a tear for old Rick? As he walked down the path, he paused again at the planter and bent over, trying to hear what Scott was saying. He thought it was something about someone not being able to hurt her anymore. Had Rick been her lover and now was Scott moving in? For the "color consultation"?

He could hear Glen LaSalle announcing at one of the orientations for new artists: "We at Campbell and LaSalle do not have affairs, dalliances, quickies, or nooners, as they might be called elsewhere. We at Campbell and LaSalle have 'color consultations.' "

Tim was trying to decide whether or not to head over to Rick's cabin and see if he could find Jane or help her find whatever it was she was looking for. Knowing Jane, he was sure she didn't know what it would be until she saw it. That quality often made her a good scout at a rummage sale— not too set in her ways, not too dead-on to the lady head vases or the souvenir bottle openers to the exclusion of everything else that was interesting. No, Janie saw all the good stuff, but unfortunately she had only one set of eyes and one pair of hands. She couldn't scoop up the first editions and the collectible LPs in one room and still be the first one to the Pyrex or the button box in the room around the corner. In fact, she could get so caught up in looking over everything that she sometimes didn't make it out of the one room she started in.

Bruce Oh had told Jane that it was her persistent looking, her openness to what there was to see that would make her a good investigator. Yes, Oh was right about that. And it made her a good picker for Tim, but he had to train her to know when to stop looking, too. He had to be able to rouse her from that trance she got into when she started going through a box of photos, a tray of old mismatched silverware. What was she always looking for? Tim wasn't sure. He wasn't sure what any of them were always looking for, except now. He was looking for Claire Oh.

Feeling more than a little silly, he walked off the path and searched behind bushes, around the rear of some of the cabins and studios. His eyes kept sweeping the property the way he wanted to teach Jane to sweep a sales room. In fact, he had used the old game show, *Supermarket Sweep*, as an example of how she was to train herself. They used to watch it when they both faked being sick on the same day in elementary school. Jane, an independent fourth grader, would be left home alone with a can of chicken noodle soup and an opener and instructions to call the EZ Way Inn if she felt any worse.

Tim would be tucked into his bed with a quilt and a tray with tea and toast. He'd have to beg his overzealous mother to go watch her soap operas in the living room because he wanted to call Janie's house and see if she had the same flu bug. As planned out the night before, Jane would be cozied under a blanket in her father's recliner watching television. Tim would call, and Janie would do the play by play.

"Oh my god, she's taking all the cereal boxes into her cart; is she nuts?" Jane would say. "Go for the hams, go for the meat counter, you idiot," she'd scream into the phone.

"You know what she'll say, don't you? But my kids love that kind and it always seems expensive and I just thought if I got enough . . . ," Tim would respond, disgusted. "What's she wearing? What's her hair like?"

Then Tim would make up a story about her and her unhappy life with her husband. "They have great kids, though," Tim would say. "They are her pride and joy."

Yes, Tim would remind Jane about *Supermarket Sweep*, and that would help her use her keen rummage-sale eye to great advantage.

Just when Tim thought he was completely over his hangover, he hallucinated. He saw a rope ladder fall down out of a tree four feet in front of him. Shaking his head and squinting and beginning to feel vaguely like Jack-in-the-Beanstalk, he looked up.

No hallucination, not even one of Tim's, ever swore like the man descending the rope.

Mickey, dressed in sweatpants and a kind of loose-fitting kimono, was letting fly with a string of expletives when he saw a startled Tim standing directly in front of him.

"What do you know about this?" Mickey demanded, holding out a chunk of gold set with what appeared to Tim to be a real ruby.

Tim shook his head, looking up to see if Mickey had indeed come down from a beanstalk after raiding the nest of a golden-Cartier-earring-laying hen.

"I built this tree house. I take care of it, and it is my sanctuary. Do you hear that? Blake and Glen have both okayed it. They know I need a place to meditate, and now I find this. There're food scraps up there, too, which, if you didn't know, I'll be happy to tell you, will bring every critter in the world into my house—*my* house," Mickey said, still holding out the earring.

Tim thought to himself that it didn't look like it belonged to any of the women in residence here, but he decided anything he said right now to the enraged Mickey might be held against him. Was this the same stoned-looking, laid-back painter who had casually dropped food all over Jane last night?

Mickey began breathing deeply—in, out. Tim could count one on the inhale, two on the exhale. Mickey was clearly trying to calm himself. He seemed to be succeeding. His face lost some of its redness; he unclenched his fists.

"I'm sorry, pal. I was out of control there for a minute," Mickey said, his voice soft and measured.

"No problem," said Tim. "If I may ask, uh, what's up? I mean up there?"

"I built it as a getaway," Mickey said. "Yeah, I know, I know, Campbell and LaSalle is a getaway, but I just need a little more, you know. I'm tenser than the average bear, and I like to have a place where no one can find me. Hardly anybody even knows about this place, but . . ." Mickey let his voice trail off, then shrugged. "I brought Martine and Silver out here last night, and we got pretty loaded. When we left, I must have left the ladder down. So someone was up there, and it just bugs me, you know."

Yeah, Tim did know. It would be like someone finding your secret clubhouse.

"Anything missing?" Tim asked.

"Like my dope?" asked Mickey with a laugh. "Nah. Looks like someone just wanted a place to crash." Mickey opened his hand and looked at the earring. "With his lady, I guess."

"That lets me out," said Tim with a smile. He took off his sunglasses, a dark and mirrored pair that had protected his bleary bloodshot eyes from the early morning light.

"No interest in stargazing?" asked Mickey.

"No lady," said Tim.

"Well, turn around while I hide the ladder so I won't put you on my list of suspects if it happens again."

Obediently Tim turned around. Holding his sunglasses just so in front of him, he watched in the reflection as Mickey pulled a rope hidden on the other side of the tree that hoisted the ladder high up into the leaves. Mickey then wound the pulley rope around a hidden branch and poof, no more beanstalk.

It wouldn't take a genius to figure out that system, thought Tim, looking around at several vantage points from which they could be seen. They were in plain sight of the deck of the art gallery and the rear of two of the cabins. There were two telescopes that Tim knew about—one on the deck of the lodge and one in the gallery library of the barn. Mickey's little secret was probably known by every resident and guest of Campbell and LaSalle, even the ones he hadn't brought up for a little taste of stoned stargazing.

Tim left Mickey mumbling to himself and shuffling off toward his own cabin. Scott had mentioned last night that Mickey was angling to become Blake's right-hand man now that Rick was gone, but Tim didn't think he had a shot at it if Blake knew he was a doper. And Mickey didn't look like he was trying to keep that fact a secret.

Tim decided to go back to the lodge and meet with

Jane. It would be time for lunch soon. They hadn't made a plan on where to rendezvous, but Tim had never known Jane to miss a meal. He could ask her how she was doing on her research assignment, and they could wander out to the porch rockers. She could tell him all about what she had found in Rick Moore's cabin, and he could tell her all about not finding Claire Oh.

He wasn't returning from his search entirely empty-handed though.

He knew that Scott and Annie were special friends and that Annie had been crying. He knew that Scott needed a root canal. He knew that mellow Mickey had quite a temper when he thought his space was being violated. And he knew about a charming little hideaway that someone who didn't want to be seen on the grounds could use without being seen herself. He was also sure that when he and Jane did find Claire Oh, she would be wearing only one ruby earring.

13

When I carried out to the alley my first box of throwaways, I was shocked at how quickly people gathered to pick through my rubbish. I had a vision of all of us, picking through rubbish every time we enter a shopping mall. After all, isn't it all eventually refuse washed up on the shore of our wants and needs? The coast of our base desires?

—BELINDA ST. GERMAIN, *Overstuffed*

Jane made a quick stop at her cabin. If Claire Oh needed a place to hide out during the day, wouldn't she feel safest in Jane's place? And even if she hadn't wanted to stay in such an obvious location, she might have left a note, perhaps something a little less cryptic than the lipstick on the mirror.

But Claire Oh wasn't hiding under the bed or in the closet or behind the shower curtain. Jane lightened the load in her big leather bag by taking out the Westman book. She could go over what she had learned from that source later. The rest of the papers she had picked up at Rick's she kept with her. After tucking his Birkenstock sandals out of sight in her closet, she left for the lodge. It was almost lunchtime, and she was sure that Tim, over his hangover by now, would not want to miss a meal.

Approaching the front porch, she saw a new visitor talking to Roxanne. She could only see him from the back, but he looked familiar. A tall, slender man, he carried himself almost regally. He had a small duffel in his left hand and was gesturing with his right. If one looked quickly, it might appear that he was patting Roxanne's shoulder in a kind of "there, there" gesture, calming her; but looking more closely, Jane could see that he was patting the air. It had the effect of a "there, there" or a "don't worry about a thing" but it was more respectful, less familiar or patronizing. The man didn't know her so would not presume to touch her. Even that gesture seemed familiar to Jane.

She was only a few feet behind him when she heard his voice.

"Please don't trouble yourself. I'm only sorry Mr. Moore didn't give you my message. I can see how it must be an inconvenience, me showing up like this."

"The room in the lodge is quite nice, it's just that it's smaller than the guest cabins. We can have it ready after lunch, and I'll make sure you can meet with Mr. Campbell after tea this afternoon. We keep a silence after lunch you see . . ."

Again, the man patted the air. "Please, you are being so kind, and I am the intruder. I will leave my bag in the car," he said.

"No, no. I'll put it in my office, and it will be in your room after lunch," Roxanne said, taking the bag. "Jane, come and meet Mr. . . ."

"Oh," said Jane, as the man turned to her with a small smile and extended his hand.

"Mr. Kuruma. And you are?"

"Jane Wheel," she whispered.

He was wearing tan dress pants and an unstructured silk-and-linen sport coat in a rich brown with a thin windowpane of robin's egg blue running through it. Against his pale blue shirt hung an incredible tie. On a tan background, shiny blue-and-green cicadas were scattered, so colorful and vividly detailed that the design seemed three-dimensional.

"Are you a restoration artist, Mrs. Wheel?" he asked.

"No, a . . . student," she answered, trying desperately to remember how to speak a few more words in English.

"Call yourself an apprentice, Janie," said Tim, walking up behind them. "It's more in keeping with the spirit of Campbell and LaSalle. Right, Roxanne?"

She nodded and began to introduce Tim to the newcomer.

"Tim Lowry, meet Mr. Kuruma." Jane said the name at the same time as its owner, who thrust out his hand toward Tim.

"Oh," said Tim. "Hello."

"I'll leave you all for a few minutes, if that's all right. I want to make sure that Mr. Kuruma's room gets made up. See you at lunch.

"Can you please tell me about these studios?" asked Mr. Kuruma, so much better known to them as Bruce Oh, escorting the two of them off the porch. As he pointed and gestured, looking out at the grounds, he quickly and quietly told them that Claire was still missing.

"When she didn't come home, I looked over a few things in her office. She has a phone record printed out every month from her business phone, her cellular, and I saw that she had called Campbell and LaSalle the night of the antique show, at seven-eighteen P.M. Which would be right after Horace Cutler had come to her booth and made such a scene. In her calendar notebook, she had written down that she had called C & L and explained the problem to Rick. I decided to show up here and say that my secretary had called to say to expect me this day, this time, and that she had left the message with a Rick Moore. Sadly, I knew they wouldn't be able to check with him to see if I had called for a meeting and tour of Campbell and LaSalle."

"So Rick Moore knew that the Westman chest had been exposed as a fake," said Jane.

"Yes." Oh nodded. "And over there?" he asked loudly, pointing to the art gallery and studio behind the lodge.

"Did Claire say how specific Horace was when he yelled at her about selling him a fake? Did he mention that it was a Westman chest?" Jane asked.

"Claire told me that it was lucky he was so mad. He just sounded like a sputtering old man. No specifics. She was relieved. Just talking about a Westman chest would have called so much attention to the controversy."

"So as far as we know, only Claire, Horace, and Rick Moore knew about the Westman chest," said Jane. "No one here has mentioned it."

"Which doesn't make sense at all. They all peer over each other's shoulders here, dickering over which brush to use, whether or not they should make a hand-hammered hinge to match, or go off and scout one. They're all in each other's pockets," said Tim, then he remembered his news. "By the way, was Claire wearing chunky gold earrings last night, big ruby in the center?"

"She owns such a pair," said Oh, evenly. "I don't know if she was wearing them when she left."

Jane didn't know whether to be impressed with Oh's composure or shocked at his coolness. "Why, Tim?" she asked.

"I didn't find her, but I know where she slept last night. And that she ate well. She apparently left crumbs and an earring in Mickey's tree house. He was furious, but he has no idea that we have a stowaway," said Tim.

Oh nodded. Was he smiling? Jane wished she knew what the microscopic changes in the rise and fall of the corners of Oh's mouth really meant? Did he have a facial tic, or did he have feelings?

"Mickey has a tree house?" she asked, turning her attention to what Tim had discovered.

"Very possessive about it, too. He thinks someone spirited one of the gals up there for a liaison last night."

"Why last night? How does he know . . . ?"

"Because he was up there with Silver and Martine getting high after the memorial service. And when he went back this morning for his salute to the sun, or whatever the hell he does up there, he found the earring and dinner remains."

Oh cleared his throat and went into Mr. Kuruma mode. Martine was descending on them like a funnel cloud.

"You cannot monopolize our new guest, my dears," she said, brushing off Jane and Tim like gnats. "I am riveted by Asian culture and sensibility, and I insist you allow me to absorb some of your"—Martine gazed upward and around, looking for that pseudospiritual teleprompter that she seemed to call upon at will—"innate knowledge."

Jane watched Martine sweep Oh away from them.

"Close your mouth, Jane," Tim said. "It's a catch-and-release program with her. She'll throw him back when she finds out he has no money, no publishing connections, and no desire to take her to bed."

"Publishing connections?" asked Jane.

"That's why she latched on to Silver. She thought he knew people in the book biz. She told me she was shocked to find out Silver didn't have an agent. Some life coach guru type stayed here, and she and Martine talked a lot of bullshit; and then the 'protégé,' as Martine referred to her, went off and wrote a bunch of self-help books and made a fortune. Martine wants a piece of that pie. She said she was terribly disappointed that Silver didn't seem to understand anything about publishing. So she's given him the gate."

"The old heave-ho, Silver?" Jane asked.

"Awa-a-ay," answered Tim, taking her elbow and pushing her toward the lodge and lunch.

Jane and Tim quickly realized that it would be impossible to fill each other in between bites of lamb ragout and a pear-and-Roquefort salad. It was much easier—and quite entertaining—to watch Martine turn up the charm for Bruce Oh. Since she ran on a fairly high wattage regularly, the effect of adding more power was blinding.

Mr. Kuruma had introduced himself as a collector and a journalist for a new art and antiques journal. He had been careful to describe it as being in that fragile start-up phase where he couldn't really talk about the details, the investors, or the people behind the scenes. Still, it gave him enough of a cachet that the artists surrounding him at the table treated him as if he were an important restaurant critic, and they were all chefs.

Only Silver seemed removed from the feeding frenzy. The metaphorical feeding frenzy anyway. The poet was taking lunch quite seriously. According to the count Jane was keeping in her head, he had helped himself to four plates of the ragout and three salads. How hungry *was* this man? Since his caftan contained pockets, Jane was certain he lined them with plastic bags so he could stock up for later. Perhaps, as a poet, he had learned to take advantage of the generous table when it presented itself as a hedge against the lean times. Or perhaps, Jane thought, sizing up his ample frame robed in a brocade tent, he was simply a man with an appetite.

The thought crossed Jane's mind that Mickey must have built himself quite a tree house if he could entertain both Silver and Martine. That pair plus Mickey would be quite a test of the structural integrity of the tree house floor, not to mention the quality of hemp used to make the rope ladder. Considering hemp quality prompted Jane to wonder if there were Campbell and LaSalle residents who needed extra money for drugs, for publishing ventures, and, glancing at Silver's once again full plate, she added food to her list, desperately enough to want to profit by pulling the old switcheroo with antiques that came in for repair.

Her use of "cahoots" and "switcheroo" within the same hour—even though it was well within the boundaries of silent notes to self—prompted Jane to consider getting herself a word-a-day calendar to improve her vocabulary, which seemed to be based much too much on old movies and conversations with Tim. She also might ask Nick to tutor her on more updated slang.

Years ago, Jane and Charley had had neighbors, an

older couple, whom they liked very much. They noticed, though, when talking over the hedges or carrying in groceries at the same time, that both the man and woman had curiously formal and old-fashioned ways of speaking. After trimming a tree and offering some of the firewood to Charley, Carl suggested that Charley measure the width of the fireplace and have "your frau call my frau."

Jane and Charley decided that what their neighbors most sounded like were two observers from another planet who had learned to imitate earthlings by reading a how-to manual. Jane now realized that what they had really sounded like were middle-aged people.

Rooted in the slang and casual speak of their youth, they had only an acquaintance with contemporary pop culture because their age allowed them only limited access, classic Catch-22—another reference Jane doubted would make sense to Nick's generation. Carl and his "frau" probably would have preferred sounding young and hip or at least like Earth-born earthlings, but no one had bothered to tell them how to do it—or pointed out that they didn't sound "groovy" for that matter. And now Jane and Charley were there—middle-aged, a faraway planet, next stop, Frauville.

"Please?" whispered Silver.

Jane realized he had asked her something. From the pained look on his face, it was clearly something important.

"Sorry. I was lost in space," said Jane.

"Butter," said Silver, louder and with a slightly exaggerated articulation, as if Jane might be a bit hard of hearing.

Jane passed the pale slab of what appeared to her to be fine Danish butter. She wanted to ask him how he could possibly be putting away a thickly spread hunk of bread, after everything else he had eaten, but as Jane Wheel, girl detective, she knew that wouldn't be the way to his heart or to wherever he kept any information that might be helpful in finding out what had happened to the Westman chest, Horace Cutler, Rick Moore, or Claire Oh.

Jane thought maybe she knew the way into his heart.

"I'm getting coffee. Can I bring you back a plate of those cookies from the sideboard?"

He gave her a great big buttery grin and nodded.

Jane arranged six cookies, two of each of the three varieties—peanut butter rounds, chocolate-studded oatmeal cookies, and dipped macaroons—on a pink depression glass plate and brought it to Silver. He looked at her with such bald gratitude that she was taken aback. What must his poetry be like? Lots of food metaphors and themes of emptiness and hunger?

"Working on a new collection?" asked Jane. "Or is that a bad question to ask a poet?"

"Not a bad question, I just have a sad answer," Silver said, brushing crumbs off the sleeve of his robe. "Block," he said, pointing first at his head, then at his heart.

Jane wasn't sure if he meant he had writer's block or he was telling her something about his arteries. He had, after all, just downed a quarter pound of butter.

"I've had great difficulty reentering my artistic space. I am working my way back to the word, so to speak," he said.

With a fork, not a pen, Jane thought, while she said, "Interesting."

"Martine is helping me," Silver said. "Coaching."

Jane wondered how one went about coaching a poet. Writing seemed like a highly personal endeavor, and writing poetry the most personal of all. How did a life coach figure into his literary work?

"Martine is good at opening up the channels," said Silver, "helping me redirect my energies."

"How?" Jane asked, truly curious, but realizing as soon as the question was out of her mouth that it might sound insensitive.

She needn't have worried. Silver was eager to share his new wisdom. He described his regime of walking and meditating, his clearing away the extraneous in his life, his elimination of the negative, his paring down of worldly goods.

"I only have two caftans, one pair of sandals. I keep one notebook for journaling and a separate one for poems. I have two sharp pencils and two pens. I use the same pen and pencil for poems, and I don't use them for anything else. They are my sacred instruments, and I keep them for my work."

Silver stopped talking and ate three cookies in rapid succession. No wonder the guy was hungry. Martine had taken everything away from him. Eating was the only thing he had left. Jane figured Martine would have him on a juice fast within the month. She was going to make him pay for not having an agent who could get her a two-book deal.

Silver picked up the small, hand-lettered card that announced the day's meals. Jane was appalled that he could even read about food after the amount of it he had just consumed. He looked giddy with delight though as he read aloud the description of dinner.

"An Evening in Provence will be tonight's theme. We will begin with a silky seafood bisque . . . ," he read, enraptured with the words that would so soon be realized as a source of satisfaction. Jane stopped listening after the first line.

That was it. That was the missing piece to this puzzle. What was it that Claire Oh had told her about the Westman chest? She'd spotted it in the basement of an estate sale. It was being used for tools or junk by the home owners. No one had even known it was there. No one had bothered to put a price on it.

That's the part she had not thought to question Claire about. She really had to find Claire Oh; it was time to stop playing games. Silver was droning on about heavy cream and a soupçon of this, just a dash of that. Hell, he probably devoted more heart and soul to the reading of this menu than he did to reading his own work. Unless, of course, he had published a cookbook in iambic pentameter. Not a bad thought, every recipe in sonnet form or something close. Jane's mind was racing as he spoke, but she hadn't really heard a thing after the first line.

"A night in Provence." Provence. Provence. Why hadn't she thought of it until now?

So what if the carving looked exactly like the work of Mathew Westman? Without piecing together some kind of history, some kind of explanation of how that particular chest had ended up in that particular basement, the chest could not be authenticated, not definitively. Even if an authority such as Glen LaSalle or Blake Campbell had declared the carving to be Westman's, without a clear time line on the piece, it would be a tough sell to make this the find of a lifetime.

Jane had been so enamored when Claire had showed her the piece that she hadn't thought to ask about the owners. How had the piece gotten into the basement? Had it been there when the owners moved in? Who had lived in the house before them? Any living family members to question? Was there anyone who could help them trace that piece of furniture?

Jane was a rookie, so it was understandable that she hadn't thought to ask. And as soon as she had dragged Tim up here, they had found Rick Moore dead, which provided a major distraction. But if Claire had brought the chest up here to be worked on, surely everyone would have been trying to trace the history of such an important find. A third Westman chest? This was museum time, major acquisition time. Jane hadn't wanted to mention the Westman connection to anyone until she found out more about the people here. Why hadn't they been talking about it to her though?

Horace Cutler's murder had been reported in the paper. Claire Oh's name was certainly mentioned. Wouldn't anyone here remember that she had just picked up the Westman chest? Wouldn't they be wondering what had really happened?

Jane stood up then realized that Silver was still reading to her, and she sat back down. She couldn't drag Tim and Oh away from the table to discuss this with them and get their take without arousing a good deal of curiosity. She cleared her throat to interrupt Silver, so she could make a polite exit. He was lingering over the description of the *pots du crème*, when he was stopped by someone other than Jane.

"May I have your attention, please?"

Officer Murkel had returned to the lodge, this time with several uniformed officers. Apparently whatever warrant Roxanne had advised him he would have to have, he had.

"We are reopening our investigation of Rick Moore's death here at Campbell and LaSalle. We will need to question everyone here, and we ask that no one leave the property without our okay. We'll be setting up an office in the gallery. The barn workshop and Mr. Moore's cabin and truck are strictly off-limits," said Murkel, ignoring the low muttering that began to grow louder at his last statement.

"May we see you now, Mrs. Wheel?" Murkel asked, phrasing it as a question, intoning it like a statement.

Jane stood up. She tugged the menu out of Silver's loving grasp and asked if she could use the pen sticking out of the patch pocket of his robe. Without waiting for an answer, she took it and wrote something on the card, and tossed the pen back on the table in front of Silver. By the stricken look on his face, she realized that she had taken his poem-writing pen, defiled his sacred tool. Martine would have her work cut out for her this afternoon. Did she do exorcisms?

On her way out, she slipped the card in front of Tim who was seated to Oh's left. *Let them get started on some of the work,* she thought, making sure Tim couldn't miss her alteration to the menu. The title of the theme dinner no longer read "A Night in Provence." Jane had amended it to—"A Night in *Provenance!!!!!!!*"

14

A place for everything and everything in its place might work for some. For the truly clutter-mad, the stuff junkies, simple sayings won't do. You must strip down to bare essentials. No spares. Do not own one thing more than you need. You do not need more storage; you need to have nothing to store.

—BELINDA ST. GERMAIN, *Overstuffed*

The word "provenance" describes the source and history of ownership of a piece of art, a piece of furniture, any object of note or value. It is a word tossed around on the *Antiques Roadshow* almost as much as "patina" and "veneer." Jane and Tim had long ago decided that if they ever had an imaginary son to keep their imaginary daughter, Patina, company, they would name him Veneer. And even if asked directly, they vowed to keep little Patina and Veneer's provenance a secret.

Jane berated herself as she followed Murkel to the gallery office set up by the police. Why had she not asked this before? How had Claire been planning to prove that this was a Westman chest? She would have had to have it authenticated by experts—they at Campbell and LaSalle could give it credibility; but before they did, they would need to know as much as possible about the discovery. Yes, valuable pieces had been found at sales and auctions, even thrift stores, far away from their birthplaces and original owners; but generally there was a paper trail, or at least an oral history, that could be discovered, that gave credence to a piece's authentication.

If, for example, a bill of sale for a third Westman chest had been found among Mathew Westman's papers, one could attach a name to the original owner. Say the Smith family had purchased a sunflower-carved chest from Mathew Westman. Research might show that the same Smith family, a few years later, had moved west to Chicago. Over the course of time, descendants scatter throughout the Midwest. Some pieces of furniture scatter with them; some, perhaps, were lost in the great Chicago Fire. Maybe the Smith family fell on hard times and their possessions were sold at auction. On a whim, a Mr. Jones bid on the now-worn and beat-up chest. He paid a few dollars for it, brought it home because he thought it looked interesting and well made, but his wife thought otherwise. It was sturdy, so they decided to put it to use, out of sight. Maybe they threw some paint on it to brighten it up. Perhaps the Westman chest was separated, its top shelf the perfect size to serve as a small side table in a child's bedroom and the bottom set of drawers, which were too ornate to be fashionable, ended up holding cans of paint and old brushes in the basement. Fifty more years passed. The Joneses' grandson's estate sale was held, and Claire Oh spotted the chest, which was so buried in the basement it was a throwaway.

Improbable, but not impossible. Jane was sure that Campbell and LaSalle would have tried to check the provenance of this piece as thoroughly as they would have examined the oxidation patterns on the undersides of the drawers and the marks of the carving tools on the sunflowers.

If Campbell and LaSalle had given their authentication, this piece would have the all-important "provenance." Somewhat questionable, perhaps—not what every dealer and collector hopes for, a pure line of ownership, a piece passed down through the same family since its creation—but still, a possible scenario that might satisfy a well-heeled collector of Early American furniture.

If Campbell and LaSalle had not found any paper trail or oral history that might give the piece of furniture credibility as a Westman-made chest, it would be far less valuable. It would not necessarily, as Horace Cutler had accused, be a fake, not if it were simply being sold as a fine old Early American chest, carved in the manner of Mathew Westman; only if it was a fine new American chest, carved in the manner of Rick Moore, being passed off as the former.

Jane couldn't believe she had not quizzed Claire Oh about the owners of the estate. Or asked about what the experts had said about the chest when she brought it in. They must have authenticated it; otherwise she would not have delivered it to Cutler or, at least, not been surprised when he denounced it as a fake.

She was so lost in thought that Jane had to ask Murkel twice to repeat his question. Even then, she felt a bit lost. Was it only yesterday that she and Tim had arrived at Campbell and LaSalle?

"I asked you, Mrs. Wheel, if you were aware of any kind of odor, a chemical smell, when you entered the barn yesterday?" Murkel asked.

Jane tried to remember her first impression of the barn when she entered it. A beautiful workshop, well equipped and laid out. She remembered seeing the cans of paint and varnishes and solvents along one wall, but she couldn't remember seeing any of them opened. She mentally sent herself back up the stairs to the gallery library. She could not remember any smell. The windows were open, though, so why would she have smelled anything?

"I don't remember a smell. The windows were all open, though, and there was a breeze, so it might have freshened the air," she said.

"You remember a breeze?" Murkel asked.

"Yes. Actually I do. When I was in the library, I noticed a book open on one of the tables. It had a bookmark in it, but the breeze had blown a few pages over it, past the marked page. And there was a little table-tent-type card that said something about the fact that Campbell and LaSalle did painstaking research on every piece brought to them for . . ." Jane stopped. That's right, further proof that someone knew the truth about the Westman chest before Claire picked it up. They wouldn't have restored it without getting its story.

"Yes?" asked Murkel.

"I remember the breeze blowing through," said Jane. "If there was a smell, I didn't notice it."

It struck Jane that no one had said why the investigation was being reopened, but considering what she had seen in Rick's truck, the carving tools, the imitation Westman sunflowers, she thought she might have an idea.

"Was Rick Moore murdered?" she asked.

Murkel smiled without the slightest trace of good humor. "What makes you think so?" he asked.

"I asked the question. I didn't say I thought anything," Jane said, beginning to think quite a lot about the sandals back in her cabin and the envelope of papers marked important.

How much trouble was she going to be in for taking all of this to study on her own?

Jane was surprised to see Murkel plant his elbows on the desk, rest his chin in his hands, and lean toward her. He looked ready to confide a deep and dark secret, so Jane prepared herself to listen.

"I know you're a detective of sorts, Mrs. Wheel, and I think you came up here following the same trail that I am now following. Don't you think we should share information?"

Jane was astonished. She was quite sure that, cartoon-like, her eyes had popped out of her skull and her chin had dropped to the floor. Since she was not sure she *was* a detective, how could a police officer in another state lean on his elbows and act like he wanted to dish the dirt with her?

"Don't be coy, Mrs. Wheel. You found Rick Moore's body. Didn't you think we'd at least check your name through our computer? It comes up in a few other recent murder investigations," said Murkel.

"You googled me?" Jane asked, incredulous.

"Police don't have to google, Mrs. Wheel, but it's the same idea."

Jane did not want to fail this test. She wanted to learn what Murkel knew without revealing what she knew, which wasn't all that much. Or was it? Lots of worrisome questions with no definitive answers. For example, where was Claire Oh? Why had she risked so much to come up here and hide in a tree house? What was in that envelope that Rick Moore had marked important? And what was the big secret of Campbell and LaSalle? That they had built a fake Westman and switched it, or that they had provided false authentification for what they knew was a fake? Or had they simply made a mistake that they needed desperately to cover up? Was someone desperate enough to kill Horace Cutler to shut him up? Oh yeah, and now the new jackpot question: Who killed Rick Moore?

If she could just satisfy Murkel for the time being, she could get out and put the right questions to the right people. Maybe Bruce Oh, if he'd been able to ditch Martine, and Tim, if he had been able to read her scrawled "provenance," were already out there getting answers. She needed to be with them, now.

"Officer Murkel, I have an idea about those windows in the barn," Jane said, trying to think one second ahead of her actual speech. "Maybe someone saturated the air with something, poured it on cloth, and put it in with Moore while all the windows were closed. I mean if he wasn't in there to cure wood, he might not have opened them. Then when he staggered out, that person led him to the stream, easily held him in the water, then went in and opened everything up. It wouldn't have taken that long, and during quiet . . ."

"Yes, during quiet time, I know. Everyone just disappears, and no one has an alibi for anything," Murkel said with a sigh. "I don't know. The windows are hinged at the top and push out easily. Maybe . . ." Murkel stopped and sighed again. "Maybe we should start at the beginning. Have you found out anything about Horace Cutler's murder since you've been here?"

Jane felt like she could answer with an honest no, since she certainly had nothing definitive to say; but before she could even get that syllable out, Murkel went on musing, finishing his thought. "I mean, besides the fact that Rick Moore killed him."

Murkel smiled when he saw Jane's face. "I'm sure by the time you leave this office, everyone will be talking about it," he said. "I explained it, in part anyway, to the secretary here when I stopped in this morning. An eyewitness puts Moore and his truck at the scene of the murder. Cutler was holding on to some strands of hair that match up with Moore's. There's a boatload of stuff on my desk that all point to him. The woman they questioned has been cleared, her story checked out."

Jane reeled, but just a bit. She must be getting better as a detective because her reeling time was getting shorter. Rick Moore had been murdered. Jane knew that. But perhaps it wasn't because of his carving skills or his knowledge of furniture forgery. Perhaps it was to cover the tracks of Cutler's murder? But weren't they Rick Moore's tracks? Why not just let him get caught? Jane was relieved at the convoluted thinking here. Maybe she *could* be a detective since the bad guys seemed to be even more confused than she was.

Murkel was treating her like a professional. Jane couldn't leave the office without giving him something. It was a matter of pride.

"I have Rick's shoes, his sandals. They were in the library under a chair. I'm pretty sure he was up there reading until something drove him outside."

Murkel nodded. "Anything else?"

"I'll let you know," said Jane, feeling guilty that she was keeping Rick's papers a secret from the first person to treat her like she was indeed a private investigator, not guilty enough to give them up until she'd had a chance to look them over, but guilty nonetheless.

Jane left Murkel shuffling some papers, still looking like he wanted to rest his head in his hands. Jane felt just the opposite. She was ready to put on her deerstalker cap and head for a gaggle of Campbell and LaSalle artists and fire questions. Claire Oh would come out of hiding soon, as soon as she heard she had been cleared. Jane guessed she'd send a squirrel with a message tied to his tail up to the tree house and let her know she could come out and play. The fact that she had been lurking around on the grounds might seem suspicious, but she didn't have anything to worry about here. She was at home when Rick Moore took his last drink of water.

When Jane went back to the lodge, she was surprised to find it empty and quiet. She had expected Martine to be organizing a séance or something. Shouldn't everyone be buzzing about the murderer among them? No one was going to be allowed to leave for a while, so shouldn't they all be standing around casting suspicious glances and shouting accusations? At least one of them should burst into tears and be afraid. But, no.

It was quiet time. Jane half expected that somewhere she would find one of those small, hand-lettered, table-tent signs that would say, "We at Campbell and LaSalle respect the quiet hours even when a murderer is running amok." Jane set off to find Oh and Tim. She was quite sure they were not keeping silent, although she knew it was possible that Tim might be running amok.

The barn was supposed to be off-limits, but Jane thought she'd just walk by it on her way back to her cabin.

That's where Tim and Oh would be or where they would leave her a note. The barn was taped off, and she could see a uniformed policeman standing at the door. The windows, she noticed, were open. They were large windows on the ground floor, hinged at the top. It was easy to tell from far away that they were open since they were simply pushed out and held with a wooden bar. The higher windows, the ones that provided light and air to the gallery library, were open as well.

"Officer, is it possible to retrieve a book from the library? That's the second-floor gallery," Jane asked.

He shook his head, as she knew he would, and she shrugged, bit her lip, and walked on, circling around to the back as if she were taking the path to one of cabins that faced the stream. Annie was in one of those, and maybe Geoff and Jake, Jane wasn't sure.

When she got to the back of the barn, she looked at the back door. It was hardly noticeable as an exit or entrance because on the inside it didn't open up to the main work area. It was at the foot of the backstairs, the ones that led down from the gallery and offices. It was the one she had left by yesterday—was it only yesterday?—when she'd wandered down to the stream and found Rick Moore. Was it possible that the police didn't even realize that this door existed? There was no guard.

Jane was ten feet away from the door when it opened. She froze, hoping that the man exiting the barn would not turn her way. He did not turn at all but walked quickly down the path. Jane followed at what she hoped was a safe distance.

Just before the trail that led up to Annie's place, he turned off the path and went into a heavily wooded area.

He knew where he was going, turning left then right until Jane was quite confused about what direction she was going. When he stopped, she stopped and watched him open a door to a large metal shed. It was so cleverly concealed within the trees that one could walk by it a dozen times and not see it. However, it was so far off the path that Jane doubted anyone would happen upon it by accident. She could see at the other end of the shed that there was a roughly cleared access road leading to a kind of loading-dock door. Jane was too turned around to know whether it was the same road where Rick Moore parked his truck, and the one he used for his secret trips in and out of Campbell and LaSalle.

The man had disappeared inside the door but left it open. He wore a baggy barn jacket, a fishing hat pulled down low, and what looked to Jane like large, blue-tinted safety goggles. There were no windows, so Jane crept up to the door and peeked in. There were several pieces of stunning antique furniture in the room. Jane scanned the space quickly to see if she could spot the real Westman Sunflower Chest. Perhaps this was where they had hidden it when they swapped it for the forgery delivered to Claire Oh. She stopped her inventory when the man pulled out a lovely butterfly table. He pulled out the delicately shaped supports that gave it its name and rubbed an appreciative hand over its surface. He knelt to feel the exquisitely turned legs. Jane noticed there was an open toolbox near his feet, and she leaned farther into the doorway to see what he was bending down to retrieve from it. When he again stood over the table, he had in his hand an old wooden mallet. Jane thought perhaps there was a peg he had to gently tap into place and she smiled, enjoying her peek at a master craftsman fine-tuning his work.

When he brought down the mallet on the table with all his might, Jane involuntarily screamed. The smashing of the tabletop was so loud that he went on with it, not hearing Jane react as if it were she being struck. Jane watched in horror as he continued to dent and pound the once-perfect wooden surface. Has he gone insane?

Jane was almost ready to go embrace him, make him put down the tool he was brandishing as a weapon, when she smelled something. It was sweet at first, then she took a stronger whiff and every bit of space in her throat was filled. It was if her head and body were made up of many rooms, and she actually heard the doors slamming shut. Eyes, ears closed off, clear thinking was now definitely closed for business.

Everything was this smell, which, she realized for just a moment then forgot, was coming from a drenched cloth that had been draped over her head from behind. The cloth was not tightened. It didn't need to be. The chemical fumes became vaporous hands that choked off every bit of air and life. She staggered backward. Air, she needed air, and water to get this out of her eyes.

The cloth fell off, or at least she thought it did. She tried to run and maybe she was running, but she couldn't tell. She was blinded, but she didn't know if she was truly blind or if her eyes had closed so tightly against the fumes that she simply had forgotten how to command them to open again. Was someone following her? She couldn't tell. She couldn't breathe. She needed something cool, something clean. She would like someone to teach her how to breathe again. She was quite certain she used to know how, but the talent was now clearly and completely gone.

She heard a raspy, choking sound. Was that the person following her? Horrible noise. It must be some kind of monster chasing her. She heard giant gasping. Who was this bearing down on her, retching and gulping? She heard the gurgle and sucking and death rattle and then wished desperately that she hadn't realized that the horrifying sounds were coming from her.

This was not fair, this breath being taken from her. She willed her lungs to fill, but they were clearly behind one of those closed doors inside of her. She wanted to breathe for Nick and for Charley; she had to breathe for Nick and Charley. She managed one tiny intake of air that did not cause her chest to cave in and felt a small bubble of hope. As quickly as it rose, it popped and disappeared when she felt two hands holding on to one of her elbows, propelling her forward. "We have to get you to the stream," she thought she heard someone say, but the voice was so far away, far behind one of those closed doors.

She fought being pushed, being led, or thought she did, but she knew that whoever was guiding her was in control. In one plaintive, lucid moment of thought, she wondered why it was that the last image she would have on earth was the bizarre scene she had just witnessed . . . a Campbell and LaSalle artist destroying an Early American butterfly table. *How very odd,* she was thinking, as she passed out. *How very odd.*

15

The feng shui practitioner will tell you to empty all trash cans daily so that you are not surrounded by stagnant energy. I suggest that these pockets of stagnant energy lurk on every surface, on every shelf, and in every closet. Be aware and beware.

—BELINDA ST. GERMAIN, *Overstuffed*

Just as Jane had heard and felt the doors within her slam shut, closing her off from the conscious world before she passed out, she now felt them opening one by one. Hearing came back in a rush, a roar, loud voices. An argument? Her eyes had been closed so tightly against whatever toxic cloud had chased her from the warehouse that opening them, actually seeing light filtering through the tree canopy, was painfully bright. She closed them.

"... coming around ... too late ... what you do ... situation ... facedown ..." Two men were talking, and Jane knew she should keep her eyes closed and listen. If they were trying to decide what to do with her, it might give her the Girl Scout advantage of being prepared. She was pretty certain they wouldn't try to dump her facedown in the stream, since Murkel and his officers might be even more suspicious about the goings-on at Campbell and LaSalle if there were two drownings in two days in ten inches of water.

Jane breathed as deeply as she could without calling attention to the fact that she could now breathe, and it felt damn good. She wanted to drink in the air, gulp it down, but she settled for small sips and tensed her muscles, hoping she would have the strength to strike out as soon as one of the men tried to touch her.

She heard someone walk toward her, the rustle of leaves and twigs much louder she realized, when one is lying on the ground. She felt the sun blocked from her face by someone kneeling next to her, bending over her. As she sensed the face getting closer to her own, she balled up her fist, opened her eyes, and struck Tim Lowry so hard on the side of his head that he fell over backward. Although she had missed his eye, where she might have done some damage at such short range, she had grazed his ear, which he now held, shouting, "What the hell are you trying to do to me?"

Jane sat up, still feeling dizzy but more clearheaded with every breath.

"Is that how you always wake up? Jeez . . . am I bleeding?" Tim asked, turning his ear toward Jane, then toward Bruce Oh, who stood over them both.

"I admire someone who, even at their weakest, prepares to meet her enemy," said Oh, bending to help Jane, who was now trying to stand.

Jane opened her mouth to say loudly to Tim what she thought of those who cried over a little slap upside the head, but all that came out was a whispered, "Baby."

Jane's head cleared quickly, and her throat began to feel

better after a few sips from Tim's water bottle. She was in such a rush to tell them all she knew that they had to keep stopping her, questioning whether it was something she'd learned from her clandestine visit to Rick Moore's cabin and truck, her lunchtime conversations, her interview with Murkel, or her little adventure straying off the path in the woods.

Bruce Oh and Tim told her that Murkel had been right about everyone having the information about Rick Moore. Word had gotten out rapidly after lunch that Moore was almost certainly responsible for the murder of Horace Cutler. Everyone was shocked or seemed to be. Geoff and Jake were the only residents who hadn't known Cutler personally. Those who had dealt with him called him a fussy, meticulous curmudgeon, who often complained about their prices, but after grumbling, always paid his bills. No one seemed to be aware of any particular argument between Rick Moore and Cutler.

"What about the Westman chest? Has anyone brought it up?" asked Jane.

"Of course not," said Tim. "Wouldn't that blow our cover? Keep us from getting the inside info?"

"Yeah, because we're getting so much of that now," said Jane.

"I mentioned it," said Oh, "indirectly. I identified myself, not only as the money behind a new art magazine, but I mentioned that Horace Cutler had recommended that I do an article on Campbell and LaSalle. And I told them that Horace had recently found a special carved American chest for me. I asked if they had worked on it."

"Who did you talk to?" Jane asked. "What did they say?"

"I mentioned it only to Roxanne when I checked in,

and she said she'd have to check the files. She was sure they didn't have anything of his at the moment."

"It wouldn't be his piece, though. Not on paper anyway. Your wife would be their client," said Tim.

Jane recovered fully enough to insist that they try to find the warehouse where she had witnessed such strange behavior. Tim suggested that she might have already been attacked with the chemicals and hallucinated. "No one here would knowingly damage a good piece of furniture," he said, when Jane described the utter destruction of the tabletop. "It had to be the rag you got smoked with." Oh had said nothing. He shushed them silently with a finger to his lips when he parted a branch and pointed out the warehouse. The door was closed. This time they all stayed back. Listening intently, they heard a rhythmic beat. Hammer on table. Jane arched her eyebrows at Tim and nodded. "He's still at it," she whispered.

As soon as she said it, the noise stopped. They heard what sounded like a garage door open in the distance.

"Come on, it's the door on the other end," said Jane.

Under cover of the trees, they circled to the back of the shed. The large door was up, and a battered pickup was parked in front of it. Two old rusty window-unit air conditioners sat in back of the truck, along with a doorless refrigerator, a few old mattresses, and some broken chairs. It was an alley picker's truck, filled with the trash that people hope and pray someone will haul away when they get it from their house to the back. An old man wearing a filthy plaid shirt stood next to the table, which now had one beautifully turned leg cracked. Jane also saw that some kind of paint or solvent had been spilled over the entire surface. She hadn't noticed it before, but from this angle, she could see the discoloration.

"If you're sure nobody here wants it?" they heard the old man say.

They couldn't hear a response or see the mad hammerer from where they stood, but he must have thanked the old man for taking it because he responded with a "No, thank *you*. I'll sure find somebody who wants it, can use it."

"TOM'S TRASH AND TREASURES," Oh read aloud from the side of the truck. "Do either of you know Tom?"

Tim and Jane both shook their heads.

They waited for their man to come back out the door and onto the path. Jane came out from behind the bushes when she heard two car doors slam shut. "He's leaving with him, with Tom." She moved around to the end of the building in time to see the truck drive around the curve in the road that led back to the main entrance of Campbell and LaSalle.

"Whoever it is is going to be back at the lodge long before we can get there on foot," said Jane.

"Do you think he saw you at the door? Did he see or hear you get attacked?" asked Oh.

"Not necessarily," Jane said. "I was all the way back at the door, and it was really loud in there. As soon as I had my first whiff of the stuff, I staggered backward and tried to run toward where I thought the path would be."

"Someone's coming down the path. That way," Tim said, pointing beyond the warehouse.

Quickly they walked back to their hidden spot around the other side of the building just in time to see Mickey and Annie. She was shaking her head and wiping her eyes, and Mickey was speaking nonstop into her ear.

Without one word, Oh put his finger to his lips and

signaled them to take two steps backward and stand perfectly still.

"We are trees," Jane heard him say, almost silently. It was less than a whisper, slightly more than a pantomime. They stood perfectly still. Mickey and Annie walked past them, close enough that Jane could have plucked the handkerchief out of Annie's hand. They remained silent, watching them as they disappeared from view.

Jane looked admiringly at Oh. He had saved them, bailed them out. She and Tim would have bumbled their way in front of them and would have had to make up some ridiculous story. What kind of ancient wisdom did Oh draw on? What could she say to him that wouldn't sound stupid and coy?

"Brilliant strategy. 'We are trees.' Is it from tai chi or something? I mean, it was almost mystical," Jane said. She walked ahead without waiting for an answer.

"What? What did you say about trees?" asked Tim, turning to Oh, who lifted his shoulders slightly and shook his head.

"Nothing. I said I don't think they'll see us."

Back at her cabin, Jane realized that what she wanted more than anything at that moment, more than answers, more than the identity of the person who had almost poisoned her with lethal chemicals, more than a Grey Goose on the rocks, which was something she wanted pretty badly, was more clothes. She wanted a great big suitcase with lots of shirts and sweaters and more socks. Yes, she had been reading a page here and a page there of Belinda St. Germain's

Bible, and she even felt like some of it made sense, but this six-item packing challenge was a crock, at least when you're in the middle of the woods being gassed and rolling around in pine needles. She needed a bath and clean clothes.

She started the tub, pouring in the lavish rosemary mint bubble bath provided by Campbell and LaSalle, and walked into Tim's cabin next door without knocking.

"I don't want any lip; I just want some clothes. Nice clean clothes," she announced.

Tim nodded. He took out an olive green T-shirt and a maroon cashmere V-neck from the chest by the bed. Rummaging in his closet, he pulled out a pair of olive linen drawstring pants. She took them all in her arms without a word. He dangled a pair of silk boxers, and she tried to give him a withering smile.

The bath was really helping. Especially since Tim went all the way up to the lodge, poured her a drink, put in six olives, and stumbled into her bathroom with one hand over his eyes to put it on the side of the tub.

"Is this Grey Goose?"

"Right country. It's Ciroc. From France, multiply distilled from grapes instead of grain. Smooth. More like grappa, yes?" Tim said, holding up his own glass.

"Grappa, shmappa. Don't go all yuppie wine tasting on me. It's good," she took another taste, "very, very good."

"Are you relaxed enough to hear something without freaking out?" Tim asked, standing by the door, his eyes still closed.

"Maybe," said Jane, sipping her Ciroc.

"I found your phone near where you fell. It was off, dead battery, and I know how you like to always be in touch. It's plugged in, recharging now. I figure you've only been unreachable for about two hours," he said.

"It's okay," said Jane. "Nick's with the good parent, so he wouldn't be upset if I didn't pick up the phone. He wouldn't even be trying to call me."

"Janie, stop being so hard on yourself. It was a permission slip for a field trip for god's sake. You didn't abandon him in a basket in the bullrushes. He got to go on a better trip with Charley, and you get to solve a mystery."

"Oh, I'm doing a bang-up job of that. Do you have a clue as to what's going on here? Besides the fact that I almost got"—Jane said, thinking how to describe what had happened to her—"ragged to death?"

Jane and Tim both started laughing. They were so loud in fact that at first they didn't hear the faint "Jingle Bells" coming from the bedside table.

"Phone's charged," said Tim, as he went to get it. Checking the caller ID as he brought it to Jane, he smiled, forgetting that he was supposed to be covering his eyes, "It's Nellie."

"Oh great. Now I *do* get ragged to death," said Jane, setting them both off again.

"Yeah?" said Nellie, responding to Jane's hello.

"You called *me*, Mom," Jane said, unable to stop giggling.

"What the hell's going on?" asked Nellie.

"Well, I'm in the bathtub drinking vodka and Tim is lending me some clothes and I can't come home from Michigan because I found somebody who was murdered here and I almost got killed today by a rag soaked in some kind of chemicals. How's the toe?"

"What the hell is Tim doing in the bathroom with you?" shouted Nellie.

"Not looking," said Jane.

"I am too looking," said Tim, raising his voice. "I'm looking, Nellie. I'm looking right at her. All my scheming pretending to be gay has finally paid off."

"Now you listen to me, both of you!" yelled Nellie, loud enough that they both could hear her. "It's dangerous to drink in the bathtub. You can goddamn drown or worse. Tim Lowry, you just stay homosexual, you hear me? You're fine the way you are. Jane, you leave him alone. Where's Charley?"

"Oh great, now it's me trying to seduce you," said Jane. "Mom, Charley and Nick are in Rockford. They'll be back home tonight, but I won't. Maybe tomorrow. How's your foot?"

"I told you, Don, she's still at some furniture farm somewhere with Tim. Oh hell, you can't fit a square peg in a round . . . oh damn, I don't know what I mean either. I just think she shouldn't be taking a bath with him. I suppose you think that's all right?"

Jane held the phone over the water.

Tim reached over and took it from her, made a quasi-believable static noise from the back of his throat, and said in a high-pitched whisper, "You're breaking up, Mom. Call you back later from a real phone." He pushed the "end" button.

"How'd you learn to make that noise?" Jane asked.

"Three years of Sunday night calls to my dad in his Florida condo and then to my mom in hers. The only compelling reason I can think of that they should have stayed married is that it would have saved me one phone call per week—156 phone calls. Static imitation has saved me many a time," said Tim.

"Is it about time for Oh's meeting with Blake to be over? I'm dying to hear what he comes up with," Jane said, then stopped when the bathroom door creaked slowly open.

Tim and Jane both froze.

Slowly peeking around the door was a very dirty, very tall woman wearing elegant high-heeled boots.

"Is this where you investigators solve your cases?" asked Claire Oh. "Because if not, and you can do it on dry land, perhaps I could have a turn here in the famous detective school. I could really use a bath."

16

There are those who will tell you that certain corners of your house, certain areas of your life, need to be cleared before you can channel your energy and be successful. I am telling you that if any corner of your life is left cluttered and blocked, you will be locked in a permanently stalled position.

—BELINDA ST. GERMAIN, *Overstuffed*

"I think she's fabulous," whispered Tim, handing Jane a belt so she could cinch up his linen pants. He rolled up the cuffs for her and stood back. "You look pretty cute in a thirties/forties Hollywood musical my-dad's-got-a-barn-let's-put-on-a-show-after-I-plow-the-field kind of way."

"Pretty haughty, if you ask me," Jane whispered back. "We're out here risking our necks for her, and she just waltzes in . . ."

Claire Oh walked into the main room of Jane's cabin, wrapped in Tim's bathrobe, Jane's spare towel wrapped around her wet hair. Jane realized that no one looked that haughty when they were all wet, and Claire, without her heels, looked almost approachable.

"You must be starved," Jane said. "Maybe we can get some leftover tea sandwiches . . . they said dinner wouldn't be until nine tonight." Jane turned to Tim, "Did they have tea today?"

"I don't know. I was rescuing you, remember?"

Jane remembered. She asked Tim if he could go and charm a plate of food out of the kitchen since they had over an hour until the dinner gong would ring. She also whispered to him to give Bruce Oh a heads-up that Claire had surfaced. Oh's meeting with Blake was certainly going on long. Tim promised to do his best, saluted, and went off to forage.

Jane watched Claire comb out her wet hair. Jane tried to think of a way to open the conversation without just launching into the twenty or so questions she wanted to fire at her, but Claire beat her to the punch.

"You must have a million questions," Claire said. "I'm ready for them, but I might not have very good answers."

Claire was definitely deflated, certainly approachable. It made sense that she would be relieved to know she was no longer a suspect in Cutler's murder. Would it last? Jane tried to compartmentalize quickly. She wanted to ask all of her questions while Claire was still wet. Who knew what would happen after she was dressed and her hair blown-dry. Jane, in her former career, had watched enough actors and models transform themselves through makeup, hair styling, and costuming; she knew it was important to strike while the iron was hot or, in this case, while the heels were off.

"Is that why you raced up here last night? To find out your own answers about what happened to the Westman chest?"

"Not only the chest. Look, I knew Rick Moore hadn't choked on chemicals. He's been working around these solvents and finishes for years. He might have lost a few brain cells, but he had enough left to remember to wear a mask and keep those windows open. Besides, it was too much of a coincidence. He was the one I talked to when I called up here that night, after Horace came down on me. And he worked on the restoration of the piece, I know he did. He's the only one Blake would have trusted with it," said Claire.

"Is Blake the one you met with when you brought it up here?" Jane asked.

"He wasn't here. I talked it out with Glen, who knew all about Westman, too, of course, and he agreed that it just might be the real deal. He said he'd go over it with Blake, and they'd call and keep me posted. They didn't call back right away, so I called them. I talked to Rick then, and he was thrilled. He said he'd seen it in the barn and had already done tons of research on the wood and carving style. Couldn't locate information about it through the Westman files though, no record of a third chest.

"Rick said he'd called the house sale people and they'd told him the chest had never come up with the owner, although he had left listings and descriptions of other valuable pieces in the house. The person in charge of the sale told both me and Rick that she hadn't even noticed it. It was only after boxes of sale stuff got removed from the top of it that it came into sight at all," Claire said, sighing. She thought it must have been an old built-in. "I was just in the right place at the right time, I guess."

Claire smiled hopefully at Jane. Jane really wanted to ask her why she had put on such an act when they had first met, but, once again, Claire beat her to the question with an answer.

"I'm sorry I was such a . . . so unfriendly when you came

to the house. I was . . . I don't know . . . embarrassed? I mean, here I was, such an expert, an art historian as I always remind Bruce, not a junk picker." Claire stopped, then smiled at Jane. "I love junk and I don't mean anything by that, it's just that Bruce is so . . . spare, you know? So I tried to make my work match up, measure up . . . then getting fooled like that, it just made me furious and I become a snobby bitch when I get mad. Does that make any sense to you at all?"

Jane thought about the many times she had snapped when poor Charley had simply looked sideways at the boxes she'd brought in from a sale. Charley, with his scientific names for everything and his special containers and his labels and his graduate students and his damn credibility. She reflected on her own defenses, her elaborate explanations of the psychology of print aprons from the fifties or souvenir salt and pepper shakers, her crafting of stories that went with her auction purchases that rivaled any university anthropological text.

"Yes," Jane said, nodding and inwardly wincing at how pretentious she must sound when she justified buying a box of advertising combs. "I think I can understand."

Jane asked Claire if she had any paperwork at all that mentioned the chest, and Claire looked up and blinked.

"What kind of paperwork? A bill of sale?"

"Yes," said Jane, "that or something that says the name of the people who owned the house. Do you have the address and all? Because if that chest had been there for a while, maybe through a couple of owners, perhaps we'll find a plausible explanation for a Westman chest being there."

Claire stopped fussing with the towel and her hair for a moment and looked straight at Jane. "I didn't even think about that," she said. "That's the strangest part of this whole thing."

"What?" asked Jane.

"No one here asked me for that kind of paperwork. No one asked where the chest came from—except Rick. He called me to get the name of the estate sale company so he could follow up a bit. Didn't even make it a big deal. In fact, he said it was just so he could go through the basement and look for old hardware since he had found a few interesting nails and knobs in one of the chest drawers. No one else asked for a bill of sale," said Claire.

"They know you, right? They wouldn't think you were bringing them stolen goods, so maybe . . ."

"They always asked a million questions. For the same reasons you asked . . . not because they were worried about me stealing it, but because they wanted to establish some kind of plausible provenance. That's why you bring something to Campbell and LaSalle—because once they sign off on it, it's established. They're like museum curators. But this happened so fast. I already had a buyer. Horace snapped at it when I called. I was so excited, did lots of research myself on Westman and how he worked, but I never realized that they weren't asking me anything."

Jane remembered the envelope she had taken from Rick Moore's truck. Maybe that had some research in it that would shed some light. He had marked it important. Jane drew it from her bag and looked at it. It was just a few pages listing a lot of Web sites. The first page, though, had an elaborate drawing of a large wooden armchair on it. Printed underneath was a capital B.

"What the hell does this mean?" Jane asked aloud,

turning when she heard the door open. It was Tim, playing the victorious hunter, carrying a plate of sandwiches, some sodas, and bottled water.

"Let's write everything down," said Jane. "It'll be a start. You bought the chest at the . . . ?"

"McDougal estate sale. It was run by the blondes, you know?"

Jane knew. They were ruthless. They often left things unpriced just so they could see how badly you wanted it when you brought it to them. They'd charge their own mothers to buy back their wedding silver. How could they be the ones to give Claire Oh the chest for free?

"They didn't want to," said Claire, when Jane asked. "They called the owner, just to make sure it could be sold; they had some strict orders about some of the stuff apparently. The owner insisted they not charge. I was standing right there and heard the guy's voice over the cell phone. Believe me, if I hadn't heard and mentioned that I'd heard, they would have put some price on it. That's what was so sweet about this whole deal."

"Who was the guy they talked to? McDougal?" Tim asked, reaching for his third sandwich.

"No, it was a real estate sale. McDougal was dead. No wife, no kids. He had been a gentleman scholar of all kinds of subjects. By the looks of his house and possessions, I'd say he was old money with lots of good taste, but everything had grown old and shabby around him. He had a magnificent library that was swooped down on by the book guys and a great basement with lots of old paper. Theater and opera programs, torn tickets, old college notebooks . . . ," said Claire. "Junk, but smart junk, you know?"

Jane knew. She was salivating. How had she missed this sale?

"I think the man on the phone was the heir. A nephew or something. He was strong-willed, to say the least, with a loud voice. He said that under no circumstances should they sell that old chest but just have it hauled away. And he said to remind the customer that it would be at her own risk in case it falls apart on her when she's taking it out. I remember him yelling it into the phone," said Claire. "In fact, I asked about him, and Blondie number one said she had never met him, had done everything by mail and phone, and she never wanted to meet him. Said he sounded like a bastard. And that's something coming from such a bi— Hello, Bruce," said Claire, standing.

"Well," said Bruce Oh.

They stood looking at each other for a moment. Claire then apologized for running out, and Bruce nodded and said he was sure she had a good reason. Then they smiled at each other. At least Jane chose to believe that Bruce Oh was smiling. His mouth gave every indication of movement, even if it didn't exactly move. Claire was definitely smiling at her husband.

"Good tie," she said.

Bruce nodded.

Holy Toledo, what kind of marital dispute was that? If only she and Charley could fight and make up like that. Jane and Tim exchanged glances, and Jane realized he was about to make her laugh so she looked away. Now *that* was a marriage. *How come the damned grass always looks so much greener?* Jane thought. She could answer that. *Because you're not the one who has to mow it.* Knitting a sweater, crocheting a snowflake, decluttering a closet, organizing, maintaining a healthy relationship all looked so easy when someone else was doing the purling, knotting, labeling, and listening. She really needed to call Charley.

"Before we go to dinner, maybe we ought to finish talking about what we know and where we're going with this?" said Jane.

Jane held up the notebook where she had written— chest found at McDougal estate—and underlined McDougal. "This is where it starts," said Jane. "Claire calls Horace first?" Jane looked at Claire for confirmation and when she nodded, Jane continued. "Okay, so Horace checks it out as a possible Westman. Then Claire calls Campbell and LaSalle, makes arrangements with Rick Moore, and he's the point man on all this? You never talked to anyone besides Glen and Rick?" Jane asked Claire.

Claire had taken out a day runner from her purse and had been checking her calendar as Jane talked. "I checked the piece in with Glen, left two messages for Rick or Blake with Roxanne. When I wanted to check out stuff I had found over the Internet, like finishing details, I called her. Rick was always the one who called me back. And when I picked the chest up, I talked to Rick. He and one of the caretakers helped me load it into my truck. I brought it back and left it with Horace's assistants and didn't talk to him until that night when he stormed in at the show."

"Did anyone here at C & L know that Horace was your buyer?" asked Tim.

"I don't remember anyone asking," said Claire. "Rick did ask me when I picked it up if I was selling it as a Westman. I asked him what he and Blake had finally decided about it, and he shrugged and said he'd leave it to Blake. Blake was going to send me his written report on the piece," said Claire, then she stopped and looked up from her calendar. "That was odd, too, now that I think of it. The report should have been given to me when I picked the chest up. It's supposed to describe the condition of something when it was brought in, with pictures, then they inventory everything they did for restoration.

"When Campbell and LaSalle does this, they list everything, the brushes they used and the number of strokes used to apply the finish. Every detail they can think of. I thought it unusual that it was going to come later, but I was in such a hurry to get back for the show, I let it go. Rick gave some excuse that Blake had had a family matter to tend to and was behind on paperwork."

"So Rick was really the only person you dealt with on the pickup, and you had no signatures from anyone here verifying anything they did?" asked Jane. "What if Rick wasn't supposed to release it? Or what if he had made some kind of substitution on his own?"

"Ah, the old switcheroo theory?" said Tim. "Interesting, but why? Claire's check was made out to Campbell and LaSalle, so there was no money there to steal and . . ." Tim stopped. "But of course, he'd have the real Westman to sell."

"With all the paperwork," said Jane. "That's why he didn't give it to Claire."

"Why did Rick kill Horace Cutler then"—asked Bruce Oh, sounding very much like he already knew the answer— "if he had the real chest and the verification?"

"To shut him up about a fake Westman chest?" offered Jane.

"But I don't think he even knew about Horace," Claire said. "I never mentioned his name. The chest was already back at our house. No one would have spotted it at Horace Cutler's shop; he had turned it right around back to me after looking at it. Bruce received it at the house. Besides, I'm the one Rick would have had to shut up. I'd be yelling my head off if I found out a real Westman had showed up on the market through Campbell and LaSalle. He'd have to . . ." Claire stopped.

"Kill you," Jane finished. "And that's exactly what he was going to do. He was coming to kill you. It wouldn't take much to find out that you brought pieces back to the safe at the antiques mall on your way home from the show. Rick was a clever enough carpenter and handyman to break into the building without tripping the alarm. Horace, waiting in the parking lot to have it out with you, blundered right in behind him, setting off the alarm and still yelling his head off about a fake Westman. Rick *had* to kill him. You were the one Rick was after, though."

Bruce Oh nodded at Jane. She felt an odd sensation. In another time, in another incarnation, he would be a nun in full habit, sticking a gold star on her forehead. She shook that feeling off and sat down on the bed.

"So who killed Rick?" asked Tim.

"Someone else who wanted the Westman?" asked Claire.

Jane looked back down at her notebook. She had jotted down a lot of events and questions that puzzled her. That warehouse in the woods? The destruction of the table? What was that about? And who had tried to suffocate her with chemicals? The only one she could safely eliminate was the guy too busy with his hammer to even notice. For all of its free artsy laissez-faire here at C & L, both she and Tim had noticed a certain amount of disgruntlement among the old-timers. What was that Tim had said about his talk with Scott . . . seems "we at Campbell and LaSalle" are in need of a dental plan.

"Possibly," said Bruce Oh. "Or perhaps someone who didn't want Rick Moore to have it."

"A lot of people feel the need for some extra money right now," said Tim. "Scott wants health insurance, and Martine wants a book contract."

"Silver just wants three squares a day," said Jane. "What about Mickey or Annie?"

Tim shrugged. He said he thought Mickey might be content as long as he had his tree house to himself. "You're lucky he didn't catch you up there," Tim said to Claire, "he's pretty protective of his little home away from home."

"Oh, I moved around, one step ahead of him," said Claire. "He uses all of them, not just his."

" 'All of them?' " asked Jane.

Claire told them there were at least eight tree houses on the property. "Maybe more," she said. "Blake and Glen had a contest one summer. Everybody got to design and build one. Everybody hid them, made secret entrances. Some are quite elaborate."

"Is there one by the stream?" asked Jane.

"Yes, by Annie's cabin. And one deeper in the woods off the path," said Claire.

Jane looked at Tim, Claire, and Oh, who nodded to her. "Go on, Mrs. Wheel," Oh said.

"Rick got hit with the same chemicals I did, or something close. But if he just got out and blindly wandered in the woods, there was a chance he'd get enough air and come out of it. Whoever got to him wanted him dead and led him down by the stream and pushed him under. I mean they'd only need a few minutes for his lungs to fill, wouldn't they? For him to drown?" asked Jane.

Oh nodded. "Three or four minutes at the very most."

"He'd be so groggy that it wouldn't be a trick to hold him under, but how do you leave the scene without anyone seeing you? If Annie did it, she could just run into her cabin; but if it were anyone else, they'd have to walk past some of the cabins, the barn, even the lodge. Even though it's quiet time, not everybody sleeps or bangs up furniture. So the murderer drowns Rick, then . . ."

"Climbs a tree," finished Tim.

"Right," said Jane, "and waits until we come along and then maybe even joins in to help sound the alarm. Who would notice where anyone came from?"

"Excellent job, Mrs. Wheel," said Oh.

"But we don't know who," said Claire.

"I'll bet it was the same person who tried to rag you this afternoon, Janie," said Tim.

Jane nodded. That's how someone dropped the rag on her, from above, from a tree house. Why, though? Because she saw someone pounding a table?

"Claire, do you know if there's a tree house out by the access road where Rick parked his truck?" Jane asked.

Claire nodded. "A nice one, with piles of cushions and a great view of the sunrise," she said.

Jane thought she saw Oh's eyebrow go up. As always with him, it was impossible to tell.

"Someone watched me, I'll bet. I searched Rick's truck

and found an envelope filled with papers." Jane walked over to her bag to show them, but stopped at the sound of footsteps on the wooden porch between Jane and Tim's cabins. Claire, understanding that her presence would upset whatever shreds of an investigation they were gathering, quietly went into the bathroom.

Bruce Oh sat down in the desk chair, his face the mask of Mr. Kuruma paying an innocent call on another C & L visitor. Jane started to put Rick Moore's envelope back into her bag, but thought better of it. If someone had seen her take it from the truck, they might be looking for it among her things. "We at Campbell and LaSalle" didn't believe in door locks for the cabins, so she quickly passed her notebook and Rick Moore's envelope over to Bruce Oh. Without any wasted motion, he smoothly slipped them into the worn leather briefcase he was carrying.

Jane was only a foot from the entrance when the visitor kicked the doorframe. Jane jumped, just a little, and looked back at Tim and Oh. Tim raised an eyebrow, and Oh nodded and gestured for her to answer the door.

She hesitated only a second then reached out her hand as another kick was planted and a low voice growled, "I know you're in there. Open up."

17

Will your relationships with people change when you have decluttered your living space? Yes, indeed. You will find yourself removing the dead wood of tired relationships and cutting through to the core of what makes a friend a friend.

—BELINDA ST. GERMAIN, *Overstuffed*

"Did you think you were going to get away with it?" Scott asked.

Scott had the same look Jane had seen several hundred times as she was growing up. Peeking out from the EZ Way Inn's kitchen door, it was the look on a man's face that said, I've put away a lot of alcohol and I've lost every possible control I might have had over my thoughts, my words, and my body. I am capable of anything right now . . . outrageous lies, outrageous truths.

Most of all, Jane remembered, it was a look that said to others who had the eyes to see: Be very careful. Tread softly. Right now, I laugh with you and love you because you are my best friends. In less than a second, I can, and will, turn on you like a snake because you are my worst enemies. Those were just some of the lessons Jane had learned from the EZ Way Inn, some lessons from the darker text of her childhood.

"Do you have any idea how much this Ciroc cost me?" Scott asked, waving an expensive-looking half-empty bottle. He pronounced the Ciroc with an exaggerated shhhh sound, which led his body into a kind of physical slithering into the cabin.

"Do you have any idea how hard it is to get? Here in the Michigan woods at the bum-fuck end of bum fuck? I mean, my dear people, we at Campfuckingbell and LafuckingSalle are situated, quite appropriately I might add, at the ass-end of nowhere."

Jane had seen many drunken people in her day, and she rated Scott Tailor as one of the most articulate. You might not approve of the language, but his diction was impeccable.

She hoped that his articulateness was an anomaly, and that his senses were as impaired as they all assumed when they gave their collective sigh of relief. It was only a disgruntled Campbell and LaSalle craftsman, their outtakes of breaths seemed to say. It wasn't the murderous resident who had dropped a chemical bomb on Jane's head and who had led Rick Moore to his drowning after, perhaps, conspiring to kill Claire and/or Horace Cutler. Or was it? Where had their drunken friend Scott been when Tim and Jane arrived? He had told them at the memorial, but Jane couldn't recall. She looked at this reeling wreck of a man, whose face she felt she had rightly appreciated when she had first met him. *He is a warm and kind man,* she had thought. Now she saw him as a bit overdone, his jollity when sober hiding the blur of dissolution when drunk.

Maybe Nellie was right. Maybe drinking was the ruination of all. Even as she served up the beers and shots, Nellie would wag her finger in the faces of factory workers, exhorting them like a Baptist preacher. "You've had enough!" she would shout. "Go home to your wife, and save your paycheck for groceries."

"That's why all the wives trust us," she'd tell Jane. "They know, at the end of the day, I'm sending those boys home."

She would have made a great army commander, Jane thought, not for the first time; Patton as played by George C. Scott in a helmet, as played by Nellie in an apron.

Jane turned her attention to Tim. It was up to him to get rid of Scott, to appease him and lead him out of the cabin so they could safely send Claire back into hiding. After all, it was Tim who had cracked open the Ciroc. Scott might not know Tim as well as Jane did, but he knew him well enough to suspect him as soon as something fine went missing. Tim's excellent tastes were the first thing people noticed about him. His appreciation for good fabric and well-cut suits, his knowledge of the best chefs and late-opening kitchens in several cities, and his impeccable eye for furniture and china made him a great dinner partner, a swell drinking buddy, and a girl's best friend. On the other hand, he'd always beat you to the last drop of Dom in the best Waterford flute.

Tim accepted his duty. With a smile for Jane and a nod at Oh, Tim put his arm around Scott and suggested they stop by the trunk of his car.

"We might be at the ass-end of nowhere, my friend, but my trunk and its state of the art cooler have been noted as a wonder of the world. Let's go check my roving cellar, shall we?"

As soon as their voices faded, Claire emerged from

Jane's bathroom, fully dressed in a Ralph Lauren striped shirt and tan linen pants. She had belted the pants with her own long, silk scarf and managed, between Tim's fine threads, and her own ingenuity, to look radiantly chic. Tim's tall, lithe figure matched Claire's inch for inch. With her hair dry and combed and a slash of lipstick across her mouth, Claire, once again, looked regal.

Jane looked down at her own small body drowning in Tim's clothes. Claire looked like she had been form-fitted, and Jane looked like she had done the best she could out of the Goodwill box on the corner. Oh hell, even if she had brought more than "six easy pieces" à la Belinda St. Germain, her own clothes wouldn't have done for her what Tim's extras did for Claire. Jane swore that when this was all over, she'd cultivate some vertically challenged friends.

In the meantime, what to do with Claire? Even though she was at home in Evanston when Rick was murdered, Murkel would want to know why she had been sneaking around. And neither Jane nor Oh wanted to be compelled to reveal their real reasons for being there either. Since someone had been spying on Jane and might want to track down Rick Moore's "Important" papers, her cabin was no good as Claire's hiding place.

"Why don't I just go back up a tree?" Claire asked. "I can stay out of sight and meet you back here whenever you say."

Jane was glad to see that the dry, dressed, and coifed Claire had remained warm and approachable. And, Jane had to admit, she was a pretty good sport, heading off to a tree house and leaving her husband and his partner—Jane still loved the sound of the word "partner," even when she was using it herself and, for that matter, talking to herself—to go off to a gourmet dinner.

"Anything more to share, Mrs. Wheel?" Oh asked, turning away from the door, where he was watching his wife disappear into the woods and/or up a tree.

"Your turn," Jane said. "What did Blake have to say?"

"A great deal," Oh said, "but nothing that led to the Westman chest. He is a complex man."

While Jane waited for Oh to go on, she gathered up the odd bits of paper Claire had taken out of her bag when they were talking and sat down at the desk.

"He is very proud of this place. Proud of the work they do, the quality of the work. Modest, though, about its reputation. Gives all the credit to Glen LaSalle and the artisans who make up the staff—and to Roxanne, who he says makes everything work.

"I asked about having some pieces made, some chairs to match three genuine ones that I have collected. He offered to look at them and take them on if they presented a challenge. If not, he mentioned that Geoff and Jake were wizards at reproduction furniture. He said that their work will be collected in less than a hundred years, and we laughed about what would become my multigenerational collection."

"You liked him?" Jane asked.

Oh cocked his head slightly and paused before he spoke. "I listened to him, Mrs. Wheel."

Jane remembered Moore's envelope that they had shifted into Oh's hands when Scott burst in on them. If Oh was going to be the good listener, she would be the good reader.

Looking through them again, she was struck by the intricacy of the sketch. She knew what it meant to draw something lovingly, to embrace a subject. This drawing, on a throwaway piece of lightweight paper, was done with an eye for detail, a complete appreciation of every twist and turn of the legs, every turn in the spindle back. The *B* printed underneath was done in a kind of calligraphy that suggested something to Jane. What was it? How odd. That one letter, a carefully drawn *B*, made Jane think of old parchment, something written on old parchment. The Declaration of Independence?

She tacked the page up on her bulletin board, a small affair above the desk framed in the same rustic twigs that outlined every photo, every mirror in the compound. She checked the nail upon which it hung and felt the round head of a modern nail. Roxanne had been here. The small board would not slide off the wall. Now the sketch was in plain sight, but even if someone came looking for it, they wouldn't expect it there. Besides, Jane had committed it to memory.

The other pages contained nothing but the listing of Web site addresses. No magic had changed them during their short stay in Oh's briefcase into an essay on who murdered Cutler and Moore and why. Even Oh didn't have that power, good listener though he was.

"I have a laptop with me, and the rooms in the lodge are wired. I'll visit these sites as soon as possible," Oh said.

He looked at the drawing, then at Jane. "What do you see, Mrs. Wheel?"

"Someone who is in love," said Jane.

"Now you *are* listening," he said.

Jane, cinched and wrapped in Tim's finery, and Oh, back in his Mr. Kuruma persona, had not talked much at first on their way to the lodge for dinner. Jane was mulling over what Oh had told her about his meeting. Mr. Campbell had been the consummate craftsman, had talked about pieces in which the "hand" was revealed. The mark of the hand was what seemed to intrigue him, and it was what he expected everyone who stayed and worked at Campbell and LaSalle to appreciate. He viewed their enterprise as a return to the Arts and Crafts movement. He told Oh that it wasn't about expensive materials or rare woods or precious metals. It was the *work* that was important, the *hand*.

Oh, taking notes as a real editor/feature writer would, confessed to Jane that if he were writing an article for his new phantom publication, he would probably title it *The Mark of the Hand*. Jane agreed it was a good title. She also remembered what Claire had repeated when Jane had first viewed the chest—the carving showed the hand of a master. Perhaps, Jane had suggested to Oh, *A Master's Hand* would be a better title, and for their separate moments of serious consideration, Jane was once again a creative director and Oh a publisher.

Before they reached the porch, Jane confessed that she was disappointed that they had so little information, so little *confirmation* of what they had conjured up and surmised about the Westman chest. Jane had hoped for some indication from Blake that he had made a second chest or even that he enjoyed copying famous works.

Oh was so gentle in his remarks to Jane that it was as if she were thinking of it all herself.

"Mrs. Wheel, I know that in the television program, by now, someone would have blurted out something. A dying man might whisper or a witness on the stand might break down. But," he said softly, "in my experience, the guilty of the world have nothing to confess. The bad guy in a television program might weep and ask forgiveness, but from what I've seen in the world, those who act badly, evilly even, feel no guilt. They feel that they are right, perhaps even that they are doing a good thing when they fire the shot, drop the bomb. In their own movies of their own lives, they are the confident heroes, not the villains. What have they to whisper or confess?

"That is why we listen to what remains unsaid. Rick Moore was certainly killed because of what he did, what he knew. Horace Cutler, for what he said. And my wife is in danger for what she *might* say. The unsaid," Oh repeated. "And you, Mrs. Wheel, it is you who have taught me to listen to the objects, also. The 'stuff' as you call it, that makes up people's lives."

Jane, thinking back on the past few days—her mistake with Nick, the snippets of the Belinda St. Germain book she had leafed through at odd hours, and the lack of conclusions drawn so far—murmured that she for one had perhaps been listening to the wrong stuff, but her companion seemed not to hear.

Oh stopped for a moment and raised his hand slightly, as if to create a sense memory. "I watched you and my wife touch the flowers on the chest so I, too, touched the flowers," he said, "but I noticed something unusual. On the left side the flowers were fully articulated, sharp. Standing with pride? Is that how you say it?"

"Proud," Jane said. "Standing proud. That indicates a left-handed carver. Handedness usually shows in the carving. The side where a carver works backward, with leaves, vines, whatever, is sometimes a bit flatter."

"Yes, I remembered my wife telling me about another piece," Oh said.

"So the wood told you we are looking for a left-handed carver?" Jane asked, pleased that she and Oh had both heard the voice of the inanimate object. Thrilled that they were listening to the same station now, she said, "That's great. That's perfect. Now all we have to do . . ."

"No," Oh said, holding up his hand again, "I'm afraid that would be that television moment. My hand told me that the right side was equally sharp, equally proud."

Jane shook her head. "Two carvers? If it's two carvers, they must live inside each other's pocket. Those carvings were perfectly matched."

"Live inside each other's pocket," Oh repeated, liking the phrase, "or lived."

Jane and Oh couldn't continue their conversation so close to the porch without attracting attention. Indeed, Martine swept down the stairs and with a "My dears," she swept Oh back up the stairs with her, leaving Jane admiring her skill at turning a plural word into a singular action.

The dinner bell, which, naturally enough at Campbell and LaSalle, was not a simple bell, but a hand-hammered copper gong affair, had not rung or been gonged or whatever the "we at Campbell and LaSalle" terminology was for summoning the troops. Because of the police presence, the questioning and searching that had gone on during the day, the later-than-usual dinner hour meant everyone had had time to get drunker than usual. Jane decided to take a quick detour before entering the lodge.

Jane needed to keep her wits about her. She hadn't really had a moment alone to allow herself any feelings about her chemical dousing. And now, instead of being scared like she really thought she should be, she found herself getting angry. Why was it that she never felt only one emotion, purely and simply? Whatever she felt was always coupled with vague guilt or unease because she suspected she should really be feeling some other emotion. She knew it was silly. Her Aunt Maxine, Don's wise and warm younger sister, had tried to warn her away from the "shoulds" thirty years ago.

"Whenever you start to say that you 'should' do something, or worse yet, that 'they should' do something, just stop it," Aunt Maxine had said, sipping her hot water and lemon. "You either will or you won't, and whatever 'they' do is beyond your puny controls anyway."

Jane smiled remembering, then immediately felt guilty. "I should call Aunt Maxine," she said aloud. "Oh, my god, and Charley and Nick! And Nellie! She's got a damn broken toe, and I haven't even thought of her all day."

Normally, the woods and paths would be dark or, at the most, dimly lit, but Officer Murkel and his men and women had lit up Campbell and LaSalle like a stage set. Jane found a bench—carved, of course, with intricate spaniels standing guard at each upright post—directly across from the barn. The windows on the ground level were all open; shutters swung out from their top hinges. The light coming out from the windows pooled on the ground around the barn, small spotlights for the odd chipmunk or racoon that ventured out on this uncharacteristically warm fall night.

Jane looked up. Tim was right about the lights on the ground destroying any chance of seeing a star-filled sky. It was too early anyway, but Jane knew that the only constellation she'd see tonight would be some dizzying celestial pattern on one of Silver's caftans. Jane wasn't only looking for Orion's belt. She wanted to make sure there was no tree house above the bench where she was sitting. Claire had described the locations with which she was familiar, but Jane needed to see for herself. She had been growing angrier and angrier at the proponents of "we at Campbell and LaSalle" think-and-speak, and this whole tree house revelation did nothing to assuage her resentment. Not only did they act like they were above you on the ground; several of them, at any given time, really were above you. Jane hated metaphors that actually came to life.

Satisfied that she saw only sky above her, Jane settled herself between Fido and Fido and dialed Charley. Prepared to leave a message, she was caught totally off guard at the sound of his voice, not the one on tape, but the warm and husky real-life voice. No one could have been more surprised than Jane herself to find that she was more than caught off guard, she was speechless. And, feeling her face with her left hand, she found she was also crying.

"Jane? Jane? What's the matter? You might be cutting out, so if you can hear me, dance around a bit and try to . . ."

"No, Charley, I can hear you. I just . . . ," she began, "I just didn't expect you to be there."

"Sweetheart, you called me. Hey, Nick, Nick! It's Mom, come on over," he called. "We're poolside here. Tomorrow's an institute day, remember? So we're staying over. Did you get my message?"

"What message? Where?" Then Jane remembered that it was Sunday night. Charley would expect her to be at home. And she would be expecting them back because it was a school night, except it wasn't a school night. How could she have forgotten what day it was; how long they had been at this place? She knew that "we at Campbell and LaSalle" were not slaves to calendars or clocks—witness this nine o'clock dinner hour—but Jane shouldn't have been seduced by this timelessness. She, of Charley and Nick and Evanston, should have been home hours ago, cleaning, storing, filing, and making dinner. And packing a decent lunch for Nick to take to school. Should, shouldn't, should. Except it was a holiday tomorrow.

"Right, Charley, I knew Nick had tomorrow off, so Tim and I decided to stay another day," Jane began, then remembered that she couldn't have left anyway. Murkel wasn't letting anyone leave Campbell and LaSalle just yet, especially the visitor who had found Rick Moore spoiling the hand-carved landscape. "It's a captivating place here."

"Janie, you sound a little odd. Is there anything wrong?" Charley asked.

"Absolutely not, why should anything . . ." Jane stopped herself. Why did she get so defensive? Charley had never tried to stop her from being a detective. Charley had never tried to stop her from being a picker. Charley had never discouraged her from anything. Jane just always expected him to do it and defended herself before he had a chance to open his mouth.

"I just miss you, Charley. And I'm so grateful that you bailed me out with Nick. And I had a close call today, but I'm fine. Tell Nick I love him, okay?" Jane said.

"You're cutting out, honey, what did you say?" Charley was shouting the way everyone does when they themselves can't hear. "What?"

"What was your talk about? Tell Nick I love him. I love you," said Jane. Those were all the important things she had wanted to get out.

"All I heard was blank blank my talk about. Blank blank blank hoaxes," Charley said, cutting out on every two words or so. "Fake fossils. Blank blankologist blank so jealous of blank, blank salted blank site clank blank mishmosh of fossilized bones blank blank rival blank blank blank announce blank of blank find that blank could blank debunk by . . . ," Charley said, the connection finally failing entirely.

As soon as Jane pressed "end," her phone rang. "Charley?" she answered.

"You're still not home with your husband?" Nellie said. Her voice was clear and the connection perfect. Jane heard every accusatory syllable.

Jane understood, clear as a hand-hammered gong. Nellie had installed the shoulds and shouldn'ts; and even if others—Charley, for example—never imposed themselves on Jane's free will, Nellie, working from her remote control, could flip the switch in Jane's brain so that actual spoken words from others, like "Hello, Jane, how are you?" were heard by Jane as, "Why on earth are you wearing *that*?"

"How's the toe, Mom?" Jane asked.

"Never mind my toe," Nellie said, "how's your husband and how's your son? Remember them?"

"They are splashing away at an indoor water park in Rockford. All is well. Their names are Charley and Nick, and I'm sure I'll recognize the faces when I run into them in the upstairs hall when I get home. Satisfied?" asked Jane, knowing in her aching heart that the great gaping maw of Nellie's righteous indignation was never satisfied.

"Sure," said Nellie.

"What?" asked Jane.

"As long as you're satisfied, I'm happy," said Nellie. "Want to talk to your father?"

Oh, my god, Nellie had learned some new kind of trick, some new kind of torture. It wasn't enough that she had faced a chemical weapon that afternoon, now Nellie was coming in for the kill with psychological warfare.

"Tell me about Michigan, sweetie," said Don.

"You tell me about Mom. She's never given up the phone to you without hand-to-hand combat. What's going on?"

"Sounds beautiful," said Don, his voice loud and hearty. "Can you still hear me, Jane?" he asked, changing to a whisper.

When Jane whispered back that she could, her father told her that he had sneaked one of Nellie's prescribed pain pills into her rice pudding, and that ever since lunch, Nellie had been happy and content.

"Nothing they can do about the toe. It'll heal on its own, but she's supposed to stay off her feet and the only way I could think of to get her down was to, you know, drug her," said her straight-arrow, crew-cut father.

"Why didn't I think of that in high school?" asked Jane.

"She's coming back. Insisted on making some soup for dinner, but in between stirring and tasting, she actually lies on the couch. I've got her all propped up with pillows, and I went out and got her some nut clusters from Fannie May," said Don. "You ought to see this, Janie, it's quite a sight."

"What's a sight?" Jane heard her mother ask. "Go get me a comb and brush, Don; I haven't fixed myself up all day.

Nellie took the phone back after Don told her good-bye. Jane could hear her father whistling as he went to fetch her mother a hand mirror and brush.

"Get my lipstick out of my purse, too, Don. It's out in the breezeway."

Jane smiled, picturing her mother propped up on the couch, applying lipstick and eating chocolates. It pleased her to think that Nellie was resting, that she was calm and happy. Even if it took the tainted pudding, it sounded like it was worth it.

"Mom, I'm glad you're resting and doing what Dad and the doctor ordered. I'll probably be back in Evanston tomorrow or Tuesday if . . .," Jane began, but was interrupted by Nellie whispering furiously, "You get yourself home, young lady. Charley and Nick need you there, and Tim doesn't need you anywhere. I have tried to tell you about the square peg in a . . ."

At least she called her "young lady." That didn't happen so often these days. Poor Don. Right in the middle of his bowl of soup, Nellie was going to produce that little pill and accuse him of trying to poison her with her own rice pudding. For the first time in two days, Jane was happy to be where she was, right here at Campbell and LaSalle. Sure, there might be a murderer hanging around, but Jane thought maybe she might have a better chance against whoever that turned out to be than Don was going to have against Nellie, broken toe or no.

"You didn't take the pain pill, huh?" Jane asked.

"I don't need any pill to put me to sleep and turn my

brain into mush. Working at the goddamn EZ Way Inn for forty-five years is doing that anyway. What does your father think he's doing anyway?"

"He thinks he's buying you candy and bringing you pillows and taking care of you, that's what he's doing. Why don't you sit back and appreciate it, for god's sake?"

"Why don't you? You're off with the peg head Tim instead of your own husband . . . ," said Nellie.

"What does this 'round peg' thing mean anyway? It sounds sort of dirty, Ma, if you want to know the truth," said Jane.

"Look," said Nellie, "I'm trying to say that you don't belong with Tim or that detective. You belong at home. You're always trying to be something you're not, Jane. That's all. And you can't be something else until you're what you're supposed to be in the first place."

"Oh," said Jane. "Now I get it."

"I don't have a college degree to explain it, honey, but I just think you do a lot of running around looking for the wrong stuff and trying to do things that don't make sense. Seems to me you've had the right stuff right in front of you. I don't see how that makes a life," said Nellie. "Oh, thanks, Don," she said, her voice softening. "Soup's almost ready. Go give it a stir, but don't taste it yet. It's a surprise."

Jane didn't know whether to laugh or cry. Her mother had managed a "young lady" and a "honey" in the same conversation; and despite the fact that she made no sense, she made perfect sense. Jane was profoundly touched. Even though she suspected her mother was wrong in her analysis, Jane so appreciated the effort. Along with this unusual surge of warmth toward Nellie, she was also filled with dread. Her mother was about to do something terrible to her father.

"Mom, what's in the soup?" Jane knew her mother had a little experience. Not that long ago, she had cooked up a valium-laced breakfast for some kidnappers and told Jane, with an evil grin, that it was as easy as taking cotton candy from a baby.

"No pills. Too easy to spot."

"Mom!"

"Never underestimate the effect of chili pepper, jalapeño, and cumin on a man expecting a mild tomato lentil," said Nellie. "It won't kill him. Where's the fun in that?"

Where indeed? Jane knew she couldn't get past Nellie to warn her father. She told Nellie not to hide all the antacids and hung up. It wasn't a pleasant thought, picturing her mother as a berserk cat who liked to play with the poor mouse before going in for the kill. On the other hand, she knew her father wasn't a mouse, and she had seen him put a lot of Tabasco on scrambled eggs. They'd work it out.

It was better to think about what else the conversation with her mother held. Two terms of endearment. Jane would accept. And even though Nellie was off-base about Jane's friendship with Tim—Nellie had just been born too early to believe men and women could be friends, best friends—she was on target when she talked about Charley. He might not have to hide a pain pill in her rice pudding, but Jane did find it hard these days to accept loving kindness when it came from Charley. What was wrong with her? She hit middle age and suddenly every time Charley offered to get her a drink of water, she took it as meaning he thought she was too old and infirm to get up and get it herself. She had always considered herself fiesty, now she was acting plain paranoid. Oh, my god, was she really turning into Nellie?

Jane had never wanted to hear a gong so much in her life. Lack of food was making her delusional. What else had Nellie said? Oh yeah—that she was a round peg in a square hole. Maybe so.

Maybe so. Jane jumped up so quickly that her cell phone fell to the ground. She picked it up and went over to the barn. The front entrance was still taped off so she went over to a side window. They were low, these windows, easy to climb in and out of, but that wasn't what Jane wanted to do. She leaned in and saw Murkel talking to a young woman in a uniform, who was nodding and showing him her notepad. From where she stood, she could see the balcony where Rick Moore would have been slouched in a chair, his Birkenstock sandals tucked underneath. There were two stairways leading up to the balcony library, one from either side. A row of shelving right under the balcony had cans and jars of solvents, finishes, and strippers. Two small table fans were there, too. A large floor fan was next to the shelf. Jane assumed that workers used them to dispel the fumes and dry applications even faster. Masks and coveralls hung on pegs. If someone opened the right can or a combination of two or three and aimed one of the small fans right where Rick had been sitting, he'd have felt the effect pretty strongly.

Jane pictured him blinking, eyes watering, stumbling down the stairs, heading for the nearest door, the one in the rear, concealed by the offices. One of these push-out windows was right there at the foot of the stairs. Did he throw his weight against it, trying to open it and hang his head out, gasping for air the way Jane had this afternoon? The murderer had had time to close up the chemical can, turn off the fan, and wearing the filtered mask, guide Rick out the back door and down to the stream. Pressing his nose and mouth into the water, it would only have taken a few minutes for Rick's lungs to fill.

Jane had asked Oh—only trace amounts, if any, of the inhaled substances would remain in his blood. They would dissipate while he was busy accidentally drowning.

Jane leaned into the window, running her hands around the trim and deep sill. They were perfectionists at Campbell and LaSalle. Even the wood they used for finishing and trimming the windows of the barn workshop was chosen because it was beautiful and unblemished.

The swelling melodic note that sounded might have been inside Jane's head it was so loud and clear. Dinner at last. Jane was ecstatic. There would be good food, good drink, and she fully expected that everyone would have imbibed just enough not to notice that she was wearing her friend's extra set of clothes. And if she could pry her partner, Bruce Oh, away from Martine long enough, she might be able to dazzle him with her dinner party conversation. She was, after all, becoming a crackerjack listener.

10

Are you going to use the tablecloth Aunt Ida left you in her will? Has it been in a drawer for more years than you can count? Stop deceiving yourself, darling, and practice the three Ds—Don't Deceive, Discard!

—BELINDA ST. GERMAIN, *Overstuffed*

Jane walked into the lodge smiling. Poker was not and would never be her game. She might not know all there was to know about Rick Moore's death yet, and "yet," she knew, was the operative word. She was close. She could see it from here. Oh had told her when they first met that solving a crime was like building a house of cards in reverse. A crime was not usually built on a rock-solid foundation. It was a fragile construct, layered with doubt and coincidence and luck and fear.

"No glue holds a crime together, Mrs. Wheel," Oh had said. "It is woven with that invisible thread of hope and guile. When a man has done something wrong, he holds his breath. If he is not discovered right away, he begins to exhale, tentatively at first, then with more confidence. It is this confident air that often blows through his house of cards. All fall down."

Jane wasn't ready to knock down the entire house of cards yet, but she was ready to remove a few from the top.

She thought she knew how Rick Moore had been smoked out of the barn and led to his death. And if she could just talk to Oh, the *how* might lead to the *who*.

"And of course you understand how completely incestuous the publishing world is, and I refuse," Martine said, lowering her voice and leaning into Oh's chest, eyes fixed on his funky maroon-and-olive necktie, as if speaking into his heart, "simply refuse to play by those rules."

Oh nodded, but looking over Martine's head at Jane, shot her one of those minor eyebrow arches that Jane was beginning to recognize and decipher. This time, she figured, hearing Martine, whose quieted voice was still a stage whisper, the eyebrow was raised in confusion. If Martine did not want to play by incestuous rules, why was she leaning in so close to one of the alleged family?

"Mr. Kuruma, Martine," Jane said. "Any news from Officer Murkel?"

Martine placed her hand on Oh's chest as if to steady herself to turn and see who was interrupting her moment. "Janet, how dear you look! A little retro Annie Hall, yes?" Martine gushed. "With Mr. Kuruma's tie, I think you could step right into the role."

"Jane," Jane corrected.

"Martine," Martine said back, daring Jane to continue the conversation.

This one would take way more energy than Jane wanted to expend to win so she smiled and turned toward Tim. He and Scott had staked out an old-boy sort of conversation area. Two leather club chairs flanked a solid chunk of wood, squared and waxed to be used as a table, and beneath them, a dark green-and-gold rug. Jane squinted and imagined them with brandy and cigars; but when she opened her eyes wide, she saw that they sat with glasses on the table, legs crossed, holding a smoke-free and seemingly sober conversation.

Had Scott drank himself sober? Although Jane didn't totally believe it was possible, her father Don claimed that he had witnessed the phenomenon many times. He could name names of those who, after a long night of carousing, just kept up the alcohol intake through the wee hours on a slower, steadier pace, like an IV drip, and were able to get over to Roper Stove on time for the 7:00 A.M. whistle.

Those stories always made Jane feel relieved that Roper built kitchen appliances rather than cars or robotic surgical arms. It might be an inconvenience to have the knob marked left actually control your right stove burner, but it seemed an easier fix and a less lethal mistake than an incorrectly installed airbag.

There was of course the possibility that Scott had not been drunk at all. He could have been outside Jane's cabin, listening to their conversation and deciding to break in at the moment he did because . . . because . . . Oh well, Jane would figure that out soon enough.

Martine had been able to fend Jane off ably enough because, Jane knew, she'd allowed it to happen. Jane didn't want to get trapped into one of those three-way conversations where she was expected to nod at every third remark made by the alpha dog, in this case, Martine. No, mingling was the right strategy for tonight. It might help her solidify some of her thoughts as to what had happened. Silver, though, had no other place to be, no other task to accomplish, and Jane noticed with considerable pleasure that he was fighting for territory next to Martine and Oh. It probably didn't hurt that a large copper tray of appetizers was parked near them. Oh excused himself from the two of them for a moment and walked over to where Jane stood alone next to the fireplace.

He slipped two pages out of his jacket pocket and with a vague smile consulted them as if they were a timetable and set them on the mantel next to Jane's drink. She had ignored the Ciroc in favor of the Grey Goose, not wanting to reinflame Scott. Oh, with the blandest of smiles and looks, told Jane that he had gone up to his room to get a jacket for dinner and managed to print out a few pages from the list of Web addresses. He then reached past her, taking a handful of wasabi-spiked almonds and excused himself. Jane noted that he had dropped a napkin over the folded pages and again marveled at how effortless his actions appeared. Jane picked up the napkin and neatly folded pages and slid them into her pants pocket, grateful for Tim's good taste in clothing and his penchant for deep, usable pockets.

Jane did not rush to the dinner table. She actually wanted to see who sat next to whom, what alliances had remained strong during this topsy-turvy day at Campbell and LaSalle. Not too surprisingly, Glen and Roxanne walked to the table together and took up posts on either side of Blake. Jane wondered if Blake was even aware that he had two sentinels on duty. Was he so used to being the king of the castle that he no longer paid attention to those who made up the court? Was he even aware of the physical presence he possessed? Blake certainly seemed undemanding—perhaps, Jane thought, he had had his position thrust upon him. He only seemed regal because of the way Roxanne and Glen deferred to him.

Jane had sensed a certain assurance, a confidence from all the C & L residents when she had first arrived. It was in the air—eau de I-know-something-you-don't-know. Jane half envied it and wanted to belong and half disparaged it, seeing it as snobbery of the worst sort. Now, she found, she missed it. It was that supreme confidence that made a place like this run. Yes, this was a substantial old lodge, built out of solid, rough timber, but what really held it together was the unerring sense that everything and everyone belonged. Who hated enough, demanded enough, was lost enough to commit murder on these hallowed grounds? Who among these people would have dared upset the balance?

Mickey wanted to step into Rick's place. He had been following Blake around and begging for a position ever since Jane had found Rick in the stream. Did he want Rick's position enough to have erased him from the picture? Scott wanted more money, complained about being broke. If he got his hands on the Westman chest, he could afford all the root canals he wanted.

Annie seemed to be crying all the time. Even now, her eyes had that puffy, tired look. Jane picked up the bowl of almonds and walked over to where Annie perched on the arm of a chair sipping herbal tea.

"These nuts are great. Have you tried them?" Jane asked.

"Spicy. I'm so out of balance, you know emotionally, that I can't eat any heat-generating foods," Annie said.

"Yeah, it is out of balance," said Jane, not knowing what the hell Annie was talking about. "Rick's death probably pulled everything out of whack," Jane said.

"Not at all," said Annie. "That was the beginning of a rebalancing. I've laid out a compass."

Jane might be new at the detective game, but she recognized a crossroads when she came to it. How she chose to play out this scene with Annie, this moment of opportunity was important and she had to use all those instincts that Oh seemed to think she had. She could either nod sympathetically and fake understanding, hoping that Annie would continue, or she could admit total ignorance, hoping that Annie would rise to the bait and want to educate her.

Jane plunged into the middle of the pool, nodded her head sympathetically, and turned her palms up to the sky. "I haven't a clue what you're talking about," she said, leaning in toward Annie and taking her hand, "but it sounds fascinating."

"Aren't you something to be so honest?" said Annie, triggering immediate reflex guilt in Jane. "I practice feng shui. I dabble anyway. And when Rick was here, I could find nothing to counterbalance the disturbance he created."

"Was he a difficult person to get along with?"

"He was unpredictable. Which can be good, you know, exciting," Annie said, demonstrating a charming ability to spin positively, "but there was no counterbalance. He had a lot of anger, his cabin was poorly situated, and that foul, dirty truck blocked the energy flow to my cabin. He was year of the rat—seemed loyal, could have been loyal, but chose to be opportunistic."

"It sounds like you knew him well," Jane said, reflecting on how little anyone else had said about Rick Moore.

"I know this," said Annie, with a sweet smile. "He was fucking with everybody's chi around here."

Mickey asked Annie to come sit with him at dinner.

She stood and held on to Jane's hand for a moment. "You're a rabbit, aren't you?" she asked.

Again Jane turned her palms upward and shook her head. The cluelessness seemed to work well for her. "Next time you eat at a Chinese restaurant, check your place mat," said Annie. "That's what got me started."

Jane took a seat next to Geoff and Jake, who, Jane was noticing, might as well have been joined at the hip. "The boys," as most of the residents referred to them, were studying a drawing as they ate, each taking turns putting marks on it.

Jane took out the paper cocktail napkin she had picked up with the pages Oh had given her. From her bag she took out a black, fine-point pen and drew from memory the chair in Rick Moore's sketch. She wasn't sure she had gotten the back exactly, but the turned legs looked right. She took a bite of her salad, romaine, thinly sliced onion, and orange slices perfectly chilled, glistening with a sour cherry vinaigrette, perfectly composed on the plate. Chewing slowly, she added the finials to the back uprights.

Geoff and/or Jake had stopped looking at the drawing they were making and turned to Jane's. Jane could feel his, then their, eyes on the napkin, studying and measuring. Maybe this was the only way they communicated. She pushed it in their direction.

The two of them nodded, and the one closest to Jane took his pen and added three turned spindles to the back of the chair. Then the other one added in a double foot rail in front. They both nodded then and pushed the sketch back in front of Jane. At the risk of breaking up what was for them a rapid-fire dialogue, Jane felt compelled to shatter it with words.

"Worked on this chair here?" she asked, cutting her sentence down as much as possible. Perhaps later they would all go out and rub sticks together or do some cave painting.

Geoff and Jake looked at her even more blankly than they had looked at her before when introduced. Then Jane's encounter with them took an even more extraordinary turn than the curve that brought her to using Etch A Sketch as a language. They began to laugh. Heartily. Geoff slapped Jake on the back, then Jake slapped Geoff on the back or vice versa, then they both slapped Jane on the back and pointed and guffawed. Jane didn't really want to break the moment by asking what exactly was so funny, so she laughed with them. They pointed to the sketch and laughed again. Then, as suddenly as it had begun, it ended; and they went back to drawing for each other. Jane, totally clueless about what had just happened, folded the napkin and put it back into her pocket.

Glen tapped on his glass for attention. "I know we've all put in quite a day. Everyone here has had to speak with the police, and by now I think everyone knows that we at Campbell and LaSalle"—Glen paused here and Jane listened for any irony, but there was none—"we at Campbell and LaSalle did not know Rick Moore the way we thought we did. Or perhaps we did know the real Rick Moore, and the Rick who committed this terrible murder was the aberration, the dark side of him that we had never met. I can only say that the Rick Moore I knew was not a murderer. He was a craftsman, artist, and friend."

Jane noted that Glen was speaking more positively about Rick now than he had at the memorial service. Jane did not remember anyone having anything intimate or warm to say then. They had let Martine keen and wail for them. It was strange that now that he had been labeled a murderer, he had become Glen's number-one guy. Was Glen in a bit of denial, or was he just laying it on a bit thickly to patch up any chinks in the armor? After all, if Rick were murdered, it was important to be perceived as his friend, not his enemy. Jane looked at Annie who sat on the other side of the table, and she gave Jane a knowing shake of the head, mouthing the word, "rat." Jane wasn't sure if she was referring to Rick again or Glen.

"It is my belief that Rick, in his guilt and in his grief, probably took his own life when he realized what he had done," Glen said, then sat down.

Jane could not see Oh's face, but she could see Tim, who, with Scott, sat across from her at the wide dinner table. She was determined not to react to any facial expression, any mouthed word, any gesture Tim might send her. The only trouble well-behaved Jane had ever encountered in elementary or high school was when she reacted to Tim Lowry's instigation. Curiously, this time Tim kept his face completely blank as everyone at the table sat in shocked silence.

Did Glen really believe that Rick had run down to the stream shoeless and thrown himself in? More precisely, thrown his face into ten inches of water?

Tim continued to stare at Jane, but his face remained expressionless. Then he started to smile as everyone looked first down at their own bags and pockets, patting them or shaking their heads. Then Jane heard it, too. The tinny notes were faint but unnervingly close to her. This time, it wasn't "Jingle Bells" but the catchy, unforgettable notes of "I'm a Believer" by the Monkees.

Tim and Scott began the silent shoulder shaking that

gave Tim away. He had changed the ring, of course, and Jane knew that when she excused herself to answer it there would be no one there. The small screen would inform her that she had missed a call, and the number shown would be Tim's. He had pushed the one number code for her phone with his hand in his pocket, knowing he had changed the ring, and he had found the perfect moment to showcase his prank. He didn't need to roll his eyes when Glen made his outlandish statement. He let the Monkees express his ironic detachment. Jane excused herself, picking up her bag and fishing out the phone, as she walked quickly to the front porch.

Jane sat on the glider, its oilcloth-covered cushions reminding her of one her parents had had on their back porch when she was a child. She pulled her knees up to her chest and stretched the bottom of Tim's cashmere pullover until it covered all of her down to her toes. It had gotten chilly and the ridiculously expensive sweater was warming, but the reason behind this fashion statement was all about the stretching. When she tossed it back to Tim tomorrow, she was confident he would have little choice but to toss it right into what Belinda St. Germain would call the "Definitely Discardable" pile. It was the least Jane could do.

She tried to work up more steam at Tim's practical joke, but Jane was actually relieved to be outside. Glen's pathetic speech felt like the last gasp of someone who knows that he's lost everything. Jane hadn't thought about him much. He was the smart one, or at least the smart-looking one. Blake was the front man, the billboard, but Glen was the professorial backup, the one who convinced everyone of the Campbell and LaSalle quality. Glen gave their stamp of approval its credibility.

Glen LaSalle was the expert who gave all the special lectures or "booth talks" at the major antique shows around the country. When the photo appeared on the society page with the benefit cochairs who had sponsored the preview party, however, it was Blake Campbell, handsome and rugged in his tuxedo, his arm around a Junior League president in a black strapless gown, who represented the "face" of Campbell and LaSalle.

And that face was going to end up with egg all over it soon enough. A murderer among them, who in turn is murdered by a second murderer among them? There had to be some kind of snappy headline that could be fashioned from that. Plus, a scandal about furniture either stolen, forged, switched, whatever had been done to the Westman chest. It would probably be the crime against the Westman chest that would bring Campbell and LaSalle crashing down even more than the murderer-within-murderer scenario. What had Tim called the murder in his shop in Kankakee? Midnight in the garden of good and stupid? Well, this was indeed murder in the garden of good and greedy. The lifestyle here was good, but fragile, and someone had seriously wanted Rick Moore to stop fucking up all the chi.

It wasn't hard to tell who of the head honchos would fare the worst if Campbell and LaSalle came crashing down. Glen might land on his feet professionally because of his authorship of books on nineteenth-century landscapes and Early American silversmiths, but Blake, the craftsman with the movie star good looks, would be the one in demand for appearances on the *Antiques Roadshow*.

Since Blake always seemed quiet, Jane couldn't tell if there was any change in his behavior during dinner. He only seemed mildly interested in what Glen was saying to the group at large, but then again, Jane thought Blake always looked a little disinterested. Jane wished he wasn't so handsome. She was afraid it meant he was guilty of something. After all, if a handsome movie star was the guest on a television show, the surprise ending was never a surprise. No big star is going to guest on a weekly program if he or she isn't given something big to do, and big on television means solve or commit. Since the series' stars solve, the big-name guest stars commit. Blake was clearly the big-name star here.

Watching Roxanne, a beautiful and poised and talented woman in her own right, hover around him only added to his stature. She was clearly no one's fool, and if she thought Blake was more than a pretty face and worth her time, Jane wanted to believe it, too.

Oh came out on the porch, and Jane waited to speak until she was sure that Martine wasn't following close behind.

"She's gone to get me a chapter of the book she's writing," Oh said, answering the question Jane hadn't yet asked. Oh looked off toward the trees, as if imploring his wife to come down from her tree house hideaway.

Jane took out the napkin and unfolded it to show Oh. She thought that he might be interested in the Geoff/Jake interaction that had gone on.

"Officer Murkel came in and asked for you," said Oh. "He mentioned that he wanted to speak to everyone for a moment after dinner, but he wanted to talk to you privately.

"Why? He couldn't have . . . ," Jane said.

Oh shook his head. "I think he wants to explain what

is still off-limits. Maybe, too, he wants to see some reactions when everyone is together, maybe drop a few hints about what someone said, causing another to react a certain way."

"No, I think it's going to be like *The Mousetrap*, and he's going to reveal . . . ," said Tim, who had come up behind them, humming the Monkees' song.

"Shut up, Tim. I've never seen it," said Jane.

"You've never seen *The Mousetrap?*" asked Tim. "And you call yourself a detective."

Oh smiled his almost-maybe-smile.

"Do you, Mrs. Wheel?" Oh asked.

"What?" asked Jane, still trying to stare down Tim, who was back to humming.

"Call yourself a detective?"

Jane looked down at the napkin on her knee. Before she could answer, Tim stopped his singing and leaned over her shoulder. "Why do you have a picture of the Brewster chair?"

Jane and Oh both looked at Tim.

"What's the matter? I just asked why you have a sketch of the Brewster chair?"

"I give up," said Jane, "why *do* I have a picture of the Brewster chair?"

"Am I supposed to know what the Brewster chair is?" asked Oh. "Is this one of those popular culture questions that Claire says everyone except me could answer?"

Tim shook his head. "Not exactly common knowledge, but Claire would recognize the sketch, I bet. It's a famous piece. I mean it's famous and infamous," said Tim. "Is that a sketch of the real deal or the copy?" he asked.

Jane held the napkin up. "You tell me. It's a copy of a drawing that Rick Moore had among some of his papers.

I was doodling it at the table, and the Geoff/Jake duo added a few lines," said Jane, pointing to the spindles in back and the foot rail.

Tim picked it up and studied it for a moment.

"The Brewster chair was one of the earliest chairs made in America. Experts can say America for sure because it's made of ash, native here, not to England. It wasn't supposed to be comfortable; it was just supposed to be the biggest frigging chair in the room. You know, the king had his throne, but Elder Brewster had his chair. Two are known to exist. One is in the Metropolitan and one, I think, is in the Pilgrim Hall Museum in Plymouth," said Tim.

"No wonder Geoff and Jake got such a bang out of me asking if they'd worked on the chair," said Jane.

"They got a bang out of it because of the copy, which is just as famous as the chair," said Tim.

Oh looked over Tim's shoulder. "Let's walk and talk, Mr. Lowry. We'll hear better if someone comes up behind. I think, for the time being, you should just be educating Mrs. Wheel and me."

The three of them got up, Tim taking out a cigar. Jane was shocked since Tim rarely smoked. He shrugged at her look and told her that Blake had offered him one of his Cubans, and no one turns down one of those. Besides, Tim had said, it would explain why they were outside. They stationed themselves around one of the carved meditation benches. Oh made sure Tim was facing the lodge so he would be able to stop talking if Martine or anyone else sought them out.

"Murkel will certainly have someone ring the gong if we're needed," Oh said. "Now, please, Mr. Lowry."

"So there are two Brewster chairs known, but there's always been a rumor of a third. Every dealer in New England at one time or another probably had a dream of finding that elusive chair," said Tim.

"So someone made fakes?" asked Jane, smoothing the napkin over her knee.

"A fake," said Tim. "A beauty."

"But he was caught?" asked Oh. "When did all this take place?"

Jane knew Oh was sensitive to Martine's hunting instincts, since he rarely interrupted anyone with questions. He would normally be cautioning her to let the story unravel. If Martine only knew what a tribute to her tenacity Oh's questions were.

"I've read a couple of versions of the story, but the quick and dirty one is this. There was this artist in the sixties see, who one day goes to some museum with his buddy to view some Early American furniture exhibit. They're both builders, craftsmen you know, and they're wearing work clothes and want to see the underside of the chair. So they're on the floor looking at the chair or table or whatever, and a curator comes in with a tour and sees these guys who look like local farmers or something lying on the floor talking about the sloppy workmanship of these museum treasures. Well, the curator gets all snooty and tells them off and embarrasses them, throwing them out of the museum. This artist, Armand LaMontagne, is plenty pissed off," said Tim, finally getting the cigar to stay lit.

"He plots his revenge on snooty museum curators by building the perfect fake. Something that would fool the experts. And he doesn't go after something small. He decides to make a Brewster chair. I heard that he drilled the holes for the legs with a modern drill and saved the shavings of wood, you know, so he could prove later that he had built it. Otherwise he made it so true it could fool a museum—used the right wood, then aged it, then dunked it in salt-water. He even broke off one of the bottom rails to make it look like it had been kicking around for a while, you know?"

"Wait a minute," said Jane, "the sixties this is?"

"Yeah. That's when he made it, but then he has a friend of his put it in his antique store with a low price on it, like the dealer doesn't know anything about it. Dealers come in and out and spot the chair, make him low-ball offers so he won't know what he's got, and it finally gets sold to some-body who resells it. Each time the piece gets resold, the price gets higher, and finally the thing goes for a lot of money to a museum. The Henry Ford in Michigan, I think," said Tim.

"So the artist was waiting for . . . ?" asked Jane.

"Satisfaction," said Tim. "He had the chair rung and the shavings from drilling the holes for the rails and spin-dles. I think the newspaper story broke in the late seven-ties."

"What incredible patience," said Jane.

"Yeah, but in some ways, it backfired. I mean, he's a noted sculptor now, but everybody always asks him about the Brewster chair. He says he was just a kid, and kids do crazy things."

"But that guy who embarrassed him, what hap-pened . . . ?" asked Jane.

"Who knows? I mean some museum official probably lost his job over this, but it wouldn't necessarily have been the original guy. You know, a lesson was learned, I'm just not sure if whoever learned it was the one who deserved such a comedown," said Tim. "On the other hand, I'm not sure it ever is."

"Is the artist still in prison?" asked Jane.

"What law did he break?" asked Tim.

"Yes," said Oh, "he never represented the piece as authentic. It sounds like he allowed others to name the chair for him."

"Wow," said Jane. "I think I'm in love."

"Really?" said Tim. "With someone who spent all that time faking it, huh? Boy, you think you know someone . . ."

"It's the passion," said Jane. "Think about the work that went into making that chair. And the incredible patience waiting while it all played out. And creating the story of its past and imagining its future. If someone doesn't take me seriously about something, I mean if someone laughs at me when I'm trying to make a point, I'm furious. And that's in private. Imagine the public embarrassment in that first museum. And here he was, an artist just studying his craft. And then to have someone not take him or his talent seriously . . ." Jane stopped. "Seriously," she repeated.

"Sergeant Murkel at six o'clock," said Tim with a smile.

Jane turned and saw him approaching: a man with a plan.

"Mrs. Wheel, may I have a word?"

Tim and Oh nodded to Jane and wandered back toward the lodge, Oh glancing up, scanning the trees, and Tim puffing desperately on his cigar.

Jane had nothing concrete to report to Murkel. The

story about the Brewster chair was interesting, but she didn't know yet if or how it added up to Rick Moore's murder. She told him that someone was banging up furniture in the large storage shed on the fringe of the property, but she hadn't figured out what that had to do with anything yet either.

"I think another night of reflection on the events here might get someone remembering something from the afternoon of Moore's murder. If people get restless, they start looking at each other a bit more suspiciously," said Murkel.

"You might want to check the tree houses," Jane said, deciding that she really needed to trust Murkel. He was, after all, the police. "Someone tried to knock me out this afternoon." Jane quickly described the warehouse, went over the destruction of furniture again, and the attempt someone had made to close her eyes to what was going on. She hadn't even planned on telling him, but once she started, she couldn't stop.

Murkel chided her for not coming to him directly, but he agreed to send his crew up into the treetops. As he started back to the lodge, Jane stopped him, remembering that Claire Oh might get trapped up there.

Murkel cut off her explanation. "Mrs. Oh is in your cabin. Her husband told us to get her down before it got too dark," he said.

"Yes, we know that Bruce Oh is Mr. Kuruma," Murkel added. "He remains more valuable as Kuruma—someone who arrived after the fact and would be of little interest to me. It isn't so strange if I seek you out, Mrs. Wheel. You found the body, and I might continue to have further questions. If I gather together Mr. Kuruma and Mr. Lowry and you to talk to, you all lose your anonymity and the other residents might treat you a bit more warily."

Murkel left Jane and went to ring the gong to gather everyone in the lodge. He announced that they would be staying on the grounds, available if anyone remembered anything he or she might have forgotten to mention earlier. Jane, standing in the back of the room, didn't know if she had become paranoid and suspicious as a detective or whether her observations were true and objective, but she sensed that something was going on among the residents. There was a palpable excitement. She noticed Mickey passing a note to Annie, who passed it to Scott. Geoff and Jake were, of course, always passing a paper between them, but this was more unusual behavior on the part of the others. Even Roxanne peered over Scott's shoulder and read the note, slightly smiling when she rocked back on her heels.

Scott whispered to Tim, who grinned broadly and nodded. Martine had tossed her head and looked disinterested when the paper came her way. No one bothered to pass it to Silver.

As soon as Murkel finished his little speech, Tim came over to Jane and escorted her out the door, whispering in her ear. "Go to the cabin and get an extra sweater and make sure you have all your cash with you. Oh says Claire is there, so bring her, too. Walk directly to the visitors' parking lot on the other side of the craft classroom space. Oh and I will be in the car, but we won't have the lights on. We have to get out by the access road on the other side. I'll explain as soon as you get there, but hurry."

Jane stood still for a moment, thinking that she had just made a tacit agreement to work with Murkel, and perhaps this wasn't the way to keep her end of the bargain; but Tim gave her a push and she knew if she didn't just do what he said, she'd miss out on something good. It was vibrating in the air around him.

Claire was sitting at the desk reading Belinda St. Germain's book.

Before Jane could tell her to grab another sweater, Claire was up and tossing one to Jane. "I know. I've been waiting."

"Good," said Jane. "You can tell me what this is about."

Outside as they ran for the parking lot, Claire pointed up to the sky. "It's a full moon, the harvest moon."

"Yes?" said Jane.

Jane heard other footsteps. Everyone seemed to be running for their cars in the distant parking lot. Murkel had someone stationed on the main road in and out of Campbell and LaSalle, but not on the access roads or in the parking lots. This was a small Michigan town, and he had a small staff. He couldn't have anticipated a mass exodus on the night of a full moon. Claire had whispered that they'd all be back by sunrise.

"From where?" asked Jane.

They got into the backseat, Tim and Oh were in front, and Tim drove off the road and onto a gravel path that he said connected with the highway in a little less than a quarter mile.

"Moonlight Market," said Tim.

They bumped slowly along the path, using only the parking lights. Once they were out of sight of the main lodge, Tim turned on the headlights. He was grinning ear to ear as he sped up and jumped them onto the main road.

"It's a tradition," said Claire. "I've only been to one, about five years ago. I got those two Chinese vases, remember, Bruce? I sold them for a huge profit to that couple from Barrington?"

"Moonlight Market is held all night, starting around midnight, on the night of the last full moon in the fall. Summer season's over, so all the resort town antique dealers drag stuff out that they want to turn over, junkers come from three states, pickers are here from all over, it's the last big score before people go south for the winter and the sales dry up until next spring. People park in the lots at the consolidated high school and sell out of their trucks or the trunks of their cars. Some people set up tables on the grounds with candles or oil lamps. It's fabulous," said Tim, practically licking his lips.

"What about Murkel?" asked Jane, checking to see how much cash she had in her wallet.

"He's a smart man," said Oh, "and has lived here a long time. He knows about this market and will figure that people are going—he will expect us to keep an eye on everyone."

"You've talked to him?" asked Claire.

"I listened," said Oh.

Pulling into the parking lot, Jane could see that it was every bit as fabulous as Tim had described. Some vendors had set up lights, giving their tables and boxes the look of theatrical set pieces. Others, with their wares illuminated by the glow of candlelight, gave their pieces romantic cachet. Jane fished her flashlight out of her purse, and Tim nodded his approval.

"You don't want to buy a vase that's mint by candlelight and crazed by daylight," he said, referring to the network of fine lines and cracks underneath the glaze that devalued so much older porcelain and pottery.

Jane and Tim agreed to split up, circling the grounds from opposite directions. Bruce Oh said he'd tag along with Mrs. Wheel, and Claire, already sprinting toward a truck with furniture, said she'd meet them back at the car in a few hours.

"Claire seems to have recovered from all the police business," Oh said pensively. He looked at Jane, who was already in her flea market trance, carefully using her flashlight to go through two red-haired women's trunkful of vintage kitchenalia.

Jane hit paydirt at the third table. By candlelight she fell in love with a grouping of typewriter ribbon tins. She had a few at home that she had collected accidentally since they were being used to hold pins and hook-and-eye fasteners in an old sewing kit she had purchased. She had realized when she examined them that the small, round tins, with colorful designs and great graphics, were great collectibles in their own right. This sweet old man, wearing a T-shirt that identified him as the "tin man," dealing out of the trunk of his car, was willing to part with all the tins for approximately four dollars apiece. Jane realized that meant that half were underpriced and half were overpriced. What decided her about the purchase, though, was a small, round, Kelly green "Typ O' Typ" tin that had random letters around the sides of the container. It was a gem, and Jane was a sucker for anything named something o' something. She probably would have paid twenty-five for that one alone, although she would have had to answer to Tim for it later. She counted out Tin Man's money and asked if he would throw in some of the mechanical pencils he had in a jar, and he told her to pick two. Jane was practically dancing, discovering two laminated Bakelite pencils in the jar, both advertising Michigan taverns. She took her folded plaid shopping bag out of her large, leather tote and shook it open.

"I'll throw this in, too, honey; it's a cutie and looks good with the Typ O' Typ. End of the season and all," he said, handing her a small rectangular tin, green with red corners. It was a tin for 7/16-inch "push thumbtacks."

It was a cutie. On the bottom was a graphic of a girl in a turn-of-the-century skirt and middy blouse holding a picture she wanted to hang. Jane started. The manufacturer was the Moore Push-Pin Company of Philadelphia. The slogan was "Moore Push, Less Hangers."

"You think Rick Moore is sending me a message to get back to business?" asked Jane, showing Oh the tin.

"I never dismiss anything, Mrs. Wheel," said Oh, "not totally anyway."

They saw Annie and Mickey and Scott making their way around the grounds. Annie was carrying a large, two-handled basket overflowing with ribbons and old packages of rickrack and seam binding. She had a few remnants of fabric or tablecloths in it as well, and Jane asked her where she had found them. A quick gesture toward the other side of the parking lot, and everyone was off again.

This was where all of these junkers, restorers, craftspeople, and recyclers came alive—the marketplace of the forgotten and worn and worn out. From several yards away, Jane watched Glen LaSalle unroll paintings on canvasses that were all jammed into cardboard boxes scattered around a U-Haul truck. They watched Blake hold old wooden-handled tools first in one hand then in another, hefting the weight back and forth, checking for balance and feel. It was a gift, really, to see everyone at their most vulnerable, everyone wanting something.

Jane had filled her plaid bag with silver dessert spoons, crocheted pot holders, the typewriter tins, and two large jars of buttons. She had laughed out loud when she picked up a small wooden box that held at least two dozen elongated pennies, the kind you made yourself in a machine as souvenirs. Jane spotted a Mount Rushmore and Yellowstone picture among them and felt that she might have happened on a collection that belonged to one person, one family. Maybe she would be able to track their every summer vacation by laying out their reasonably priced souvenirs, hand cranked out by the kids at every stop along the way.

Oh wandered over to a food truck where an entrepreneur from two towns over had come to sell coffee and doughnuts when word got out that Moonlight Market was being held. He brought Jane a coffee, and they paused in the middle of the frenzy for a momentary recharge.

A woman with wildly curly hair gathered on top of her head in antennaelike ponytails asked Oh if his tie was for sale. He shook his head.

"I get that all the time," he said to Jane. "Claire says I should name a price and make some money. She is confident she can always find more."

"But you don't like getting caught up in the buy and sell?" asked Jane.

"Gifts, the ties are gifts from my wife, so I could never sell them. She says it's the only sentimental thing about me, but it doesn't seem sentimental. Seems impolite to think about not keeping them. Even if they are," he looked down at the tie he was wearing, "sometimes silly."

Jane sipped her coffee and looked left and right. This was marvelous, a moonlit madness that everyone here shared. There was the hope of finding your heart's delight, whatever it might be. The one thing you wanted and needed and had to have, and tonight, because you were in the right place at the right time, would have. And for however long it lasted, that romance of the marvelous thing would make you happy.

Jane was about to explain this whole love story to Oh when she looked straight across the field at a truck illuminated by two work lamps clamped to the sides of the bed.

Broken furniture and old air conditioners, alley pickings of every sort, were piled high. Sitting on top of Mount Debris was something else, though. It looked like a well-made table, what once might have been a valuable antique, now a dented and broken throwaway. Tom, of Tom's Trash and Treasures, was lifting it down for two people to get a better look.

Jane hurried across the field with Oh following. She managed to tell Oh that it was the table she had seen earlier. Behind the couple who were looking at the table was another man, pretending to be totally enraptured by an old turquoise high-fi set with detachable speakers, but Jane could see that he was studying the table and listening to Tom and the couple discuss it.

"Nah, it was a throwaway, too. Found it in the alley. It's a good one though. Anyone can see that's solid wood, not one of your new glue-and-sawdust models."

The couple wandered off, but the dealer who was

feigning interest in the speakers and disinterest in the table stayed close. He watched others come and tap the table, look underneath, examine the legs. He was joined by someone who looked like he could be his brother, just a taller, thinner version of the same man.

"Well," he whispered, "is it a Thornbury?"

"Might could be," he answered. "If it is, the old man doesn't know it, though. He wants to get rid of it for twenty-five dollars."

"Buy it," the tall version hissed.

"I can get it for less," the other one answered.

"Shit," said the brother or the partner. He had only glanced away for a moment, but the couple from earlier had come back and given Tom a twenty and were now carrying the table to the parking lot.

"You cheap bastard, now I have to go to work," the tall man said, following the couple to their van. Jane and Oh followed, too, pausing long enough to look at various tables, hoping to deflect anyone who might suspect them of stalking the table and its buyers. Jane saw Claire a few tables over and asked Oh to go get her so she could size up this piece of furniture.

"Looks like a Thornbury," she said. "Hard to tell, though, without looking at the construction. It's in bad shape."

"Would it be worth speculating on for twenty-five dollars?"

"Honey, anything's worth speculating on for twenty-five dollars. Tim's got you on way too small a budget," Claire said. "If it's the real deal, a Roger Thornbury–made card table, it's worth thirty thousand at auction, even in that shape."

Jane, Claire, and Bruce watched tall man cajole and wheedle the couple, brandishing a tape measure like a sword. He seemed to be trying to convince them that he had run to measure the space for this old table in his summer cabin; he had an odd, awkward space to fill, and his wife was going to kill him if he didn't come home with it since she had said it would fit—he had been the one who'd insisted on measuring. He didn't know how much they had paid, but he was willing to give them fifty dollars just to spare himself the aggravation.

Jane admired the young couple; they remained impassive during the whole speech. The wife whispered something to the husband, and he told tall man that his wife was suspicious. Was he an antiques dealer who knew something they didn't know? The man laughed uproariously. He was good, Jane gave him that. He insisted he didn't know a Chippendale from a chipmunk; he just knew he wouldn't be out of the doghouse for months if he didn't come home with that table. Would they take a hundred dollars?

The couple took $125, and the wife shook her finger at the man and told him they better not turn on the *Antiques Roadshow* and see him standing between the Keno brothers. He laughed again and shook his head.

As soon as the couple had walked away, Claire walked up to the man. "Is it a Thornbury?"

"I don't know," he said slowly, "but I have to find out."

"Do you have a card?" asked Jane.

"Ask my stupid, cheap brother over there. I don't want to do anything dealerlike while that couple might be watching. She'd come over here and peck my eyes out."

"Would you take five hundred for this right now?" Jane asked.

"No," he said, "although by tomorrow I'll probably be kicking myself. Do you have a card?"

Jane shook her head. She was beginning to think she'd better get some. Jane Wheel, PI, picker-investigator.

"How will you authenticate this table?" Oh asked, as he offered to help him carry it to his truck.

As they walked away, Jane heard him telling Oh that there was a place nearby called Campbell and LaSalle . . .

A little after 4:00 A.M. they were headed back to Campbell and LaSalle. They had fished out the market and were happy shoppers; but more important, for Jane, she had seen the Brewster chair plan in action.

She knew as soon as she saw the table on Tom's truck that it was the one she had watched being "distressed" earlier that day.

And scanning the crowd, spotting another interested party watch the drama of the tall dealer scam the young couple out of a potentially valuable antique, she saw him. Standing tall, hands shoved into his pockets, hat pulled low, Jane could picture him as she had seen him earlier that day, wielding a hammer against that poor, defenseless table.

The problem, she now realized, with figuring out who at Campbell and LaSalle might have a reason to carry out a forgery plan, to make such elaborate copies and set them free in the world, was that she had thought there had to be a money motive. For someone to have fooled Claire with the fake Westman chest or pulled a switch when she picked it up, Jane had believed someone had to be looking for a profit. Hearing the story of the Brewster chair, however, expanded the possibilities.

What if someone wanted to make these forgeries for

fun? Just to prove he could do it? He wouldn't sell them; he'd just release them into the dealer/shark-infested waters of country antiques and watch them swim back to Campbell and LaSalle for restoration and authentication.

No one was sleepy when they got back to the compound. No one even looked tired. Everyone who had sneaked out now filed into the lodge with their purchases, hoping that Cheryl and the staff had been tipped off about Moonlight Market and planned breakfast to begin even earlier than normal. The coffee was on and a basket of muffins and scones sat on the sideboard. The kitchen hummed with activity, and there remained an excited buzz among those residents who had gotten away with something by sneaking out.

Since Jane had been semirecruited by Murkel, she was surprised she didn't feel at all guilty about sneaking out or seeing everyone else sneak out. Well, why should she? It was Jane's job, as she saw it, to help Murkel make sure no one got away with murder. The Moonlight Market had provided the perfect opportunity to piece the puzzle together.

She hadn't said anything to Tim, Oh, or Claire in the car on the way back though, because there was one more piece that she had to figure out. If someone wanted to play a trick, work a scam like the Brewster forgery, and didn't care about making money from it, why would anyone be killed over it? Why had Rick Moore killed Horace Cutler, and why had someone killed Rick Moore? What was at stake?

Jane had begun telling Oh some of her thoughts when Tim and Claire brought coffee over to the table.

"What would Belinda St. Germain say about that bag

of stuff, Janie?" asked Tim. "Looks to me like you've violated your parole."

"No, I was reading that book while you all were at dinner," said Claire, "and as long as you get rid of an equal number of objects, you can have new stuff."

"I'm afraid you don't know Jane very well; she can't get rid of anything," said Tim, laughing.

"I'll get rid of twelve things in my purse right now," said Jane, "while I figure something out."

Jane pulled a handful of odds and ends from her purse and stared down at them. Solving this murder was going to be easier than sorting out this stuff. She made each card, each pencil, each highlighter, each key ring, each yo yo (where had she picked up two yo yos?), each notebook stand for one of the Campbell and LaSalle residents.

She knew who wasn't taken seriously, who might want to prove himself as a master craftsman, and who wouldn't have to care about making money from it. That was easy. She made her Bakelite compact stand for him. It was at least as well carved and attractive as Blake's handsome face.

"May I have your attention, campers?" said Murkel, who had come in from the office. He was the only one in the room who actually looked like he had been awake all night. Oh nodded at him and gestured slightly toward Jane Wheel, who was laying the contents of her purse out on the table. Jane nodded, too, as if to say, I'll have this worked out in a minute; but Murkel did not look satisfied.

"Although I explained that no one was supposed to leave the grounds for any reason, it seems there was quite a caravan into town last night, this morning, a few hours ago."

"Moonlight Market," said Annie brightly. Jane would

make the black Bakelite squirrel call that said on the side it was made in Olney, Illinois, stand for Annie. She had wanted Rick to stop blocking her chi.

"We're all back," said Scott, fixing mimosas at the sideboard. That's the way to start a Monday morning. Jane took her green EZ Way Inn key ring and made it stand for Scott. He wanted money or at the least a dental plan.

Mickey sat down and started buttering a muffin. Mickey could be the Bakelite dice she kept in a leather pouch. He wanted Rick's spot as Blake's right-hand man. And he maybe wanted Annie, too. He'd kept his eyes on her the whole time he slathered butter on his pastry.

Jane found a wrinkled buckeye to stand for Silver and a pack of Life Savers for Martine. Geoff and Jake came in, and Jane found two pink pearl erasers to stand in for them. Jane knew that Geoff and Jake just wanted a place to do their work, Silver needed to get rid of negativity, and Martine wanted a book contract and a little Oprah glory. She wanted to be Belinda St. Germain, for heaven's sake.

Glen and Roxanne were sitting in the club chairs. When Blake took a seat at the table, Roxanne got up and came over to him and he absentmindedly kissed the top of her head. Jane hadn't seen her at the Moonlight Market, but that didn't surprise her. You only had to meet Roxanne once to know that she didn't need stuff to make her happy. She was one of those self-contained people. As long as she had this place to run and Blake to take care of, she would be happy.

"Since everyone's up and at 'em so bright and early, maybe this would be a good time to have a group discussion of Rick Moore's murder," said Murkel.

Jane found more purse detritus to stand for Glen and Roxanne. A Zippo lighter for Glen and a . . . what was it her mother had been saying constantly? "A round peg in a square hole?" Is that what she had found to represent Roxanne? Jane told Oh she needed Murkel to stall for two minutes before he started the meeting.

Jane stood up and looked at the circle of objects in front of her on the table. If Annie saw this up close, she might think Jane was laying out her own version of the feng shui compass. Jane looked it over once, picked up a few things, then excused herself.

She needed to check the direction it was pointing one more time.

19

You might think your mind is not as cluttered as your closet. Go right ahead and tell yourself that, my dears. When you are finally honest with yourself, however, you will look inside that kitchen drawer, awash in old batteries, twist ties, expired coupons, spent candles, and half-empty match-books, and you will see, instead of a drawer, a mirror.

—Belinda St. Germain, *Overstuffed*

When Jane came back in, Martine had cornered Oh, who was being defended by Tim. Murkel was talking on a cell phone; and although no one had left, the novelty was wearing off. Everyone was restless, wanting to get to their nests and look over their Moonlight Market treasures. Only Blake looked content, stirring his coffee and smiling at what he had wrought.

Martine was holding a folder over her heart with her right hand, and she patted it with her left, as if calming an infant.

"This is it, my work, my life, my heart," she said.

"Wow, all that in less than twenty pages?" asked Tim. "You are one hell of a concise writer, Martine. Been studying poetry with Silver?"

Martine was a woman who had been withering people

with a glance for years, and she was used to being able to do so at will. She narrowed her eyes into slits and directed all of her goddess/life coach/aquarian/new age/crone/coven power directly at him, but quickly found that it all bounced off his invisible, who-gives-a-shit protective shield.

Martine had met her match with Tim. He was the most unwitherable person Jane had ever met, and she had spent several years in advertising. She had worked with actors and models and clients who could buy and sell her. Yet each and every one of them were the potential victims of their egos. Jane knew that if you attack the ego in just the right way, you can start a hairline crack that can become the Grand Canyon, splitting someone in two. Jane had seen many a client brought to his knees by a supermodel, many a supermodel brought to her knees by an actor, and many an actor brought to his/her knees by a less-than-enthusiastic response to a performance. She had never seen Tim Lowry brought to his knees by anyone.

Jane watched Martine gather herself and prepare to hurl another thunderbolt at Tim. She half wanted to tell her to save her energy because Tim could not be cracked, at least not by Martine. And she half wanted to see Martine hurl herself at the brick wall of Tim's confidence just for the sheer spectacle. Neither half engaged her quite enough.

"I'd like to speak to Mr. Kuruma for a moment, if you would excuse us," said Martine, wisely choosing frosty behavior over the wasted energy of taking on Tim.

"Nope," said Tim.

"*Pardonnez moi?*" said Martine, reminding Jane of some actress. When Jane realized that the actress was actually the muppet Miss Piggy, she laughed out loud.

Was it just twenty-four hours ago that they had sat mourning Rick Moore? More precisely, was it just twenty-four hours ago when they had sat drinking and listening to Martine talk about the concept of mourning Rick Moore?

What a difference a day makes, Jane thought, taking out the printouts that Oh had given her earlier. She skimmed the stories of the Brewster chair from two different perspectives. One article was an interview with the artist, Armand LaMontagne. In it, he seemed to want to talk about his current sculpture but was unable to totally divorce himself from the Great Bewster Chair Hoax. Even though the story had broken over twenty years ago, LaMontagne was still asked about it all the time.

Tim had told the story pretty well. There were a few more interesting details here. He had made the chair out of green wood so that as it dried, it would warp and shrink, mimicking the natural aging process of a real Great Brewster aging over time. He'd swabbed the joints of the chair with a homemade blend of glue, hair, and dirt. He'd even dreamed up a three-hundred-year history for the chair, taking out one of the chair rungs because he imagined one owner liked to lean back and put his feet up.

The other printout that Oh had given her was an article by a professor on noteworthy hoaxes and forgeries. This author was far more damning of those who dared to fool the experts than the writer who had interviewed LaMontagne. Jane understood his point of view, since most of the forgeries and fakes had been fabricated for profit. But the Great Brewster Hoax was innocent enough, wasn't it? Jane might have been less admiring herself if

LaMontagne had been out for a buck, but he just wanted to make a point.

The professor who authored this paper, though, thought it was reprehensible for an artist to devote that much time and energy and craft for deception. He maintained that the artist's gratification in fooling the experts and destroying at least one curator's career without committing any crime that could be proven in a court of law must have been pretty thin satisfaction. Jane wondered if perhaps the author of this paper was a museum curator himself.

What had Charley said his speech was about? Hoaxes. The phone kept cutting out, but she had heard the term *hoaxes*; and this paper mentioned, in addition to the Brewster hoax, antique document forgery and paleontological hoaxes. Teams on digs salted the sites of their rivals with fake fossils. At best, it sent one team down the wrong path and slowed them down in their findings. At worst, it tricked a professor or scientist into publishing something that would ruin his or her career. Not necessarily illegal, but certainly not harmless either.

Tim handed Jane a glass of orange juice, and she eyed it carefully.

"What?" Tim asked, laughing. "What?"

Jane sniffed and sipped the tiniest taste. It was, after all, Tim who just yesterday had handed her iced water with olives. She shuddered thinking about it, drinking the juice and being thankful that Tim didn't like to repeat himself.

Okay, here was a profile of a prankster. Tim liked to play a trick or two, like changing the ring on her phone.

What was the harm in that? It was all just for fun, to get a laugh. So what was the harm in any of that? Laughter was good. But there was a problem, too. When that laughter came as a result of embarrassing someone else, it no longer was innocent. There was harm done. Or at least, there was the potential for harm to be done.

Blake was sitting near the fireplace to the left of Murkel, holding a brandy snifter, half full. That was Blake's glass, never half empty. Rich, handsome, talented, it probably should have been enough for him. Blake's glass was more than half full.

Jane wondered how long he had been crafting these fake antiques? Had he read the book on Mathew Westman and decided that a Sunflower Chest would be the perfect project. How long had he been banging up those tables and chairs and sending them out on the back of flatbed trucks to swap meets? It would be like starting Internet jokes and chain letters, measuring the time it took for whatever he'd started to come back to him. How did he keep score? And who knew? Had Rick Moore worked on these pieces with Blake and gotten greedy? Had he decided there was a profit in these deceptions? Or had Rick Moore been fooled by Blake's work, then embarrassed? Disappointed?

Or even more dangerous, had Rick Moore been worried for his mentor? Had he thought Blake was about to be exposed, and had Rick decided that he had to protect Blake? Jane was fascinated, watching Blake. He was playing with a cigar and lighter. No one, not even Blake, smoked indoors here; but Blake seemed to be toying with the Cuban and vintage Zippo. He was flipping things back and forth, almost juggling them, along with his drink.

"Ah," said Jane aloud. Bruce Oh had pulled up a chair next to her and waited for her to explain what she had figured out.

"He's ambidexterous," said Jane.

Oh followed her look and saw that Blake had gotten out a pocket knife with several tools attached to it. He had flipped out the scissors and was snipping off the end of the cigar using his left hand. He then picked up his brandy with his right hand and drained the glass.

"That explains the carving on the chest, anyway," said Jane, "even though there are plenty more things left to explain."

Murkel cleared his throat and, uncharacteristically, the room fell silent. Jane had been correct last night at dinner when she'd noticed some shakiness on the part of the residents. These were people who ordinarily wouldn't give a police officer the time of day, but enough events had unfolded here at Campbell and LaSalle that each of them seemed to be paying this visitor from the outside world a bit more attention than they had yesterday.

"Our interviews are now concluded here, and except for some moonlight madness, everyone has been most cooperative," said Murkel. Jane sat up a little straighter and waited for Murkel, to whom she had given her notebook, to point his finger at Blake and ask him what exactly had been going on here at Campbell and LaSalle. But Murkel was not pointing a finger, he was shaking hands with Blake, thanking him for laying the compound open to him and his people. The investigation seemed to support the preliminary findings of accidental death for Rick Moore. Then Murkel, who Jane was beginning to see had a wicked flair for the dramatic, repeated the word "seemed" and looked over at Jane.

"Seemed to be supported until Mrs. Wheel took on the case," Murkel said.

"What?" said Jane, thinking to herself at first that it seemed pretty loud for a silent self-directed question, then realizing it hadn't been silent. She also wondered just what kind of information googling her, or whatever Murkel had done, had produced. "Took on the case?" What had Oh said about her on his police reports?

Imagine that, Jane did say to herself, *I managed to get all eyes on me even without my cell phone ringing.*

"Yes, Mrs. Wheel?" asked Murkel. "Did you have a question?"

"Yes," Jane said, "I do have a question."

Jane stood up and surveyed the room. "Well, it's actually more of a comment," she said, clearing her throat. "I don't see how Rick Moore's death could have been accidental. He hadn't been working with chemicals, and if he were really trying to end it all, surely he wouldn't have chosen a stream with only . . ."

"How do you know Rick wasn't working with chemicals?" asked Annie.

"Tim and I had gone into the barn before I found him. There weren't any jars or cans opened. There weren't any projects on the floor. There was a row of solvents and a fan below the gallery loft, where I believe he had been sitting with a book," Jane said, making a mental note to take his Birkenstocks out of her closet where she had stashed them.

"Mrs. Wheel, I'm sure you're an observant woman, but

you and Mr. Lowry probably didn't go into the mixing room, next to the office. Rick told me he was going to work there that afternoon," said Glen.

This was getting exciting. *Maybe this is how* The Mousetrap *ends?* thought Jane.

"You really think he was overcome, Glen?" asked Blake. "Rick knew better than that. . . ."

The look Glen LaSalle shot Blake Campbell vibrated in its intensity. Blake seemed not to notice, but Murkel and everyone else in the room felt the reverberation.

"I mean if anybody understood the safety procedures, it was Rick," said Blake, totally oblivious.

"Mr. LaSalle, didn't you say at dinner that you thought Rick committed suicide?" asked Oh.

"I said it was a possibility, but . . . ," Glen began, but was interrupted by Blake.

"That doesn't make sense either, Glen. Rick was a sonofabitch, but he wasn't stupid," said Blake.

"Christ, Blake, shut the hell up," said Glen.

By this time, the residents of Campbell and LaSalle were dumbstruck. No one had heard these two raise their voices above a murmur for twenty years, and now they were publicly squabbling in front of guests and the local police. "We at Campbell and LaSalle"—the whole lot of *we*—were shocked.

"But, Glen . . ."

"I'm trying to save your ass, you idiot. You and your damn tribute pieces. I told you this would ruin us, but no, you wouldn't listen. You were just having a bit of fun with it, proving your genius and all," said Glen. "You arrogant asshole! Are you satisfied now?"

Not only was Blake unsatisfied; he seemed totally clueless. "Are you talking about my fakes?" he asked. "Oh, Glen, no one cares about those. Just hobbies, right, Officer Murkel?"

Glen looked like someone had bashed him in the face with a hand-turned, green-ash spindle. What was Blake doing talking to the policeman about this?

Murkel held up his hand and asked that everyone calm down for a moment.

"Mr. Campbell explained his copies of fine antiques, and he showed us his storage area earlier today. Nothing illegal going on that I can see, although I guess I'd be pretty mad if I was one of those dealers who thought I had a real one on my hands."

Blake smiled and nodded at Murkel. The sight of that, the two of them grinning at each other, seemed to cause something in Glen LaSalle to explode.

"You dumb fuck! I'm trying to save your life here!" Glen shouted. Roxanne had stood up and motioned to Annie, and the two of them were trying to get Glen to sit down, but he would have none of it. "That ungrateful little shit, Rick Moore, was blackmailing you—I saw the letters. Do you really think you're above the law? Just because this guy hasn't put two and two together yet doesn't mean he won't."

"I'm thinking with that mouth he might not be guesting on the *Antiques Roadshow* next season," whispered Tim. "Can you imagine if he disagreed with one of the Keno brothers?"

Jane looked down at the objects removed from her purse—her own feng shui compass or map. Then she looked around the room. Everything had clicked into place. She knew Blake had been making the masterful copies of museum-quality furniture, then banging them up, aging them to have a little fun with dealers who thought they had found the treasure of a lifetime. And now she knew who had killed Rick Moore. If she could get Glen LaSalle to shut up for a minute before he got himself arrested for murdering Blake Campbell in front of several interested witnesses, she could end this high drama. She caught Oh's eye, and he seemed to be giving her an encouraging look. Either that, or a discouraging look. She made a mental note to ask him later how she was supposed to read his expressions to know what to do and when—that is, if they were going to be partners.

"I think I can answer some . . . ," Jane began, then realized no one was listening to her. Glen was shouting. Roxanne was trying to get him to drink a glass of water. Scott was pouring mimosas all around. Annie was looking through her purse, claiming to have some St. John's Wort to give Glen. Mickey looked like he wanted to make a break for the door and head right up a tree, and Martine was trying to lead everyone in a series of deep breaths. Only Silver seemed not to notice what was going on. He had found a whole tray of untouched chocolate pots du crème on the dining room table and was knocking them back like Jell-O shots, lined up on a campus bar.

Jane climbed up on the seat of her chair and gave an ear-splitting whistle. Somehow she was certain that she had veered away from *The Mousetrap*. Agatha Christie would never have made Poirot or Miss Marple climb on top of a vintage Stickley chair to get the crowd's attention.

"I know what happened," Jane said, "and if you'll give me your attention, I'll tell the rest of you."

Glen stopped sputtering, and Jane took advantage of the lull.

"Blake Campbell crafted what might be taken for a Westman chest, a priceless antique," she began, and Blake nodded, almost as if he were taking a bow. "And although he usually made his simpler fake antiques here and allowed them to be carted off by junk dealers to be sold at flea markets, then possibly make their way back for restoration, he wanted a better showcase for the fake Westman," Jane said.

Jane reached into her right pocket and pulled out her small notebook, flipped to a page and nodded, and looked to Blake.

"Was McDougal your uncle?"

Blake nodded. "Uncle Mac. I was his only relative."

"Blake hired a company to dispose of his uncle's estate by having a sale, but before they came on the scene, he split his Westman fake in two and planted the pieces among his uncle's belongings. He buried the bottom half of the chest in the basement under tools and boxes, so when someone spotted it, it was unpriced. He insisted that it be given away so no one could accuse him of taking any money for it.

"The dealer who discovered it, Claire Oh, brought it here for restoration and authentication, and checked it in with Glen LaSalle, then discussed it with Rick Moore," said Jane, gesturing to Claire who was sitting next to Tim, devouring a scone. "He started to research it, and in snooping around found the evidence that Blake had made it in his private shop. . . ."

Blake held up a hand. "Very good, Mrs. Wheel, but one thing. Rick knew it was made here; he helped with it. I just don't think he liked the game. He felt that there was money to be made. He wanted to sell the Westman as a real Westman, you see, and . . ."

"That's why Rick switched drawers, right? To make Claire Oh's Westman an obvious fake when it was returned, so it couldn't be sold as the real deal?" Jane asked.

Blake nodded. "This was a long project, and Rick had become a real Westman carver. He could do the sunflowers in his sleep, but he could do the faces and all the other motifs, too. He had built his own Westman chest. I never dreamed he'd try to sell it as a real one . . . when I saw what he was up to, I got mine out. Whether it was considered a fake or a genuine one, it would muddy the waters for anything Rick tried to do."

Jane looked over at Claire. "That's what puzzled you, right? It seemed so authentic when you first found it, then, when you saw the drawers Rick had put in, so obviously fake, you couldn't figure out why you had been so sure in the first place?" Claire nodded and Jane continued.

"Rick realized that he had to stop any talk about a fake Westman on the market if he wanted to pass off the one he had made as real and drive up the auction price. He went into Chicago to silence Claire Oh and maybe even reclaim the chest. He probably figured she'd have it at the antique mall and he could steal it back or destroy it. Instead he found Horace Cutler, whom he realized also knew about it. That's why he killed Horace."

"So he really did that," said Blake. "I didn't want to believe it."

"Yes, you arrogant dumb ass, and he had a letter from you offering him money to do it," said Glen.

Blake, finally, was speechless. He had no answer for that. Roxanne left Glen to go minister to Blake, but he shook his head at her offer of a glass of water.

"That's what you mean about him blackmailing me?" said Blake, finally. "You didn't mean about the Westman; you meant about the murder?"

Glen didn't even dignify the question with a reply. He actually looked relieved that he didn't have to shout in Blake Campbell's ear anymore. When Blake realized that his silence looked like he was agreeing that he had hired Rick to commit murder, he stood up.

"No, I didn't do that. I didn't ask Rick to do anything of the sort."

"I saw the letter, dear," Roxanne said, trying to pat his shoulder as he strode away from her. "I didn't believe it at first, but Rick insisted. He said some ugly things about what he'd do to you, to this place . . ."

"Anyone here could have written that note," said Jane, reclaiming the floor. "You're all artists and copyists to a certain degree. Anyone could have gotten a piece of Blake's stationery and written a letter that implicated Blake."

Jane did indeed have everyone's attention now. She felt the change in the air. Up to now, she was pretty much saying things that they found interesting, plausible, if somewhat surprising, but now they might be implicated. Everyone here had a stake in protecting Blake's name, protecting Campbell and LaSalle from scandal and murder.

"Who did it?" asked Blake. "Who forged that letter?"

"Oh, Rick did that himself," said Jane. "I found a piece

of paper he'd practiced Blake's handwriting on. He was using it for a bookmark." She looked at Oh, who nodded very slightly. "Yes, Rick did it and showed it to Roxanne and Glen. He thought it protected him if he was your boy."

"Wait a minute," said Blake. "You were willing to protect me?"

Glen started to shake his head, muttering again about what a dumb shit Blake was. Jane thought she heard him say just another dumb, handsome blond and something about the ego of the guy.

"You were willing to protect me, cover for me?" Blake asked Roxanne. The Campbell and LaSalle residents were all looking up at him, nodding dumbly, hopefully. Would this movie they were watching have a happily-ever-after ending?

Blake nodded with them for a few seconds, then said, equally quietly, "But you believed I was a murderer?" He went over to the sideboard and poured himself a tumblerful of expensive brandy.

"I've lived with you people off and on for thirty years. You've been my family. And you believed I asked someone to kill a person?"

Blake looked over all of their heads and past their eyes as best he could until he was meeting Murkel's steely blues. "Well, Officer Murkel, I didn't kill anyone or ask anyone to kill anyone, but I'm afraid I can't vouch for anyone else here. I realize I don't know everybody as well as I thought I did."

"Poor baby," said Glen. "Poor Blake. Has your innocence been shattered? You think everyone just loved you and thought of you as the grand papa of this place? At least

I didn't have any illusions about everybody. We were a meal ticket, and a damn fine meal ticket." Glen looked back toward the dining room table. "Right, Silver? And our fine residents? They were slave labor. And they were getting sick of it, right, Scott?" Glen asked. "It was getting harder and harder to keep up the work standards and the reputation of Campbell and LaSalle. We had created a whole commune of spoiled, pretentious brats and not one of them had a health plan or job security. Anyone here would have protected you because they didn't want this place to go up in smoke or down in flames, whichever you prefer. Your little game of beat the masters was going to cost everybody. Hell, Geoff and Jake are the only ones who have a business of their own outside of this place, and everybody made fun of them, right? Workaholics, right? Instead of an alcoholic like Scott or a pothead like Mickey?" Glen wasn't yelling anymore. He sounded exhausted.

"So *you* did it?" asked Blake. "For Campbell and LaSalle, Glen? *You* killed Rick?"

Jane realized that this was what Oh had warned her about. If you let these climactic courtroom scenes play out, the guilty might never confess. They don't think they're guilty because they did the right thing. That's why the world needs detectives, Jane realized. It's what Oh had been trying to teach her. If they weren't around to make sure the guilty got discovered, things might wind around and around until the wrong person put a noose around his own neck.

Glen had buried his head in his hands, and his shoulders were shaking. Anyone would think he was crying, his whole body racked with sobs. When he lifted his head, though, he was laughing. "No, you dumb sonofabitch, I didn't kill Rick. Until a few minutes ago, I thought you had done it and were just too dumb to shut up about it. I just figured you were showing off—one more demonstration of the master's hand."

"My turn again?" asked Jane.

In the dead silence that greeted her question, Jane looked down again at her objects to be discarded à la Belinda—as soon as they stopped standing in for her suspects.

"Before dinner, I went out and looked in the window at the barn. Rick Moore had been up in the gallery library reading. The murderer went in and opened up the kind of eye-burning solvent that Rick would recognize and know was dangerous. The fan was switched on, blowing the fumes right into his face from below. He would be too blinded and disoriented to find his way down the steps and directly out the back door. Instead, once he stumbled down, he'd try to push open one of the windows. But he couldn't. He might have even moved over to the next one and tried to push it open, but he couldn't open that one either. By then, it would be easy to lead him out the back door to the stream and hold his head under for a minute or two. As soon as he took in a couple lungsful of water, all that was needed was someone to come along and find the body."

"Why couldn't he get the windows open, Nancy Drew?" Tim asked.

Jane unrolled her fist and held it out. In the middle of her hand were the objects she had selected from her bag to represent Roxanne: two nails, the nails Roxanne had left on the table after replacing the hanger for the mirror in the dining room—one a contemporary two-inch nail and one an antique, square iron nail.

"He couldn't push them open. The only person who had a twenty-first-century hammer and a handful of smooth, round nails had hammered them shut."

20

If by now you have not learned that less is more, there is still hope for you. Sit in your most cluttered room, surrounded by your most superfluous objects. Begin again with chapter 1 and this time, pay attention.

—BELINDA ST. GERMAIN, *Overstuffed*

The room had cleared quickly after Murkel took Roxanne away. She had not offered even one word of protest. She smiled at Blake; then she was gone. Then everyone was gone. Jane's phone had rung once more, and it was Nellie. Jane handed the phone to Tim, who made his static noise and hung up. Now Claire and Oh, Tim and Jane sat in front of the fireplace one last time, Tim pouring one more round of strong morning coffee for everyone.

"How are they all going to face each other again?" asked Jane. "Blake was defrocked as the high priest of antique integrity, revealed as a dangerous prankster. Glen's a mean, jealous cynic who called everyone out. And Roxanne, the one person who made this place run, who really gave to it instead of taking from it, is going to jail.

"Alcohol, food, drugs, work," said Tim. "Eventually, sex. They'll medicate for a while, then some project will come in or some new hotshot artist will arrive to give a master class in inlaid veneer or something, and this will all fade away."

"Good work, Mrs. Wheel," said Oh. "I knew Blake Campbell didn't know what had happened, but I wasn't sure who did. I always think the person who does the bookkeeping, the paperwork, is a good suspect, but I didn't have the final . . ."

"Nail in the coffin?" asked Tim.

"If I hadn't held on to these nails, I'm not sure I would have known it was Roxanne. When I leaned against the window frame, I saw and felt the holes where the nails had been hammered in. I realized that they were smooth, round holes and that the nails would have had to be removed quickly. I know those square heads are tricky to get out, and Roxanne was the only person at Campbell and LaSalle who had modern nails and a simple claw hammer to get them out fast."

"You don't seem to be that happy about solving the crime," said Claire, brushing off more tree-house debris, leaves and twigs, from Tim's sweater. She had felt more than vindicated when Jane revealed that the drawers had been switched. She had been sure she wouldn't have missed such obvious phonies when she'd originally brought home the chest from the estate sale.

"I feel sorry for Roxanne," said Jane. "She ran this place, probably loved it more than anyone, and was trying to preserve it from an unscrupulous man."

"Aha," said Oh, "as I said, she had nothing to feel guilty about so why would she confess? She had done something noble."

"Right," said Jane. "She had put on a mask and goggles and sent toxic fumes into a man's face, then led him to water and held his head down until he drowned. I know she's not a saint, but it's . . ." Jane noticed that Bruce Oh seemed to be smiling at her. He was actually giving her a genuine, lips curved upward, slight, but unmistakable, smile.

"It's complex," she finished.

Jane and Tim drove home later that morning. Neither one of them wanted to spend another minute in the cabins at Campbell and LaSalle. Jane had very little to pack, and because most of Tim's clothes had been loaned out, neither did he. She did put back all of the objects into her tote bag, and when Tim reminded her that she was supposed to be getting rid of them to make room for her Moonlight Market purchases, she shook her head.

"Maybe later," she said. She fished out the Moore Push-Pin Company tin from her Moonlight Market shopping tote, put the two nails inside, and dropped it into her bag. A new talisman to keep, to add to the wrinkled buckeye and the EZ Way Inn key rings.

Tim said he felt wide awake and didn't mind driving. Jane said she, too, was bursting with energy and curled up in the front seat, closing her eyes.

In and out of sleep, Jane kept hearing Belinda St. Germain's voice in her ear. All of the snippets of *Overstuffed* that she had tried to absorb between meals and tree houses and chemical solvents and furniture hoaxes floated through her brain, leaving her feeling much more cluttered than she had two days ago when she had vowed to remake her life.

"Why was that again, dear?" asked Tim. "Why are we doing the topsy-turvy?"

"Because I'm a bad mother. I lost Nick's permission slip."

"No, Jane, you're not a bad mother, you're a distracted mother. And even if you got rid of every McCoy flowerpot in your house and every pair of Bakelite dice and every advertising thermometer, you will still be a distracted mother. They're the best kind."

"Yeah, right," Jane said, yawning. "Like Nellie, she was always distracted, and she was terrific. A regular mom and a half."

"Hey, can you imagine if she wasn't distracted? If she'd used up all that manic crazy energy watching and following you around all the time?" asked Tim. "You'd be a basket case."

"Like I'm not," Jane said, slipping away into sleep.

"No, you're not," said Tim. "And besides, all that manic chatter is helpful. Nellie got you thinking square pegs in round holes, and that got you thinking about the nails, and you need all that stuff in your head and in your house. There's nothing you have to get rid of. Sometimes, darling, less is just less," Tim said, and reached into Jane's bag, pulling out her copy of *Overstuffed*.

Tim took his eyes off the road just long enough to glance at the author's photograph on the book jacket. "Holy shit, she looks like Martine," Tim said, and shuddered. "That's all we need, another life coach, Janie," he said, nudging her. "Janie, wake up for a minute."

"Yeah?" Jane asked. "I'm awake," she said, not opening her eyes.

Tim pushed the button on his door that rolled down Jane's window.

"Honey, you've got a great husband and son and friends. You've got to stop worrying about all the wrong stuff. Throw this out your window for me, okay?"

"Okay," Jane said, tossing *Overstuffed* onto the shoulder of the road.

"Feel better? You've gotten rid of at least five pounds of useless clutter. That's the stuff that needed to go. Right?" Tim asked.

"Yes, five pounds," murmured Jane.

"Atta girl," Tim said. "You got it."

"Okay," Jane whispered. "Got it. Got Charley and Nick and you and Don and Nellie and Oh . . ."

"Quite a cast for a dream," said Tim, smiling.

"Got it," Jane said, still sound asleep. "Got all the wrong stuff."

"Right stuff," said Tim.

"Right stuff," repeated Jane, smiling at a dream just beginning to form at the edges of her sleep.

Acknowledgments

Thank you to my family—my husband, Steve, my first and best reader, and our children, Kate, Nora, and Rob, who provide witty commentary as well as the patience necessary for having writer parents. To the following, my sincere thanks for wonderful friendship as well as various forms of expertise: Judy Groothuis, Dr. Dennis Groothuis, Chuck Shotwell, Lynn Shotwell, Cas Rooney, Lauren Paulson, Michael Swartz, and Sheldon Zenner. Thanks to Gail Hochman for being a writer's best friend. Thanks to Kelley Ragland and Ben Sevier at St. Martin's for asking all the right questions (providing more than a few answers, too), my copy editor, Marcy Hargan, and thank you, Anne Twomey, for designing such knockout covers.

Note

Two authentic Brewster chairs with excellent provenances are known to exist. The chair built by Armand LaMontagne is still owned by the Henry Ford Museum and is often loaned to other museums for exhibits on fakes and forgeries. There are no known Westman Sunflower Chests; however, I suggest we all keep our eyes open.